Hot Hand Sutras

Essays and Articles

Lawrence Shainberg

RUBY PRESS
Truro, Massachusetts

ISBN: 9798396049260

Cover design by Sasha Dorje Meyerowitz

CONTENTS

INTRODUCTION

Early in the summer of 1970, I began work on a novel—
eventually to be titled *Memories of Amnesia*—which aimed to
explore the quandaries of neurology and brain damage. I meant
the book to be both subjective and objective, as much related to
my reading in the scientific and medical literature as my
experience with Zen practice, sitting meditation, which seemed to
me a confrontation with my brain and its imperious power in my
life. Very soon, it became clear that this combination—Zen
experience and the focus on my own neurology (e.g., the brain
that was producing the book) would make the book both
immediate and chaotic. Clearly, the vision amounted to writing in
the present moment, attending to the brain that was producing
the book. In addition to the nagging awareness that my ambition
was exceeding my talent, this created extreme anxiety. I faced this
quandary every day but I persisted because I was innocent enough
to believe that the book could include the struggle or more, that
the struggle was its affirmation.

Zen practice was the motor that drove me. One doesn't sit
formally, in silence, for prescribed amounts of time, without
developing acute awareness of the seemingly autonomous activity
of one's brain and equally acute belief that the mind is not entirely

synonymous with it. It was this awareness and distinction that I meant to honor in the novel, and both, it seemed to me, required acknowledging, moment by moment, the fact that my language, memory and literary instinct originated in my brain.

As time passed and I was more and more frustrated, it became obvious to me that I needed objective experience to balance my intuition, research in the world of medicine in general and neuropathology in particular. The problem was that every sort of medical or scientific research required credentials, and I had none at all.

I was close to abandoning the novel when, in a stroke of luck, a family friend arranged an appointment for me with an esteemed neurosurgeon, chief of the department at one of New York's prestigious hospitals and the medical school associated with it. At a meeting in his office, he was so cordial and open that I ventured to describe my novel to him. Clearly disinterested, he shrugged and shook his head. "Mind-brain stuff, right? Some of the guys on my staff are interested in it, but I tend to avoid it myself."

Disappointed, I thanked him for his time and stood to leave but he had a question for me. "Have you ever seen neurosurgery?"

"No."

"Would you like to?"

"Of course."

"Are you busy tomorrow morning?"

"No."

"Can you get up early?"

"Sure."

"Meet me 6:30 at our locker room. I'm doing an interesting case."

Wildly excited, I was waiting for him when he arrived. In the locker room, I was assigned a set of surgical scrubs. A few minutes later, I stood behind the man they called "the boss" while he performed a craniotomy and exposed the object—in this case, the brain of a six-year-old boy—which had become my hopeless, tyrannical obsession. Minutes into the procedure, I knew that my impulse to get out of my office was not just correct but life-saving. No one on earth could be indifferent to the vivid reality of a neurosurgical operating theatre, but for me, it seemed a kind of ambiguous salvation, liberating me from the book on one hand and confirming it on the other. In these dire, life-and-death circumstances, it seemed wrong to be exhilarated, but I was. So much did logic and reason and professional etiquette desert me that later, as we were changing out of our scrubs in the locker room, it seemed entirely natural to ask the boss if I could write a book about him.

"Why not?" he said.

My impulse was fortuitous and life-changing. Six weeks later, after my book-proposal had won me a contract and his authority had brought me a white Lab Coat with a photo ID clipped to the breast pocket, I returned to the hospital in a different capacity. That morning, like most others for the next seven months, I entered the main lobby through the revolving doors and took the elevator to the ninth floor, where the boss and his staff had their offices, or the eighth, where most of their patients were recovering or awaiting diagnosis and surgery. The existence I'd come to doubt in my office was confirmed by the way others looked at me and checked out my credentials. With staff and patients, I had the objective identity, which, in the solitude of my office, with my intransigent book, had come to seem like a pipedream. For seven months, I had full access to patients and generous cooperation with the boss and his staff as well as access to other departments—Neurology, Radiology, Pathology, Physical Therapy, Social Work, etc.--that coordinated with neurosurgery. The book that grew from this experience—*Brain Surgeon, an Intimate View of his World*—was critically and commercially successful, and the book that had led to it—*Memories of Amnesia* —was finally possible when I returned to it.

Every serious writer understands the mysterious, alchemical voyage—from subjectivity to objectivity and back again—which made the novel possible. Developing novels are empty and formless when they're envisioned, but their realization is all about coherence and form. It's no exaggeration to say that most of the articles in this book are an implicit or explicit mirror of the trip I took from my office to the hospital and back, the lesson I've learned again and again—that for all the solitude my work requires, it can't be entirely separated from the phenomenal world without the obscuration of both.

1. GOING NOWHERE FAST

First Published in Harper's Magazine, September 1979

Of all the runners in this year's New York City Marathon, the most unusual, by any estimate, will be among the group that calls itself, "The Robert Wilson Brigade." Named after the esteemed dramatist *(Einstein on the Beach, The Life and Times of Sigmund Freud,* etc.), who is known among other things for his interest in "slow motion" and his use of tedium as a dramatic device, the Wilson Brigade is a group of runners who value slowness rather than speed. Like others in the race, they will measure their accomplishment by the time they take to finish, but these iconoclasts, recognizable by their electric-blue T-shirts with the turtle on the chest, will be the only participants for whom more is less and less more. A Wilsoner who runs the 26.2-mile distance in *less* than seven hours will be automatically suspended from the group. Several among their ranks point with pride to ten-hour marathons, and one claims to have used twelve hours, twenty-five minutes, forty-three seconds to complete the Boston Marathon last April.

The brigade was formed by T. Krishna Murphy, a thirty-four-year-old Irish-Indian (Irish father, Indian mother) from Madras. An accomplished distance runner in college, Murphy, or T.M., as he is known to his disciples, turned his attention to the marathon after graduation and, before his conversion to Slow Distance, had lowered his time to a very respectable 2:23:21 (at Muscle Shoals in 1972). The revelations that led to Wilsoning came to him in January 1974, when an interview with Frank Shorter appeared in *Runner's World*. The statement that impressed Murphy was in reply to a question concerning marathon speed. "It may well be," Shorter said, "that a slow marathon takes more out of you than a fast one. Don't forget: the slower your time, the longer you have to endure." T.M. says this statement changed his life, leading him to his now-famous theory that speed is a narcotic, a drug we use to escape anxiety. "If slow marathons are harder than fast ones, why do we reward those who run fast? I say it is because speed is an expression of our cultural disease, the embodiment of a technological ethos that makes us rush through our lives as if we can't wait to get them over. Shorter made me understand that the real challenge is to run slow, not fast."

Murphy turned his training pattern inside out. His morning ten-mile run, which three months before had required sixty-three minutes, became a fifteen-miler that took four hours. To eliminate what he calls the "problem" of his long stride, he designed a special belt that he tied to his legs and shortened gradually until, after nine months, he had brought his stride down from the forty-seven inches his coaches had admired to its present fifteen inches, which he calls "the no-stride" (this belt, incidentally, was marketed last winter by Tao Industries of Northern California under the trademark "Krishnabelt").

His new training was far more difficult, he says, than anything he'd done before. There was less physical pain (any workout that contains physical pain he calls "pathological") but in its place was an insufferable boredom that delighted him. "There are those who fear boredom and devote their energies to avoiding it," he wrote, "but not us, not Wilsoners. We welcome it! Tolerance for boredom is tolerance for anxiety, and that's what we seek to develop. Not leg strength or some brute, macho fantasy of courage, but patience, tranquility, an ability to be present in any given time and space, a freedom from the need for entertainment and distraction. That's why Wilsoners don't go to movies or watch TV. For us such behavior is merely speed in other forms."

* * *

Although just forty-seven runners will compete under the Wilson banner in the New York marathon, the brigade claims a membership of 234 from nineteen countries, including the People's Republic of China and Tibet. Murphy is confident that Wilsoners will become a substantial presence in the world of international athletics. In his view, the brigade is a revolutionary movement, a reaction against widespread disease. "People go out to track meets and cheer the sprinters. Can you imagine? That's like cheering junkies when they shoot up. Speed is the death instinct concretized! The 100-meter dash is psychodrama, an experiment in group psychosis. And the idea of running a marathon against the stopwatch is comparable to measuring sexual capacity by the speed with which you can reach orgasm. What we're after, if you like, is making love as long as possible."

Scientific support has come from Charles "Baba" Limbic, the radical Romanian neurophysiologist whose work with rats confirms most of the hypotheses that led to Wilsoning. Limbic, famous for his work on the "neurology of desire" and "impatience" and especially his identification of the particular cell-bundles in rats' brains that are responsible for "ambition," had discovered Slow Distance independently when he found that rats on slow exercise wheels were "neurologically superior" to those on fast wheels. By "neurological superiority" he meant of course that their "ambition-centers" were smaller and that they were therefore less "anxious" and more "content." Others have questioned this definition, but Limbic claims proof of it through autopsy. Indeed, last winter he published photographs taken by electron microscope that purport to compare the "ambition-centers" of rats from different wheels and to demonstrate conclusively the superiority of "Wilsonian" over "conventional" rats.

* * *

The ultimate measure of Wilsoning's success may lie in the fact that, like all important movements, it has spawned its own dissidents. The groups that have attracted particular attention are the "Giacomettis," who not only take their name from the great Swiss sculptor but attempt in races to emulate his work; the "Neurologists," who consider themselves Limbic's disciples; and the "Neurowilsoners," who claim they have joined Murphy's original vision to that of the Neurologists.

Giacomettis believe they have found the ultimate realization of Slow Distance. Says their founder, the Tibetan monk Chogyam Pumaddidas, "If the problem is motion, why indulge it?" For Pumaddidas and his disciples, the true anxiety for a runner lies in "not-running," and the ultimate drug, therefore, is running, slow or fast. Thus, Giacomettis, like other runners, congregate around the starting line at races, but take only one step beyond it, whereupon they freeze in poses similar to Giacometti sculptures. These poses, which Pumaddidas calls "asanas," will be held for lengths of time approximating Wilsonian levels, anywhere from five to twelve hours, during which Giacomettis, in order to maximize their anxiety, attempt to imagine every step of the race they are "not-running." Some are said to be so successful in this enterprise that they suffer injuries comparable to those of conventional runners. Pumaddidas himself came out of last year's Boston Marathon, which he did not run for nine hours, with a case of "runner's knee" and a severe hypoglycemic condition. Injured or not, Giacomettis—or Giacs, as they call themselves— who hold their poses for five hours or more are said to "realize" the race, and they have their own medals with which non-competitors are honored.

If Giacs have extended Murphy's laws, the Neurologists, according to their spokesman, a Japanese neurochemist who studied with Baba Limbic and has for the past few years called himself "Medullah," have revealed their ultimate absurdity. For Medullah, the problem of speed is the problem of the brain, specifically the universal condition that he calls "Here-There-Aphasia." HTA, as it is known in the vernacular, is the devastating delusion that "here," a function of the right hemisphere, and "there," a function of the left, are different places. In effect, speed is an inevitable symptom of an asymmetrical brain, for once the hemispheres are divided, animals so afflicted will rush desperately from one place to another in search of unification.

Says Medullah (whose English, according to his disciples, is not so much "broken" as "neurologically symmetrical"): "Brain problem, not speed. Not running not enough. Not speed. Not happen not so quick." After years of work, Medullah devised a series of experiments in Limbic's laboratories that led to confirmation of his theory and, eventually, to "Neurologizing." Through selective breeding, he developed a species of rat that had a brain as asymmetrical as a human being's, with correspondingly large "desire-bundles" and "ambition-centers." When released on exercise wheels, such rats (called "Olympians" in papers published by Medullah) will run with maximum speed until exhausted. Retaining one group of Olympians for control studies, Medullah strapped another into specially designed harnesses that held them in suspension above the wheel so that, while their bodies remained motionless, their feet were always "racing." The idea of course was to "fool" the rats into thinking they were in motion. "Brain thinking moving," Medullah explains, "but brain mistaking. Thinking 'here!' thinking 'there!' but look! Always here!" Kept in harness throughout their lives, these rats, upon autopsy, were found to have no "desire-bundles" whatsoever. What is more, their brains were so much "of a piece" that no demarcation could be found between the hemispheres.

Since the harness was impractical for human beings under normal racing conditions (Medullah has built several, which, used in conjunction with conveyor belts, are featured attractions at the Neurologists' training camp in the Catskills), Medullah devised a method of running that he believes will accomplish the same healing process in the human brain that the harness accomplished in the rats. Neurologists bring deck chairs to the starting line and sit in them throughout the race. They are trained to keep their eyes closed and to move no part of their bodies except their feet, which, like harnessed rats, they tap softly on the ground as if they're running. According to Medullah, this subtle action has an *uncanny* effect on the brain, setting the motor regions at war against the reflective centers, exciting in the "here-region" a continuous sense of abandonment, in the "there-region" a sense of imminent arrival. Upon opening their eyes, Neurologists— having fooled their brains completely—are said to experience "brain-wholeness" to such an extent that they are transported with joy. And those who sit out enough races, according to Medullah, will gradually merge their hemispheres until, perceiving the ultimate truth that all points in space are one, they will relinquish the delusion of motion. "How go anywhere?" he says. "Anywhere everywhere!"

Of all Wilsonian dissidents, the most extreme are those who call themselves the "Neurowilsoners" or "not-Wilsoners." Organized by a young runner named "Emile Zatopek" (he includes the quotation marks in the spelling of his name to distinguish himself from the great Czech runner, to whom he is not related), Neurowilsoners reason that, while Murphy's original insight was correct, he did not understand it himself. As a former Wilsoner who became, in his time, a Giacometti and a Neurologist, "Zatopek" speaks from legitimate experience when he says, "All Wilsonism points in the same direction. Murphy's wisdom and Medullah's experiments reveal that the problem—the root problem!—is ambition. What neither understood was that the ultimate ambition of a damaged brain is to cure itself of brain damage. How can we make progress if we don't attack that problem at its source?"

Following "Zatopek," Neurowilsoners attempt to rid themselves of all desire by doing what they desire the least. As they understand it, there is no better way to undermine ambition than running long distances as fast as possible. Since they regard this activity as pathological, they consider it an efficient process by which the brain is forced to accept its own hopeless predicament. "What we aim to do," says "Zatopek," who ran last year's Boston Marathon in two hours fourteen minutes flat, "is relinquish once and for all the belief that we can improve ourselves. Anyone who's ever seen a runner in peak condition will know that, whatever claims he makes to the contrary, this is his true goal. Let others war with brain damage! We embrace ours and deepen it in every way we can!"

2. THE VIOLENCE OF JUST SITTING

First published October 10, 1976, in the New York Times Magazine

Three hours northwest of New York City in the Catskills, 40 miles from Grossinger's and not much farther from Woodstock, markers indicate the private road into the monastery. Following a stream, the road climbs two miles through heavy forest, opens onto a cemetery they call Sangha Meadow, then suddenly veers to cross a wood-plank bridge which resounds beneath my car like gunfire. In fact, the monastery—called International Dai Bosatsu Zendo —comes into view precisely as the "gunfire" sounds. A touch melodramatic perhaps, but Zen Buddhism has never had an argument with melodrama. During my stay here, I will often be reminded of this bridge, for crossing it is not unlike driving into ambush. No great Zen master designed it like this, but ambush is, for me at least, not an unreasonable introduction to Zen monastic life.

I am not here as a journalist but as a prospector. During four years of Zen practice, the interest in its ultimate form, monastery life, has grown in me as it grows, I imagine, in all Zen students. Zen meditation—called zazen —is always solitary, but as time goes on the solitude wants to be shared. After a while, the need for community becomes intense, the idea of such community in a natural landscape extremely appealing. Dai Bosatsu, an authentic

8

Zen monastery in the Japanese tradition, open to any man or woman willing to sit in meditation with the residents and help them with daily chores, is an enthusiastic—if somewhat overwhelming—response to that need. There aren't many places where you'll find out more quickly how serious you are about your meditation, or, if you're serious, what direction you want it to take.

From this point, at the bridge, I am able to see both the monastery and the old house that belonged to a former owner of this estate, James Beecher, the brother of Harriet Beecher Stowe, author of "Uncle Tom's Cabin." Standing beside a lake, half-a-mile apart—the house, a 19th century lodge with dormer windows and natural siding; the monastery consummately Japanese, three connected buildings with mortared walls and a dark, scalloped roof—they dramatize the cultural collisions embodied by Dai Bosatsu. This is a place where students assume Japanese names; where pickled plums, a Japanese delicacy, are served along with oatmeal for breakfast; where the opening ceremony was conducted first in Japanese (for the benefit of a plane load of laymen and monks who flew in for it specially from Japan), then in English.

Buddha himself predicted the movement of his vision from East to West, but what occurred over centuries in the Far East, with form evolving slowly out of content, has happened here— superficially at least—with great, often bewildering speed. Copied from a Japanese monastery that evolved over decades, Dai Bosatsu took three years to build and cost $3 million—most of it donated by the president of a major American corporation, a student of Zen who chose to remain anonymous. The practice to which it is devoted has been around for almost 2,000 years, but it was barely known in this country until the 1960's. Where else but here, when else but now, could the money, the resources (including some 1,400 acres of open land) and the quixotic enthusiasm come together make such vision possible?

Eido Shimano, the 44-year-old Japanese master (or roshi) who founded Dai Bosatsu, did not arrive in New York until 1964, and for four years after that his meditation center, or zendo, was a small New York City apartment. The road to the new monastery began, in a sense, when that apartment became too small for the number of people who wanted to sit there, and the Zen Studies Society, of which Eido Roshi was president, bought a carriage house on East 67th St. In 1968, that carriage house became The New York Zendo, one of the largest urban Zen centers in America, and six months later the land for Dai Bosatsu was purchased.

At first the project was envisioned as a simple country retreat, but as time went on the vision grew. When the monastery opened last July 4—surely one of the more remarkable Bicentennial events—the Zen Studies Society found itself the owner of the largest and most authentic Zen temple outside Japan. At every step in this evolution, Eido Roshi has had to choose between Americanizing Japanese Zen and retaining the forms of his native country. In most cases he has chosen the latter. The architect who designed the building was sent to Japan to study: Japanese carpenters did most of the finishing work, and the central zendo is a copy of the one at the monastery called Tofuku Ji, in Kyoto. There are some Zen students who feel that Eido Roshi's choice was wrong. American Zen, they say, should be allowed to develop its own form, as it has to a greater extent, for example, at Tassajara Zen Center in California. For Eido Roshi, however, "Japanese culture" is "Zen culture." As he sees it, the practice and the culture are inseparable. "There will be plenty of time for Americans to evolve their own forms," he says. "Dal Bosatsu, meanwhile, is meant to be a place where this evolution can begin.

Most people begin the practice, I think, the way I did—sitting down for five or 10 minutes, facing the wall. It seems extraordinary at first, a quick exotic avenue to insight and tranquility, but unless one keeps the practice on a superficial level such excitement doesn't last. As time goes on, one finds that zazen is nothing more or less than attention to the present: things as they are rather than as they should or used to be. Once that dawns, many give it up. Of 25 people who show up at the Washington D.C. zendo, it is estimated that one becomes a Zen student. On the other hand, according to Eido Roshi, anyone who sits for three years will continue all his life. For me, zazen becomes mere ordinary and organic the more I do it, more like eating than eating terrific food. While this makes life without it rather difficult to imagine, it also makes the practice harder. Like others, I think, I used to help myself along by making it heroic.

What brings people to zazen? Every student I know came to it out of some form of psychic desperation, profound disenchantment with self-improvement fantasies and—this above all—an intense interest in its concreteness and simplicity. Americans have played with Zen intellectually at least since the 1940's, but the gap between Zen theory and Zen practice (which is to say, traditional Zen) is wide indeed, approximate more or less to the gap between a box score and a ball game. People who come to meditation centers, not to mention monasteries, are interested in playing the game not reading about it.

From a certain point of view, zazen is rather a simple process: You keep your body still and firmly balanced, your eyes open, your back straight and unsupported. Posture and breathing are crucial, not because good posture and breathing are thought to quiet the mind, but because, in the language of Zen, the body-mind dichotomy is absurd: To sit well and to be well are the same.

Within this posture, the silence is large, and various strategies are brought to bear on it. It is considered essential to sit with a group and, eventually, to work with a teacher, who will often assign koans—traditional, non-rational Zen problems that are used as a focus in meditation. In the beginning, however, you simply count your breath, "one" on the inhale, "two" on the exhale, continuing to 10, where you start at one again. As anyone who tries it will soon discover, it is easier described than accomplished. The brain resists focus on such a basic physiological activity, and very often the more effort one mounts the more distracted one becomes. The idea in Zen is not to resist distraction but remain attentive to it. You hear your thoughts, as they say, but don't chase after them. This attitude is called "detachment," and it is the sustaining principle of zazen.

You don't have to be a Zen student to know about detachment. It is the space we live in when our minds are open rather than constricted, the space we inhabit, if my experience is any guide, when we are laughing at ourselves. No one lives entirely beyond this space and no one lives entirely within it, but we all have our ways of seeking it. Zazen, however, is less a strategy for entering detachment than a practice which, without detachment, is impossible. No way to sit there counting your breath if your mind is fixing on things; no way to tolerate motionlessness if you get obsessed with it. This is not to say that Zen students don't get obsessed, or fixed, but that the practice is a way of sitting in the center of the mind's flight and desperation. The vision of Zen is that any attempt to escape the flight intensifies it. The only way is to sit and be attentive to it, with patience and compassion. Detachment is both the prerequisite and the result of this activity.

As Zen teachers constantly remind their students, zazen is "just sitting." For one reason or another, one decides to give up the search for solution and literally sits down in the center of his problem. Of course, the human mind being what it is, this act itself can become a search for solution, and some practices, like transcendental meditation, seem to encourage this, promising happiness, peace of mind, the whole illuminated package. Zen is disinterested in solution and unenthusiastic, even bored with the idea of happiness. There is, of course, "enlightenment" (or "kensho" or satori), but this is not a condition one seeks. In fact, the adamant belief of Zen is that we are, as they say, "enlightened before enlightenment." In other words, enlightenment is not a state to be acquired but rather a fundamental human condition. To seek it, by definition, is to deny it.

It doesn't take long to discover that, for all its innocent connotation, "just sitting" is a violent proposition, challenging most of the automatic, cognitive functions of the brain. "Just" to sit, after all, is "just" to accept one's situation without attempting to judge it, change it or explain it; "just" to be in the present without yearning toward the future or clinging to the past. In other words, to be without ambition and without ego. In fact, Zen is often called "ego-killing practice," and most of its pain and disorientation can safely be laid to ego resistance. Don't suspect, however, that Zen nurtures the romantic fantasy of ego absence, which is so ubiquitous in books on "Eastern wisdom." Its vision of the human paradox is total and uncompromising: We can't live with our egos and we can't live without them; detachment is natural and impossible; "just sitting" is both the easiest and the hardest thing a man can attempt to do. Zen is not a means of solving the paradox but of exploring and containing it. And the "ambush" of Zen monastic life may be nothing more than the experience of meeting the paradox head-on.

* * *

We are awakened at 4:30 in the morning by a resident who walks the halls with a tiny golden bell that sounds like the world's most gentle ice-cream truck. Ten minutes to get to the meditation hall. Morning service will last until 7:30, breakfast until 8; lunch is at noon, dinner at 5:30, evening zazen from 7 to 9, lights out at 9:30. The rest is mostly work, much of it demanding. There is a logging operation here (the building itself is heated by wood), a maple-sugar facility, a large organic garden which supplies most of the vegetarian menu. With monastery cleaning and kitchen work, there is never a shortage of things to do. Except for Wednesday, the day off, there is no free time at all.

* * *

Dai Bosatsu is meant to be a "lay monastery," which is to say a place where people can study Zen even if they do not wish to become monks or nuns. In summer it is open to guests who are willing to stay at least a week, but twice a year it will close for 100-day training sessions. During this time, 40 students (paying $500 each) will remain in seclusion together, following more or less the schedule we're following now and studying with the master, Eido Rosin. One week each month will be devoted to *sesshin,* the intensive retreat periods that are the cornerstone of Zen practice, the most difficult of all its disciplines. During *sesshin,* most work is suspended, and days are given over to zazen and a traditional form of study with the master, a formal confrontation called *dokusan.* After breakfast, during *sesshin,* one continues sitting, and after lunch one continues sitting. Sometime more than 14 hours per day can be devoted to zazen. In this context, the usual difficulties of the practice —the anxiety, the leg pain, the ego threat —mount exponentially. In the parlance of Zen centers, anyone who sits is a "Zen student," but "serious Zen students" are those who attend *sesshin.* Anyone who does, even for half a day, will understand the reasons for this terminology. *Sesshin* can be brutal, a kind of controlled breakdown. It is not meant for those who aren't committed to the practice.

I splash water on my face in the bathroom across the hall, then put on the old sweat pants I use for sitting. My room is about 12 feet square: no amenities except a mat on the floor for sleeping, a wonderful view of the lake and what has come to be called "Dai Bosatsu Mountain" on the other side. On the door there is a set of rules. Among them:

o Please remember that the essential purpose of Dai Bosatsu is zazen practice and the attainment of kensho and their actualization in daily life.

o Keep in mind that we are involved not just in zazen practice but the transmission of Buddhism from East to West.

o The following things are prohibited: liquor, smoking in or near the building, noisy walking, slamming doors, any kind of musical instrument, strong perfume, or colorful clothes. (The thrust of this rule, like many others here, is to make it possible for people to live together with minimal trespass on personal boundaries or the meditative atmosphere.)

o Don't leave until your stay is completed.

o When leaving, you are expected to pay your respects to the Roshi and the Sangha ("Sangha" means "the congregation of people who sit together.")

We gather in silence outside the zendo and do our best, with various forms of yoga and calisthenics, to stretch out our backs and legs. For all but 20 minutes of the next 3 hours, we will be sitting cross-legged, at morning service and at breakfast, and there aren't many, even among advanced students, who take that prospect lightly. The full lotus posture — legs crossed so that the feet are resting on the thighs—may come naturally to Orientals, but for Americans, particularly men, it is agony. Serious injuries can result if one attempts it, or even the half lotus, a slightly easier variation, too soon. It is true that American Zen teachers, unlike their Japanese counterparts, permit other positions, even sitting in a chair (if one does not move and his back is straight and unsupported). But anyone who sits understands the utility of the lotus postures, which keep the body still and balanced and help to deepen one's breath, and works hard to achieve them.

The residents are wearing brown or black robes, and some have shaven heads, like the roshi, indicating their consecration as monks (no women have yet shaved their heads up here). They are a diverse group: a former Catholic nun, a philosophy professor, a concert pianist, a welder, a journalist, a number of dropouts from college and graduate school. Though most are in their mid-20's, one is 60, another 42 and three are in their 30's. Predominantly middle-class, they are sons and daughters of physicians, psychiatrists, Army officers, businessmen, artists and musicians. Their reasons for being here run a gamut from psychological desperation to religious conviction. Some are critical of Dai Bosatsu, finding it too luxurious or too Japanese; some feel as assaulted by it as I do; but none questions that being here has been anything less than profound.

As we meet in silence this morning, I understand their feeling well. For all our divergent backgrounds, we share belief in meditation and knowledge of its difficulties. The communality is tangible here, the sense of vulnerability and friendship almost intimidating. As time goes on, much about Dai Bosatsu will confuse me, and some things will even offend me, but my memory of these mornings —our meetings outside the zendo and the meditation that followed — will remain unequivocal, the only "religious" experience I've ever known that did not seem, in retrospect, unauthentic and sentimental.

At 4:50 a line forms and winds slowly through the corridor that rims the zendo. This is kinhin, or walking meditation. One of the monks leads us, carrying at his chest a pair of flat sticks called "clappers," which he strikes at exactly 5 o'clock, signaling us to enter the zendo. We proceed to our cushions, bow to each other and take our seats.

The zendo is a long, elegantly simple room with high ceilings and Japanese rice paper screens along each wall. On each side is a row of tatami mats and black meditation cushions, and at the end, an austere altar, where a black Buddha sits in the lotus posture. Incense burns before it, and its fragrance fills the room.

Morning service is an elaborate ceremony, combining recitation in English of various Buddhist scriptures, and chanting, mostly in Chinese. Like walking, chanting is a form of meditation. Most students, even some masters, do not understand the words they chant, but that is not relevant. Although these are the Buddha's teachings, it is the sound that matters, the attention we bring to it and the uncanny sense that develops, as we chant, that all our voices are one.

For some students, I'm told, morning service is profoundly moving, but for me it is depressing. This is not my first encounter with the forms of Zen as they have been imported from Japan, but it is certainly the most oppressive. Religious ritual, organized religion of any sort, has always been anathema to me, and one of the things that attracted me to Zen was my belief that it shared this revulsion. After what I felt out side the zendo, the service seems irrelevant and theatrical, a great superstructure of form without content.

If you caught a Zen master in a rare explaining mood, he would tell you, I think, that my reaction is an expression of my naiveté and romanticism about Zen. The ritual, he would say, is part of "ego-killing practice," and its purpose is not to entertain or to stir the emotions but to provide a form in which the ego can be relinquished. That being the case, no one comes to it without ambivalence. Like the rigid schedule here, the monotonous routine and the lack of variety in the food we're served, the ritual is aimed at that part of my mind which desires variety and stimulation. It is that part of me, the master would say, which in rebellion now.

I know this argument and it makes sense to me, but it doesn't help. Maybe I am into ego resistance, but I still feel awful. Not for the first time and not for the last, I decide to leave Dai Bosatsu as soon as possible.

During morning service, we have faced each other, but now we turn and face the wall. Three times in succession a great reverberating bell is rung, and then there is silence. For the next 50 minutes, there is no sound except those occasioned by swallowing and growling stomachs, both of which seem, in this context, absolutely thunderous. The sun is coming up and light is changing in the zendo, sending streaks across the wall before us. We hear the birds awaken in the pines outside the window, the wind whistling over the lake. And we hear, of course, the particular sounds our minds are producing on this particular day. My decision to leave becomes a decision to stay, then again a decision to leave, then the argument dissolves. As often, there are thoughts about "religious ritual" and "Zen" and "meditation," each more inane than the one before. The first five minutes seem like hours, the next five like no time at all. Insight comes and goes, boredom and leg pain come and go. Like everyone else, I keep my eyes open, my knees planted firmly on the cushion, my hands in my lap, thumbs touching, one palm cradled in the other. Chances are there is a great deal of agony in this room, but no one moves. "When you are sitting in the middle of your own problem," writes Shunryu Suzuki Roshi in his book "Zen Mind, Beginner's Mind," "what is more real to you: your problem or you yourself? The awareness that you are here, right now, is the ultimate fact."

* * *

Nyogen Senzaki, a revered Zen teacher who conducted a zazen group in Los Angeles from 1922 until his death in 1958, said there was no way he could bring Zen to America because Zen was here already. Despite this implicit presence, however, an explicit historical progression can be traced, beginning with the appearance of Senzaki's teacher, Soen Shaku Roshi, at the World Parliament on Religion in Chicago in 1893, and the first American visit, in 1897, of Dr. D. T. Suzuki (not to be confused with Suzuki Roshi), who happened to be another of Soen Shaku's students. Almost alone, Suzuki—who later lectured for many years, mostly at Columbia —was responsible for the tremendous interest in Zen theory that spread through the United States during the 1950's. But the cultivation of Zen practice was left, as far as we know, to Senzaki and the First Zen Institute, which was formed in New York in the 1920's. Though himself not a roshi, Senzaki formed a deep friendship with Soen Nakagawa Roshi, the honorary founder of Dai Bosatsu, who was then abbot of the Japanese monastery called Ryutaku Ji, where Eido Roshi was a student. It was their friendship that led to Eido Roshi's arrival in New York in 1964. Quite coincidentally, half a dozen other masters arrived in the United States around that time, including Suzuki Roshi, who was to found Tassajara and the San Francisco Zen Center.

These newcomers formed the nucleus from which a truly American Zen practice began to emerge almost immediately. They were captivated by the enthusiasm Americans brought to zazen, and in no hurry to return to the comparatively staid lives of temple priests that awaited them in Japan. Soon after they arrived, zazen groups began to be formed, and, for the first time, sesshin became available to American students on a regular basis. Today, there are more than 100 Zen groups throughout the country, dozens of communes built around serious Zen practice, and established Zen centers in a number of major cities. The widespread interest in zazen also can be measured by the fact that "Zen Mind, Beginner's Mind," which many consider the finest book ever written on zazen, has sold 175,000 copies, with no promotion whatsoever, since its publication in 1970.

These days, an American student can pursue Zen on any level to which he or she might be inclined. There is a well-known roshi in New York who has half-a-dozen students and won't accept more. The New York Zen Center is a simple New York apartment, the New York Zendo (of The Zen Studies Society) is as elegant and traditional as Dai Bosatsu, and there is a rigorous Zen group with an American master on a working farm in Maine. Philip Kapleau, the first American roshi, has a large center in Rochester, Korean Zen groups have recently appeared on the East Coast, and there is a widespread interest in Tibetan Buddhism, which in many respects is similar to Zen.

Some teachers believe Americans do better in small, informal groups, and others, like Eido Roshi, consider monastic life essential. What they all agree on, however, is that zazen, no matter how long one practices it, must never become institutional or ritualistic, and must be protected from the temptations to use it as therapy, sedative or escape. Zen students, in essence, must guard against over-emphasis on Zen itself. The great difficulty, as most experienced students will tell you, is the inclination to become obsessive about the practice, too dependent on the teacher or too attached to the forms. Since zazen addresses crucial psychological problems like distraction and alienation, it is heady stuff at first, intoxicating and sometime hallucinogenic. Rare is the student who does not, at some point, consider it the answer to all his problems, and unfortunate ones never get off that track. Those more fortunate, however, will find a teacher who offers them what the great master Rinzai offered his students in the 14th century: "I say to you there is no Buddha, no Dharma, nothing to practice, nothing to prove! Just what are you seeking thus in the highways and byways? Blind men! You are putting a head on top of the one you already have!"

Of all the ritual at Dai Bosatsu, the most complex is that which surrounds the dining hall. Each resident is assigned a set of black lacquered bowls and a pair of chopsticks, all of it wrapped in a brown napkin and called a *jihatsu*. There is a prescribed manner in which the *jihatsu* is carried when entering the dining hall, a manner in which it is set down, unwrapped, laid out on the table, and —after eating — a carefully regulated process by which, at the table, it is washed and dried and wrapped again. Even the angle of the chopsticks, when set beside the bowls, is specified.

* * *

Like much of the ritual here, the overriding purpose of this one is quiet and order. Laid out haphazardly, the chopsticks would make a rough and disturbing esthetic pattern, but placed parallel to each other they form an elegant and consistent line up and down the table. Similarly, if the bowls are handled carelessly, they make a tremendous racket, but the ritual—a precise technique in which one knuckle is pressed against the bottom of the bowl while the fingers grip it from the top—makes it possible to handle them in silence.

Dining in this silence, side by side with fellow students after two hours of meditation, is no meager experience. For me, it is not only a continuation of zazen, but the point at which I will begin to understand, for what seems the first time, what it means to take meditation beyond the zendo. During the meal, sitting in zazen posture, one neither speaks nor looks around. One eats, as they say, mindfully. Bowls are passed —oatmeal, milk, maple syrup, raisins, peanuts—and one either bows his head to refuse or places his hands together in the position the Japanese call gassho before helping himself. At first, like a lot of the ritual here, this seems silly and up-tight, almost embarrassing, but as the meal progresses, it becomes clear that its effect is to focus all attention on one's food. In the context of this attention, tastes and textures sharpen, and the "ordinary" experience of eating begins to seem extraordinary. In contrast to this, it seems that in the past I've taken most food in a state of oblivion, used it for distraction and escape.

The odd thing, is, however, that this experience is not altogether pleasant. The food, to be sure, seems uncommonly delicious, but in some way, like Dai Bosatsu in general, eating in this matter is claustrophobic. I would imagine that such claustrophobia is not unusual among Zen students. How could it be otherwise when the thrust of the practice is to shut off escape routes, to create a situation in which there is nothing to do but see whatever there is to see?

Zen teachers will tell you that, for all its exotic reputation, zazen begins and ends with seeing, and that all its mystery and paradox derive from the curious effects that vision has on people accustomed to being blind. For me, the most powerful of these effects is that the better I see, the more I see things in time — changing, I mean, dissolving and re-forming. It is no great insight to say that things are ephemeral, but for me, at least, it is completely amazing to see them that way: both more and less real, more vivid and more meaningful, more ridiculous and comic. As Buddhist scripture puts it: "Things are not as they seem; nor are they otherwise." I used to think this was "advanced Zen" but I know now it is the province of anyone who sits, even from the beginning. Seeing things in this light can make life easier and richer by a lot; it can also — when the ephemeral object of your vision happens to be yourself — make it painful and disorienting. For all my ideas about detachment, I had no intention, when I sat down and looked at the wall, of applying it to myself.

No doubt such ambivalence makes me, in the case of Dai Bosatsu, an unreliable witness. I am more involved with zazen since I was there, but nowadays, when I remember the place, waves of apprehension fill me. What Mao said about revolution, I think we can say about Zen, that it is not a tea party. Everything about the practice is an assault upon the self, and Zen monasteries are its ultimate weapon. No accident, I think, that I could not wait to leave Dai Bosatsu, that I was sorry to leave, that I dread going back, that I'll probably go back soon. Why should my feelings be anything but mixed? No self greets attack with joy, and my self, when it remembers Dal Bosatsu, gets the willies. It may be that the willies are what Zen is all about, but it doesn't help to say it.

3. THE PLEASURE PAPERS

First Published in Provincetown Arts, 1992

Those who doubt that the road of science is paved with the private struggles of human beings would do well to study the pleasure controversy. According to *Conquering Pleasure: The Memoirs of Richard Pincus,* the Nobel laureate's crucial insight into the metabolism of pleasure was a direct result of his passion for eggs. If Pincus' physician, Dr. Edward Loomis, had not been disturbed by his patient's cholesterol count, the world would have an altogether different view of positive sensation. Eggs, however, were not alone in motivating Pincus. "First, it was cigarettes;" he writes, "then alcohol, then red meat. Now it was the food I loved above all others. One by one all the great ingestible pleasures had been denied me, as they had been denied so many others. It wasn't so long ago that I was told to strip the skin from chicken! Drink skim milk! Avoid cheese, butter and ice cream! But strange as it seems, even I, who'd worked on pleasure for more than 20 years, had never suspected what lay behind these prohibitions until eggs were also taken away from me!'

Pincus, as most of us know, was an expert in pleasure long before this moment. The 1991 Nobel Prize was awarded him for his proof that all pleasure derives from a small declivity—now known as the Fissure of Pincus—between the hypothalamus and the hippocampus. While other regions of the brain had vied for

24

the title of "pleasure center," and many researchers had advanced theories in support of them, Pincus's work proved that the Fissure of Pincus was the single irreplaceable link in the chain that produces, in animals as well as humans, sensations experienced as positive. Animals rewarded with electrical charge in this fissure ignore hunger, thirst and sex in order to obtain it. Furthermore, brain scans and the computer-assisted imagery they produce have shown that the Fissure of Pincus literally lights up with a measurable (in units that Pincus dubbed "pleas") intensity that varies precisely in proportion to the amount of charge (measured in volts) the animal has received. In the original Pincus equations, one plea is equal to the amount of illumination produced by .0001 millivolts of electrical stimulation in the Fissure of Pincus, 6.79 pleas the average luminosity of the Fissure of Pincus in a group of pigs two minutes after ingesting 600 grams of ground sirloin, and 8.2 pleas the average derived by the same group at the height of sexual coupling.

Armed with such knowledge, Pincus found himself in an ideal position to investigate the suspicions aroused by his physician. Other researchers had challenged specific dietary restraints, questioning, for example, research on cholesterol or sodium, but obvious though it seems to us now, no one had realized that every food or activity discredited by medical research had a single aspect in common. Writes Pincus, "How had scientists failed to notice that forbidden foods were always delicious? That not a single unpleasant taste had been forbidden us? That all of which science had shown to be unhealthy—sunlight and chocolate, coffee, marijuana, and deep-fried clams—were invariably sources of pleasure?" To investigate this theory, Pincus enlisted the cooperation of a Princeton colleague as esteemed for his immunity research as Pincus for his work in pleasure. Alexander Blemish had won the Lasker Prize in 1990 for discovering Immuno-Uno, the neuro-transmitter that diminishes immune response at a predictable rate. A by-product of this research was the development of the Blemish Immunity Test, or BIT, which made possible—by means of a "Blemish Meter" attached to the paw of an experimental animal or the fingertip of a human subject—the precise, moment-by-moment evaluation, in MicroBits, of an individual's immune response. In other words, as Pincus realized, Professor Blemish had developed not only a means by which the fluctuations of health could be determined but, if joined to his own experimental protocol, a window on the relationship of health and pleasure. In his first series of experiments, Pincus found that even "Micro-Pleas," the smallest units of pleasure, as determined by illumination of the Fissure of Pincus, have a precise, negative impact on the immune system, with one micro-plea producing a loss of .00834 MicroBits in immune response. What was more, the Pincus-Blemish equation was found to be reversible. As Pleas impacted MicroBits, MicroBits impacted Pleas. In the elegant experiments designed by Pincus—and quickly replicated in laboratories throughout the world—rats with electrodes implanted in their Fissures of Pincus were shown to experience a precise unit (1.0016 Pleas) of pleasure for every MicroBit lost on their Blemish Meters. The correlation between pleasure and health was indisputable. As Pincus noted on the day his results were published, "It isn't cholesterol that makes eggs bad for you. Eggs are unhealthy because they taste good. A high cholesterol count is a function of an illuminated Fissure of Pincus. Show me a fresh egg that tastes rotten and I will show you an egg that lowers your cholesterol!'

A self-described health-nut, Pincus did not, like some of his colleagues (Alexander Blemish, for example, who is said to have gained more than 50 pounds in the three months following these experiments) commence to eat forbidden foods with impunity. In fact, as his recently published *More Bits Diet* makes clear, his discoveries gave him a self-control he had never had before. Research which, by his own admission, had aimed to free him from dietary restraint had eliminated the need for it. "The problem of diet," he writes, "is the problem of taste. Once I understood how much the good taste of eggs could hurt me, they ceased to taste good any longer, and because of this, it was easy to avoid them!'

Guaranteed by Pincus to produce a weight-loss in excess of two pounds a week, the *More Bits Diet* is remarkably simple. "Find the foods you like least and eat them all the time. If certain foods tempt you, find a way to make them unpalatable. Vinegar and cayenne pepper are useful in this regard, provided of course that your recipe doesn't call for them. Excesses of salt, sugar or almost any other condiment will often provide the difference between a negative and a positive move on your Blemish Meter. Over-eating is very helpful, especially when you're not hungry. Always eat as quickly as possible, placing another bite in your mouth before the previous bite has been chewed. Food swallowed in large chunks is almost impossible to enjoy."

Until follow-up research began to reveal their darker implications, the Pincus-Blemish experiments were lightly regarded, even among scientists. Within months of their publication, however, Stamford's Karl Edgar Rich used them as a springboard to discredit the universally held belief that winning is better than losing. Hourly readings of Blemish Meters worn by the NBA champion Sacramento Kings revealed their immunological efficiency to be measurably less than that of the last place Detroit Pistons. Correlating these figures with concurrent longevity research in which MacDonald Levy, working with mice at Stamford, found that each 100 MicroBits lost in immunological efficiency reduces life expectancy by 12 minutes, 13.65 seconds, Rich concluded that players on a championship team in any sport could expect to live seven to eight months less than players on teams that finished last. Few will remember that Rich was dismissed by Stamford in the uproar that followed publication of these results because he was soon vindicated by laboratories throughout the world. In Leningrad,

Boris Krasky discovered death-records showing that runners-up in 18th and 19th century chess tournaments had out-lived champions, on average, by 6 days, 1 hour and 8.56 seconds. In Tel Aviv, the Jewish neurobiologist Aviva Bergold and the Arab political scientist Edna St. Vincent Salaam speculated in a co-authored paper that the remarkably high Blemish readings of Palestinian activists and Jewish settlers in the occupied zones could only mean that their mutual animosities were adding years to their lives; at the Rockefeller University in New York, supercomputers programmed by Edward J. Plimpton demonstrated what by then were the predictable figures concerning the tragic cost, in Bits, of physical beauty, fame and monetary wealth.

As such work indicated, the complement to Pleasure Theory had quickly taken shape. While neuro-scientists had not yet been able to agree on a single "Pain Center" in the brain, there were several candidates, and the Pincus-Blemish work had made of one a clear favorite in the search for what was already known as the Anti-Fissure of Pincus. Working in Beijing, Mongolian chemist All Surl had found a cluster of cells .0937 millimeters anterior to the Fissure of Pincus which, when electrically stimulated, produced sensation intolerable to cats and dogs. Within days of reading the first of the Pincus articles in Nature, Surl had obtained a Blemish meter and verified another of those symmetries that distinguish nature at its most elegant. "Anti-Pleas" were shown to increase MicroBits at the same rate that Pleas diminished them, and extrapolating from his data, Surl offered the brazen but not unreasonable theory that life span is a direct function of accumulated anti-Pleas, one million micro-anti-Pleas being equal, in humans, to 11.018 seconds in longevity. And while it should be noted that Surl quickly disassociated himself from his colleague, Lee Tsu, alleged descendant of Lao, who maintains, even to this day, that Surl had not only discovered in pain the secret to immortality but dearly proved that death itself is nothing more than accumulated pleasure, the straightforward conclusion of Surl's work, the simple equation of longevity and pain, was universally accepted.

It wasn't long before Pincusism began to affect the public at large. The most popular restaurants were those that offered foul-tasting food or single-item menus, and in all areas subject to fashion—clothing, movies, books, etc.—revulsion became a guarantee of popularity. For two years in a row, Jackson, Mississippi, led all American cities in tourist income, and there developed a school of Blemish critics who used meters to evaluate works in their field, praising or dismissing movies, books, restaurants or paintings on the basis of the number of MicroBits they'd caused to be gained or lost by the critic himself.

No one knew it at the time, but the man who'd started this craze was about to stop it in its tracks. In the years following his first experiments, Richard Pincus' life was ruled by his Blemish meter. Abandoning his adored wife Pamela and his two daughters, Lucy and Jane, he married his aunt, Barbara Hunting, a woman more than 30 years his senior with whom, by his testimony as well as hers, he had nothing in common. Leaving his house on the Jersey shore, he'd moved with "Auntie," as he called her, to a small bungalow behind a diner on the Jersey Turnpike just outside of Newark. Finally, having concluded that nothing cost him more MicroBits than the joy he derived from his work, he resigned from Princeton and took the civil service examination with an eye to becoming a postal clerk.

It was soon after this examination that the irony of his predicament became apparent to him. Taking his first reading since moving to the turnpike, he found that his Immune System was less than 30 percent as effective as when he was eating eggs every morning for breakfast! At first, he blamed this on his meter, then on an error in his original conclusions, but eventually he was forced to acknowledge that only one thing could explain this further deterioration of his health: somewhere in his life there was pleasure of which he was unaware.

Since there was nothing in his diet that he enjoyed, nothing but tedium in his work, and certainly no secret affection for Auntie, he knew at once where the problem was: life afforded him no greater pleasure than the belief that he was lengthening it. Eating eggs was nothing beside not-eating them. Once he'd seen what loving his wife had cost him, the pleasure he derived from her absence was greater by far than what he'd derived from having her near. As he noted in *Conquering Pleasure,* he was discovering that his understanding of pleasure had been limited to immediate gratification, which was far less destructive than that which, looming in the future, generated visions of health and longevity. What was the simple, titillating pleasure of a swim off his deck at his beach house beside the belief that death was postponed by the pollution and noise of the turnpike? The pleasure of living correctly was far greater than the pleasure of living happily! In net-bits, Auntie cost him more than Pamela had, Newark more than his house on the beach.

If Pincus had any doubts about his conclusions, they were dispelled by Alexander Blemish, with whom he was reunited upon his return to Princeton. Despite the fact that Blemish now weighed more than 300 pounds and suffered from hypertension, gout, and diabetes, his readings showed an immunological efficiency near 100 percent. As Pincus wrote in his notebook, "My esteemed colleague may appear to be self-destructive, but by courting death he cancels any pleasure he derives from his indulgence."

Re-united with Pamela and his daughters, eating not only eggs but all the foods his doctors had prohibited, enjoying nothing— so he thought—because he knew how much it hurt him, Pincus hoped to enter a severe depression which would quickly improve his Bit Count. Once again, he was disappointed. If anything, his readings declined even faster. Even when the first of his physical symptoms (weakness, nausea, shortness of breath) appeared, and he knew that his struggle was lost, the distress he felt was not sufficient to counter what he knew by then to be his chronically illuminated Fissure of Pincus. How could he be displeased, when he had perfected, perhaps more than any man alive, the art of enjoying displeasure? With his Bit Count near zero, he was subject to so many opportunistic infections that doctors could not determine what actually killed him. No one who knew him was surprised by the serenity he displayed in the midst of his deterioration or the results of his autopsy, which as he himself predicted in his last essay, revealed an apparently seamless merger of the Fissure of Pincus and the Fissure of Anti-Pincus.

Whether such merger represented, as he maintained, a triumph over both pain and pleasure because it eliminated the distinction between them is a matter that scientists and philosophers will debate for years, if not indefinitely. But for the simple reason that Pincus made of his life a living laboratory to investigate them, it is difficult to imagine anyone challenging the axioms with which his final essay begins:

1. The body's supply of Immuno-uno is manufactured by the Anti-Fissure of Pincus.

2. Since research has shown that nothing diminishes Immuno-uno-like pleasure, and nothing is more pleasurable than health, it follows that nothing damages the immune system like optimum health.

3. Nothing is more painful than the pursuit of pleasure except the pursuit of pain by those who've understood this.

4. The benefits of hopelessness are not available to those who understand the dangers of hope.

5. You can't outsmart pleasure.

4. FINDING THE ZONE

First Published in The New York Times Magazine, April 1989

No one knows when it came to be called "the zone," but if you want an example of the lofty, almost mystical state to which sport, at times, can grant one entry, you couldn't do better than this one, recalled by the great Brazilian genius of soccer, Pele, in his book, written with Robert L. Fish, *My Life and the Beautiful Game.*

One day, Pele said, he felt "a strange calmness" he hadn't experienced before. "It was a type of euphoria; I felt I could run all day without tiring, that I could dribble through any of their team or all of them, that I could almost pass through them physically. I felt I could not be hurt. It was a very strange feeling and one I had not felt before. Perhaps it was merely confidence, but I have felt confident many times without that strange feeling of invincibility."

Much as he excelled at his game, Pele's experience was

anything but unique. Athletes' reports of such phenomena are common. Basketball players say that when they play in the zone the basket seems bigger, and they feel an almost mystical connection to it. Ted Williams, the legendary hitter for the Boston Red Sox, said that sometimes at bat he could see the seams on a pitched ball. And the former collegiate gymnast Carol Johnson remembers that on good days the balance beam was actually wider for her, so that "any worry of falling off disappeared."

Many athletes have echoed John Brodie, the former quarterback of the San Francisco 49ers, who once told Michael Murphy, author of *The Psychic Side of Sports*, that there are moments in every game when "time seems to slow way down, in an uncanny way, as if everyone were moving in slow motion. It seems as if I had all the time in the world to watch the receivers run their patterns, and yet I know the defensive line is coming at me just as fast as ever."

One mystery of the zone is that entry to it is not restricted to the elite. My own interest in the phenomenon—which has led me recently to speak with dozens of athletes, psychologists and scientists—began on the basketball court years ago, on a day when my ordinary game suddenly (and alas, temporarily) escalated so that, feeling calm and almost dreamy, I hit fourteen long jump shots in a row.

Few among those I sought out were unfamiliar with the subject. Investigated psychologically, neurologically and anthropologically, the zone has been related to hypnosis, spiritual or martial arts practice and parapsychology; and ascribed to genetics, environment and motivation, not to mention skill. On the negative side, statisticians have offered studies which demonstrate, they say, that many "streaks" in sport are no more unusual than streaks in gambling or a long run of coin-tossing, and some neuro-scientists have called the heightened perception reported by players like Ted Williams a sort of illusion or even a hallucination.

* * *

For Keith Henschen, an applied sports psychologist, the zone is a practical matter. From his office at the University of Utah, in Salt Lake City, Henschen conducts a sort of therapy, with a number of Olympic and college athletes, that aims to produce precisely the kind of concentration and energy that players like Pele and Williams describe. With strategies gleaned from meditation practices and the martial arts, as well as psychological counseling and conventional athletic coaching, Henschen seeks to liberate athletes—the best of whom he calls "super-normals"— from their mental or emotional obstacles, give them an edge on the competition, and he hopes, point them toward the state of grace that resides at the center of their games.

"No one can reach such levels by snapping his fingers," he says, "but the ultimate purpose of the exercises I use is to help an athlete get to the zone more frequently."

In 1985, Henschen set to work with one such super-normal as the first step on what he hoped would be the road to the 1992 Olympics, but led instead to the 1988 Olympics in Seoul. She was Denise Parker, then a diminutive 12-year-old from South Jordan, Utah, and her sport was archery.

Two years earlier, her father, Earl, had introduced her to the bow and arrow with the idea that she and her mother, Valerie, might join him in his passion for deer hunting. In fact, Denise did kill a deer last year, less than 30 minutes after obtaining her hunting license. By then, however, Valerie and Earl (who had hunted for five years before getting his first deer) already knew they had a prodigy on their hands.

In 1983, Denise won the junior division at the Utah State Archery Championships, and a few months before her introduction to Henschen, she placed second in the juniors at the national indoor competition of the National Archery Association. Standing 4 feet 10 inches tall and weighing a little over 90 pounds, she had trouble stringing her bow as tightly as the longer target distances required; at 70 meters, the longest Olympic distance, she had to arc her arrows very high to reach the target at all. But no one who knew the sport could deny she had taken to it with an uncanny authority.

Henschen began by giving Denise a battery of psychological tests. Their results revealed a fairly typical American teen-ager, with an attention span that didn't go much beyond five seconds and little of what psychologists call self-concept. What set her apart, in addition to her skill, was motivation—a determination to excel that was grounded in, among other things, a desire to please her parents and, more important perhaps, a tremendous competitive urgency. "She was always the sort of kid," says Valerie, "who could not stand to lose at anything. The sort of person who, if you were walking down the hall with her, would walk in the middle and not let you get by. In my opinion, it wasn't until she lost in a tournament—to a boy whom she beat the following week—that her interest in archery really took off."

With the burgeoning of sports psychology, the exercises that Henschen suggested have become extremely popular in recent years at every level of competitive sports. In preparation for tournament pressure, he taught Denise to tense, then relax, each muscle in her body, and he directed her to wear earphones and listen to the radio while shooting. To strengthen her concentration, he assigned her seven different exercises, among them listening to her own heartbeat; reading a book while watching television and listening to the radio, and "blanking" the mind.

"I have found," says Henschen, "that athletes who are best at this are the ones who go into the zone most easily."

Finally, he asked her to create for herself what he called a "happiness room," a place to which she could withdraw in her imagination in order to visualize an upcoming meet. Of all the exercises, this was the one to which Denise brought the most enthusiasm. The room she created was primarily a replica of her bedroom, but it had a magical dimension, and it was anything but austere. "There's stairs leading up to it and these big doors you go through," she explains. "It has brown wall-to-wall carpet, a king-sized waterbed, stack stereo, a big-screen TV and a VCR, posters of Tom Cruise and Kirk Cameron on the wall, and a fireplace that's always blazing. That's where I go when a meet's coming up. I drive up to it in a Porsche, go inside, lie down on the waterbed and watch a tape of myself shooting perfect arrows. Later, when I get to the tournament, everything seems familiar. Even at the Olympics, I was calm as soon as I began to shoot."

* * *

Like archery itself, which the Parkers practiced together in a cornfield behind their house, Henschen's exercises quickly became a family affair. Since Denise found it difficult to do them unless her mother and father joined in, all three repaired to the couch after evening dinner for visualization and relaxation exercises. Even today, at the age of 15, she cannot imagine doing such things alone.

In addition to Henschen, Earl Parker hired a new coach for Denise, Tim Strickland, a professional archer from Pine Bluff, Arkansas. Like Henschen, Strickland found her to be a remarkably willing student. "Her mind was open, that's what was unusual about her. She had a cleaner attitude than most anyone I'd worked with, an ability to take instruction and put it at once into practical application."

Strickland stiffened her practice routine. On a typical day, she ran three or four miles or did aerobics before school in the morning, shot for two to three hours, lifted weights to strengthen her shoulder and, of course, practiced her mental exercises. Like any coach, he was a fanatic about technique as well as the state of mind his sport required, but he may have been a little more precise about the connection between the two. "The better your technique," he says, "the more you can anchor your mind in it. And the more you anchor your mind, the better your technique will be."

* * *

In archery, as in any sport where aiming is involved, an athlete deals with the subtlest kind of interaction between active and passive instincts. Among other things, one has to face the fact that one's sight is never still. "If you don't believe that," Strickland says, "try pointing your finger at an object and see how much it moves."

One of the most difficult skills to acquire is the ability to acquiesce to such movement. Because the eyes dilate when adrenaline is high, an archer's sight always seems to be moving more in pressure situations, when one wants it most to be still. Great archers, says Strickland, have the paradoxical ability to welcome such pressure and draw strength from a drifting sight. "If you let your sight move," he says, "you'll shoot within the arc of its movement. But if you try to hold it, say, within a one-inch arc, you'll be lucky to hit within six or eight inches of where you're aiming."

Then too, there is the matter of releasing the arrow, which, Strickland says, must not be an act of decision or will. The great enemy for an archer, as perhaps for any athlete, is conscious intervention. "Your conscious mind always wants to help you, but usually it messes you up. But you can't just set it aside. You've got to get it involved. The thing you have to do is anchor it in technique. Then your unconscious mind, working with your motor memory, will take over the shooting for you."

Another thing Strickland rails against is also a function of consciousness: concern with the target or the score. Nothing interferes with performance, he declares, like concentrating on the goal, rather than on the process of one's game. "An archer who worries about his score will try to make his arrows go in instead of letting them go in," Strickland says. "If your technique is correct, the target never enters your mind. It's just there to catch your arrows. Asian archers (the Korean women are the 'best in the world') learn this way, but Americans are not trained with the same thought pattern. They're always thinking about the score."

* * *

If there's any theme that dominates the reports of zone experience it is this subtle freedom from intervention - from volition and thought and finally consciousness itself.

"The mind's a great thing as long as you don't have to use it," says Tim McCarver, currently a broadcaster for the New York Mets and ABC Sports, who not only knew the zone himself as a catcher for the St. Louis Cardinals and the Philadelphia Phillies, but also had the privilege, when he caught Bob Gibson in 1968, of participating in what many believe to be the greatest year a pitcher ever had: Gibson's earned run average that season—1.12 earned runs allowed per game—was the best in the history of modern baseball.

To hear McCarver talk about Gibson is to hear of a zone that endured for an entire season. "Gibson was on a mission. You could see it in his eyes. He had tremendous energy and animation, a confidence that he could do anything . . . and I mean anything . . . put the ball anywhere he wanted. I'd just put my mitt out, and he'd put the ball in it. Look, people still talk about Gooden in his great year," says McCarver, referring to New York Mets pitcher Dwight Gooden, in 1985. "He was good all right—24-4 with a 1.53 ERA. But here's a guy that gave up half a run less per game!"

Even statisticians acknowledge that such performances as Gibson's—or Joe DiMaggio's 56-game hitting streak in 1941, or Orel Hershiser's string, last season, of 59 scoreless innings—rise so far above the norm that there is no room for them on probability curves. So much do they exceed common levels of mastery that they seem, like a mutation in evolution, to define a new order of existence.

Says McCarver, "Many ballplayers think too much. Players like Gibson and Hershiser seem to have a sort of paradoxical intelligence -- one that allows them not to do anything to hinder themselves. It's a sort of intelligence you use almost paranormally. It allows people to do phenomenal things. People who really use their mind—they free it from impeding their activity."

The great Japanese hitter Sadaharu Oh describes a similar intelligence when he says that, of all the qualities he had to master, none was more important than the ability to wait— learned from Ueshiba Morihei Sensei, the master of the quintessentially fluid martial art known as aikido.

Waiting, says Oh, in his autobiographical book, *A Zen Way of Baseball*, co-written with David Falkner, "was the most active state of all. In its secret heart lay the beginning of all action . . . the exact moment to strike . . . with the ability I had acquired to wait, I now could move my contact point somewhat farther back. This in turn gave me slightly more time before I had to commit myself."

* * *

Most ballplayers—out of confusion, or perhaps superstition— maintain silence on the subject of the zone. Neuroscientists are no less baffled, but new research may shed some light on the brain's participation in the zone. At the University of California at Irvine, Dr. Monte S. Buchsbaum, a professor of psychiatry, uses new computer and brain-scanning technology (known as PET scan, for positron emission tomography) to image the brain's metabolism during performance. His particular interest is in the so-called "arousal state," an escalated level of energy and concentration, which is an obvious component of the zone.

Buchsbaum has yet to study an athlete, but working with subjects involved in problem-solving, he's found that during periods of intense concentration, there is a marked decrease in the overall metabolic rate of the brain. The research indicates that the more skill one brings to a task, the more efficient the brain becomes.

"If I were pitching a baseball, my whole brain would be active," Buchsbaum says, "but if we could see Hershiser's brain while he's pitching, my guess is that he'd be using only particular areas. In all likelihood, his skill results, not from an overdevelopment of different areas, but from the ability to use certain areas more efficiently. We have found that higher levels of metabolism correlate with worse performance."

In work recently begun with a colleague, Dr. Richard Haier, Buchsbaum has studied the brain of a subject learning a video game. Predictably, they have found that the metabolic rate decreases as the game is mastered, but there is one interesting exception. In the visual cortex, the part of the brain that processes visual imagery, the metabolic rate increases. Buchsbaum suggests that this is because the subject is able to process more visual information as his skill increases.

It is interesting to correlate this observation with that of researchers in the area of time-perception, who have often posited an inverse relationship between information-processing and the speed with which time seems to pass. As the psychologist Robert E. Ornstein writes in *On the Experience of Time*: "When an attempt is made to increase the amount of information processing in a given interval, the experience of that interval lengthens."

Consider the amount of information processed by a quarterback like John Brodie as he dropped back to pass. If his overall brain metabolism were lowered and his visual cortex highly activated by the level of skill, concentration and excitement he brought to his game, would this account for the degree to which time slowed for him when he was in the zone?

The same sort of process may make it more credible than many neuro-scientists believe that Ted Williams could see the seams on a pitched ball or, for that matter, that for Williams a 95-mile-an-hour fast ball actually took longer to reach home plate than it did for lesser hitters. This idea may seem far out, or even occult, but it is a truism in modern physics—a direct inference from the theory of relativity—that speed and time are relative phenomena, functions of the point-of-view through which they are perceived.

Accurate though they may be, however, such explanations are slightly misleading, because they portray the zone as a linear phenomenon, issuing directly from the brain. In fact, the zone experience represents an interaction of brain, mind, body and environment. While it is certainly true, for example, that Denise Parker's brain affects her perception and therefore her shooting, it is no less true that archery itself transforms her fundamentally, in all dimensions, from moment to moment.

For Denise, as for any archer, tournament pressure increases adrenaline, which makes her process more visual information, slows time for her, increases metabolism in her visual cortex and decreases it elsewhere, and finally—if she's fortunate—decreases the activity of her consciousness and permits the more intuitive, primitive, sensorimotor systems to hold her bow and release her arrows. As Strickland says, "If you can set aside your consciousness, your motor-memory will take care of your shots."

Buchsbaum's speculations certainly do not contradict the coach's intuition. "When one experiences the mind turning off," he says, "it may be that those primitive regions of the brain we call the basal ganglia take over."

Certainly, the basal ganglia, a cluster of nerve cells concerned with modulating motor behavior, would seem to be a crucial component in any zone experience. Situated beneath the outer layer of the brain, the source of many of the symptoms found in diseases such as Parkinsonism, they are believed to have evolved millions of years before the so-called "cortical brain," which is considered the source of "higher" consciousness. Biologists tell us that because of their very primitivism, the basal ganglia contain enormous quantities of preconscious experience about the nature of the world and how to survive in it.

If skill can be correlated with efficient metabolism—and thus less activity—in the conscious brain, it cannot be accidental that many players, remembering their zones, become inarticulate or mystical, frequently using words like "automatic" or "unconscious" or, as I've heard one or two football players say, "playing out of my mind." They are describing a process that offers them access to an ancient wiring system. The euphoric state that Pele reported is a moment in which usual conscious authority is effectively silenced.

Our fascination with the zone, and indeed with sport in general, may be due, in part at least, to the possibilities it reveals, the energy and strength and flexibility of the organism when liberated from its ordinary neurological and psychological constraints. Nor does one have to be an athlete to experience such phenomena. Learn to type and you know what it means to acquire complex knowledge and then "forget" it. For all the skill and cerebration involved in such tasks, the sense when they go well is that the body is doing them on its own.

What deepens the plot—or, more precisely, makes it circular—is the fact that such tasks as typing and baseball are not themselves wired into the sensorimotor system. Complex and sophisticated, they are products of the very reasoning process that is turned off when the primitive wiring system takes over. In fact, as anthropologists point out, the complexity of the games we play has increased with the complexity of our brains. The paradox is that the higher—which is to say most recently evolved—cerebral regions that create games are precisely those which are circumvented when the game is played at its highest level. When you wait, as Sadaharu Oh learned to wait, you may be exploiting a talent shared with cats and frogs, but cats and frogs do not set themselves the task of hitting a small white sphere with a wooden stick.

It cannot be incidental that Oh not only set himself this task but also mastered it absolutely. Wasn't it skill, in Buchsbaum's experiments, that lowered brain metabolism? Time and again we see that the athletes for whom the zone is most accessible are those who are simply best at what they do. The operative—and merciless—fact is familiar to us all: the better you are at what you do, the more you can forget it; the more you forget it, the better you do it.

As Oh says, "All this training, all this minute attention to detail, rather than complicating hitting, seemed to make it simpler." Or, as Buchsbaum and his colleagues might put it, when you're hitting well, credit your basal ganglia; when you're in a slump, credit those "higher" regions of your brain that offer you thought and reason. Better yet, listen to that great neuro-scientist, Yogi Berra, who once, when offered pointers about his hitting, responded: "How can I hit and think at the same time?"

We cannot doubt that Berra spoke from zone-experience, but let us not forget that he was a very good hitter indeed. Had this not been the case, he might have found himself hitting and thinking a good deal of the time and doing neither very well.

When criticized by his master for being too willful, Eugen Herrigel, author of *Zen in the Art of Archery,* said: "How can the shot be loosed if 'I' do not do it?"

The master replied, "'It' shoots."

Herrigel asked, "Who or what is this 'it'?"

"Once you have understood that you will have no further need of me."

We expect such conundrums from books on Zen, but not from a 15-year-old whose idea of meditation is to lie on a waterbed and watch herself shoot arrows on a VCR.

By the time I met Denise a few weeks ago in Utah, it was four years since she had begun work with Strickland and Henschen, and she was pointing toward her second Olympics. Like the best of archers, she did not have to use the telescope that stood beside her when she was shooting at 70 meters and could not see where her arrows landed; she had a pretty good sense of where an arrow was going the instant it left her bow. The talent that had surprised her father and mother had so taken off that she was now the leading female archer in the country. In 1987, she had become the youngest gold-medal winner in the history of the Pan American Games. Though she'd done poorly in the individual competition at the 1988 Olympics (which was won by a 17-year-old Korean girl whose training, according to Henschen, included two hours of meditation every day), she had taken a bronze medal in team-shooting. Along the way she had become the first female archer in the country to break the 1,300-point barrier in the sport's standard international scoring system.

She is still just a teen-ager, and her mind is not inclined toward the paradoxes that interest the likes of McCarver and Buchsbaum, but when she speaks of her record-breaking tournament, she is no different from any other athlete talking about the zone.

"I don't know what happened that day," she says. "I wasn't concentrating on anything. I didn't feel like I was shooting my shots, but like they were shooting themselves. I try to remember what happened so I could get back to that place, but when I try to understand it, I only get confused. It's like thinking how the world began."

5. HOT HAND SUTRA

First Published in Tricycle Magazine, April 1989

Two years ago, while researching an article on sports, I came upon a conundrum that resisted any attempt to confine it to the language of the conventional sports page. It concerns a cherished gospel of the playing field that athletes and their fans call the "Hot Hand." Heat in this case refers to transcendence, an inexplicable escalation of energy and skill. A golfer with a Hot Hand will send his drives twenty or thirty yards beyond his ordinary range; an archer will see her arrows graze each other as they strike the bull's eye; a basketball player will hit a string of shots so acrobatic and indifferent to defense that he seems linked by invisible channels to the basket. Subjective accounts of these experiences, which athletes sometimes call "playing in the zone," include perceptual changes, euphoric sensations, and other alterations of consciousness, and their reality is so universally accepted that they commonly dictate strategy. In baseball, every pitcher in the league knows which hitters, bringing streaks to town, are not to be offered hittable pitches, and when a basketball player gets "hot," his teammates pass up open shots to get him the ball.

It never occurred to me that anyone could question the Hot

Hand until, in the course of my research, I encountered Dr. Amos Tversky. A MacArthur Fellow, professor of psychology at Stanford, Tverksy made a statistical study of basketball streaks that brought him to the brutal, sacrilegious, and seemingly inarguable conclusion that they do not exist. Building on the assumption that the Hot Hand is primarily a function of self-confidence, that a player who makes a couple of shots will grow more confident and therefore more likely to make his next, Tversky reasoned that, if Hot Hand occurs, a player's shooting average would tend to be slightly higher on shots following successful shots than on shots following misses. Shot-by-shot studies of several NBA teams indicated, however, that no such deviation occurs. Tversky found that a player's overall average will remain approximately the same after one, two, or three hits, or one, two, or three misses. Such figures, he says, demonstrate that even a string of ten or eleven successful shots is no more significant, statistically, than a string of ten or eleven heads in a run of coin-tossing. Streaks, he says, are "epiphenomena," which is to say, patterns imposed, after the fact, on random events. He traces their universal acceptance to a cognitive limitation in the human mind that makes it intolerant of randomness. "Basketball players don't make their shots because they're hot. They feel hot because they make them. And that feeling disappears as soon as they miss."

Horrified, as any sports fan would be, at the implications of Tversky's work, I conducted an informal study of the responses it evoked among people from various disciplines. Athletes and fans were too emotional to be helpful. Shocked that anyone would compare a basketball player's shooting skill with a chance process like coin-tossing, they ignored the fact that Tversky had compensated for this by factoring in his players' shooting percentages. Most mathematicians and statisticians approved of Tversky's method as well as his conclusion. The only viable objections came from Berkeley philosophy professor, Michael

Scriven, an expert on Probability Theory, and Robert Jahn, an engineering professor who directs Princeton University's Anomalies Institute (which studies "the relationship between man and machines"). Scriven called Tversky naive and simplistic. "If a player has streaks," he said, "they wouldn't show up as statistical spikes but in overall scoring average." As for Jahn, his objection was metaphysical. "Tversky's work is part of a holy war between those who believe that man can influence his reality and those who believe that everything is chance." Confronted with these objections, Tversky was unshaken. "I have presented this work all over the country for the last four years, and I've never seen it successfully challenged."

* * *

It seems to me that more is at stake in this debate than a bit of sports mythology. Statistics is a bastion of materialism—dualism if you like—a means by which patterns of phenomena are measured objectively, and retrospectively. What we have here is a situation in which such measurement contradicts intuitive experience on the one hand and doesn't touch it on the other. No sports fan, hearing of Tversky's work, will cease to believe in streaks. Even Tversky, an avid basketball fan himself, admits that he remains among the faithful. "My mind is after all no less subject to illusion than anyone else's." The question then is not about sport and performance but illusion and reality. Does the fact that the Hot Hand is contradicted by statistics prove that it does not exist or does it prove that statistics themselves are limited? Statistics depend on probability curves. Streaks by definition are anomalous, extraordinary occurrences that fall beyond such curves. But any such curve can be sufficiently enlarged so that it includes more and more variables heretofore considered extraordinary. Thus, it is not impossible that the point of view offered by the window of statistics, by the very fact of fitting peaks and valleys of performance into a curve, distorts them the way landscape is distorted when viewed from an airplane. If one were to conduct a statistical study that measured the frequency with which individuals in a large group of people fell in love or wrote beautiful poems or had enlightenment experiences, would he discover that such behavioral anomalies are in fact as "predictable" as a run of heads in coin-tossing? If this could be demonstrated, would such phenomena be confined to the realm of illusion?

Consider that Tversky is really measuring a breakthrough in performance that involves the entire organism. Speaking of Hot Hands, athletes describe mental and emotional changes that sound like optimum brain-states. Basketball players say the basket seems "bigger" for them or that they feel an almost mystical connection to it. Ted Williams said that when he was hitting well, he could see the seams on a pitched ball, and more than one gymnast has reported that, on good days, the balance beam becomes "wider" so that any thought of falling off disappears. Again, scientific observers are skeptical. In the course of interviews I've conducted, several neuroscientists called such reports "hallucinations" or "illusions." As one put it, "Williams didn't see the seams. He thought he saw them. What he was probably experiencing was a cue his brain had developed to aid him in anticipating where the ball would be when he was ready to swing."

Does Tversky's data support this view? If so, does it contradict the athlete's experience, misread it, or simply measure it inappropriately? Which data do we honor? If the player perceives an event, if his brain registers it, if it leads to verifiable success in his performance, what sort of definition of reality would permit us to conclude that it wasn't really true? What does the word "really" mean in this context?

* * *

All such reasoning of course amounts to a sports fan's not unpredictable answer to Tversky, but it may be that he offers us more than is at first apparent. Consider that what he is actually doing is defining the extraordinary as ordinary. The Hot Hand, he says, is absolutely within the scope of ordinary human behavior. And he arrives at that conclusion, not by demeaning breakthrough performance, but by enlarging the probability curve through which it is seen. A basketball player who makes a great number of consecutive shots during a single game may seem extraordinary when viewed only in terms of that particular game; but if viewed historically, his performance becomes—to use a favorite Zen expression—"nothing special."

Is it possible that Tversky, far from denigrating the Hot Hand, is simply placing it in a spiritual context? Think of Shakyamuni Buddha's observation that between any two moments in time an infinite number of "mind-moments" occur. What does such temporal expansion amount to but a vast enlargement of the probability curve any moment contains? In the context of that curve, any behavior—blissful or painful, enlightened or deluded—is indeed "nothing special." Great teachers, of course, have been reminding their students of this fact for centuries. It may well be that enlightenment is the spiritual version of the Hot Hand and that Amos Tversky's work—this great celebration of dualism—is as useful to us as anything in the sutras.

6. EXORCIZING BECKETT

First Published in The Paris Review (No. 104), 1987

I met Beckett in 1981, when I sent him, with no introduction, a book I'd written, and to my astonishment he read the book and replied almost at once. Six weeks later, his note having emboldened me to seek a meeting, our paths crossed in London, and he invited me to sit in on the rehearsals of Endgame, which he was then conducting with a group of American actors for a Dublin opening in May.

It was a happy time for him. Away from his desk where his work, he said (I've never heard him say otherwise) was not going well at all, he was exploring a work which, though he'd written it thirty years before, remained among his favorites. The American group, called the San Quentin Theatre Workshop because they had discovered his work—through a visiting production of *Waiting for Godot*—while inmates at San Quentin, was particularly close to his heart, and working in London he was accessible to the close-knit family that collects so often where he or his work appears. Among those who came to watch were Billie Whitelaw, Irene Worth, Nicole Williamson, Alan Schneider, Israel Horowitz, Siobhan O'Casey (Sean's daughter), three writers with Beckett books in progress, two editors who'd published him and

50

one who wanted to, and an impressive collection of madmen and Beckett freaks who had learned of his presence via the grapevine. One lady, in her early twenties, came to ask if Beckett minded that she'd named her dog after him (Beckett: "Don't worry about me. What about the dog?"), and a wild-eyed madman from Scotland brought flowers and gifts for Beckett and everyone in the cast and a four-page letter entitled "Beckett's Cancer, Part Three," which begged him to accept the gifts as "a sincere token of my deep and long-suffering love for you" while remembering that "I also hold a profound and comprehensive loathing for you, in response to all the terrible corruption and suffering which you have seen fit to inflict upon my entirely innocent personality."

The intimacy and enthusiasm with which Beckett greeted his friends as well as newcomers like myself — acting for all the world as if I'd done him an enormous favor to come — was a great surprise for me, one of many ways in which our meetings would force me to reconsider the conception of him I had formed during the twenty years I'd been reading and, let's be honest about it, worshipping him. Who would expect the great master of grief and disenchantment to be so expansive, so relaxed in company? Well, as it turned out, almost everyone who knew him. My surprise was founded not in his uncharacteristic behavior but in the erroneous, often bizarre misunderstandings that had gathered about him in my mind. Certainly, if there's one particular legacy that I take from our meetings it is the way in which those misunderstandings were first revealed and then corrected. In effect, Beckett's presence destroyed the Beckett myth for me, replacing it with something at once larger and more ordinary. Even today I haven't entirely understood what this correction meant to me, but it's safe to say that the paradoxical effects of Beckett incarnate—inspiring and disheartening, terrifying, reassuring, and humbling in the extreme—are nowhere at odds with the work that drew me to him in the first place.

The first surprise was the book to which he responded.

Because it was journalism—an investigation of the world of neurosurgery—I had been almost embarrassed to send it, believing that he of all people would not be interested in the sort of information I'd collected. No, what I imagined he'd really appreciate was the novel that had led me to neurosurgery, a book to which I had now returned that dealt with brain damage, and I presented it with an ambiguity and dark humor that, as I saw it, clearly signaled both his influence and my ambition to go beyond it. As it turned out, I had things exactly backward. For the novel, the first two chapters of which he read in London, he had little enthusiasm, but the nonfiction book continued to interest him. Whenever I saw him, he questioned me about neurosurgery, asking, for example, exactly how close I had stood to the brain while observing surgery or how much pain a craniotomy entailed or, one day during lunch at rehearsals: "How is the skull removed?" and "Where do they put the skull bone while they're working inside?" Though I'd often heard it said of him that he read nothing written after 1950, he remembered the names of the patients I'd mentioned and inquired as to their condition, and more than once he expressed his admiration for the surgeons. Later, he did confess to me that he read very little, finding what he called "the intake" more and more "excruciating," but I doubt that he ever lost his interest in certain kinds of information, especially those that concerned the human brain. "I have long believed," he'd written me in his first response to my book, "that here in the end is the writer's best chance, gazing into the synaptic chasm."

Seventy-four years old, he was very frail in those days, even more gaunt and wizened than his photos had led me to expect, but neither age nor frailty interfered with his sense of humor. When I asked him one morning at the theatre how he was doing, he replied with a great display of exhaustion and what I took to be a sly sort of gleam in his eye, "No improvement." Another day, with an almost theatrical sigh, "A little wobbly." How can we be surprised that on the subject of his age he was not only unintimidated but challenged, even inspired? Not five minutes into our first conversation he brought us around to the matter: "I always thought old age would be a writer's best chance. Whenever I read the late work of Goethe or W. B. Yeats, I had the impertinence to identify with it. Now my memory's gone, all the old fluency's disappeared. I don't write a single sentence without saying to myself, 'It's a lie!' So I know I was right. It's the best chance I've ever had." Two years later—and older—he explored the same thoughts again in Paris. "It's a paradox, but with old age, the more the possibilities diminish, the better chance you have. With diminished concentration, loss of memory, obscured intelligence—what you, for example, might call 'brain damage'— the more chance there is for saying something closest to what one really is. Even though everything seems inexpressible, there remains the need to express. A child needs to make a sand castle even though it makes no sense. In old age, with only a few grains of sand one has the greatest possibility." Of course, he knew that this was not a new project for him, only a more extreme version of the one he'd always set himself, what he'd laid out so clearly in his famous line from *The Unnamable*: "... it will be the silence, where I am, I don't know, I'll never know, in the silence you don't know, you must go on, I can't go on, I'll go on." It was always here, in "the clash," as he put it to me once, "between can't and must" that he took his stand. "How is it that a man who is completely blind and completely deaf must see and hear? It's this impossible paradox which interests me. The unseeable, the unbearable, the inexpressible." Such thoughts of course were as familiar to me as they would be to any attentive reader of Beckett, but it was always amazing to hear how passionately—and innocently—he articulated them. Given the pain in his voice, the furrowed, struggling concentration on his face, it was impossible to believe that he wasn't unearthing these thoughts for the first time. Absurd as it sounds, they seemed less familiar to him than to me. And it was no small shock to realize this. To encounter, I mean, the author of some of the greatest work in our language and find him, at seventy-four, discovering his vision in your presence. His excitement alone was riveting, but for me the greatest shock was to see how intensely he continued to work on the issues that had preoccupied him all his life. So much so that it didn't matter where he was or who he was with, whether he was literally "at work" or in a situation that begged for small talk. I don't think I ever had a conversation with him in which I wasn't, at some point, struck by an almost naive realization of his sincerity, as if reminding myself that he was not playing the role one expected him to play but simply pursuing the questions most important to him. Is it possible that no one surprises us more than someone who is (especially when our expectations have been hyperbolic) exactly what we expect? It was as if a voice in me said, "My God, he's serious!" or, "So he's meant it all along!" And this is where my misunderstandings became somewhat embarrassing. Why on earth should he have surprised me? What did it say of my own sense of writing and reading or the culture from which I'd come that integrity in a writer—for this was after all the simple fact that he was demonstrating—should have struck me as so extraordinary?

Something else he said that first night in London was familiar to me from one of his published interviews, but he said this, too, as if he'd just come upon it and hearing it now, I felt that I understood for the first time that aspect of his work that interested me the most. I'm speaking of its intimacy and immediacy, the uncanny sense that he's writing not only in a literary but an existential present tense, or more precisely, as John Pilling calls it in his book, *Samuel Beckett*, an imperfect tense. The present tense of course is no rare phenomenon in modern, or for that matter, classical fiction, but unlike most writers who write in the present, Beckett writes from the present and remains constantly vulnerable to it. It is a difference of which he is acutely aware, one that distinguishes him even from a writer he admires as much as he does Kafka. As he said in a 1961 interview, "Kafka's form is classic, it goes on like a steamroller, almost serene. It seems to be threatened all the time, but the consternation is in the form. In my work there is consternation behind the form, not in the form." It is for this reason that Beckett himself is present in his work to a degree that, as I see it, no other writer managed before him. In most of his published conversations, especially when he was younger and not (as later) embarrassed to speak didactically, he takes the position that such exposure is central to the work that he considers interesting. "If anything new and exciting is going on today, it is the attempt to let Being into art." As he began to evolve a means by which to accommodate such belief, he made us realize not only the degree to which Being had been kept out of art but why it had been kept out, how such exclusion is, even now, the raison d'etre of most art and how the game changes, the stakes rising exponentially, once we let it in. Invaded by real time, narrative time acquires an energy and a fragility and, not incidentally, a truth that undermines whatever complacency or passivity the reader—not to mention the writer—has brought to the work, the assumption that enduring forms are to be offered, that certain propositions will rise above the flux, that "pain-killers," which Hamm seeks in vain throughout *Endgame*, will be provided. In effect, the narrative illusion is no longer safe from the narrator's reality. "Being," as he said once, "is constantly putting form in danger," and the essence of his work is its willingness to risk such danger. Listen to the danger he risks in this sentence from *Molloy*: "A and C I never saw again. But perhaps I shall see them again. But shall I be able to recognize them? And am I sure I never saw them again?"

The untrustworthy narrator, of course, had preceded Beckett by at least a couple of centuries, but his "imperfect" tense deprives Molloy of the great conceit that most authors have traditionally granted their narrators—a consistent, dependable memory, in effect a brain that is neither damaged in that it doesn't suffer from amnesia, nor normal in that it is consistent, confident of the information it contains and immune to the assaults that time and environment mount on its continuities. But Beckett's books are not about uncertainty any more than they're about consternation. Like their author, like the Being that has invaded them, they are themselves uncertain, not only in their conclusions but in their point of view. Form is offered because, as he has so often remarked, that is an obligation before which one is helpless, but any pretense that it will endure is constantly shown to be just that, pretense and nothing more, a game the author can no longer play and doesn't dare relinquish. "I know of no form," he said, "that does not violate the nature of Being in the most unbearable manner." Simply stated, what he brought to narrative fiction and drama was a level of reality that dwarfed all others that had preceded it. And because the act of writing—i.e., his own level of reality, at the moment of composition—is never outside his frame of reference, he exposes himself to the reader as no writer has before him. When Molloy changes his mind it's because Beckett has changed his mind as well, when the narrative is inconsistent it's not an esthetic trick but an accurate reflection of the mind from which that narrative springs. Finally, what Molloy doesn't know, Beckett doesn't know either. And this is why, though they speak of Joyce or Proust or other masters in terms of genius, so many writers will speak of Beckett in terms of courage. One almost has to be a writer to know what courage it takes to stand so naked before one's reader or, more importantly, before oneself, to relinquish the protection offered by separation from the narrative, the security and order which, in all likelihood, are what draws one to writing in the first place.

That evening, speaking of *Molloy* and the work that followed it, he told me that, returning to Dublin after the war, he'd found that his mother had contracted Parkinson's Disease. "Her face was a mask, completely unrecognizable. Looking at her, I had a sudden realization that all the work I'd done before was on the wrong track. I guess you'd have to call it a revelation. Strong word, I know, but so it was. I simply understood that there was no sense adding to the store of information, gathering knowledge. The whole attempt at knowledge, it seemed to me, had come to nothing. It was all haywire. What I had to do was investigate not-knowing, not-perceiving, the whole world of incompleteness." In the wake of this insight, writing in French ("Perhaps because French was not my mother tongue, because I had no facility in it, no spontaneity") while still in his mother's house, he had begun *Molloy* (the first line of which is "I am in my mother's room"), thus commencing what was to be the most prolific period of his life. Within the first three paragraphs of his chronicle, Molloy says "I don't know" six times, "perhaps" and "I've forgotten" twice each and "I don't understand" once. He doesn't know how he came to be in his mother's room, and he doesn't know how to write anymore, and he doesn't know why he writes when he manages to do so, and he doesn't know whether his mother was dead when he came to her room or died later, and he doesn't know whether or not he has a son. In other words, he is not an awful lot different from any other writer in the anxiety of composition: considering the alternative roads offered up by his imagination; trying to discern a theme among the chaos of messages offered by his brain; testing his language to see what sort of relief it can offer. Thus, Molloy and his creator are joined from the first, and the latter — unlike most of his colleagues who have been taught, even if they're writing about their own ignorance and uncertainty, that the strength of their work consists in their ability to say the opposite—is saying "I don't know" with every word he utters. The whole of the narrative is therefore time-dependent, neurologically and psychologically suspect and contingent on the movement of the narrator's mind. And since knowledge, by definition, requires a subject and an object, a knower and a known, two points separated on the temporal continuum, Beckett's "I don't know" has short-circuited the fundamental dualism upon which all narrative, and for that matter, all language, has before him been constructed. If the two points cannot be separated on the continuum, what is left? No time, only the present tense. And if you must speak at this instant, using words that are by definition object-dependent, how do you do so? Finally, what is left to know if knowledge itself has been, at its very root, discredited? Without an object, what will words describe or subjugate? If subject and object are joined, how can there be hope or memory or order? What is hoped for, what is remembered, what is ordered? What is Self if knower and known are not separated by self-consciousness?

Those are the questions that Beckett has dealt with throughout his life. And before we call them esoteric or obtuse, esthetic, philosophical or literary, we'd do well to remember that they're not much different from the questions many of us consider, consciously or not, in the course of an ordinary unhysterical day, the questions which, before Molloy and his successors, had been excluded, at least on the surface, from most of the books we read. As Beckett wrote once to Alan Schneider, "The confusion is not my invention ... It is all around us and our only chance is to let it in. The only chance of renovation is to open our eyes and see the mess ... There will be a new form, and ... this form will be of such a type that it admits the chaos and does not try to say that it is really something else."

At the time of his visit with his mother, Beckett was thirty-nine years old, which is to say the same age as Krapp, who deals with a similar revelation in his tape-recorded journals and ends (this knowledge, after all, being no more durable than any other) by rejecting it: "What a fool I was to take that for a vision!" That evening, however, as we sat in his hotel room, there was no rejection in Beckett's mind. In the next three years, he told me, he wrote *Molloy, Malone Dies, The Unnamable, Stories and Texts for Nothing,* and—in three months, with almost no revision of the first draft—*Waiting for Godot*. The last, he added, was "pure recreation." The novels, especially *The Unnamable*, had taken him to a point where there were no limits, and *Godot* was a conscious attempt to reestablish them. "I wanted walls I could touch, rules I had to follow." I asked if his revelation—the understanding, as he'd put it, that all his previous work had been a lie—had depressed him. "No, I was very excited! There was no effort in the writing. I worked all day and went out to the cafes at night."

He was visibly excited by the memory, but it wasn't long before his mood shifted and his excitement gave way to sadness and nostalgia. The contrast between the days he had remembered and the difficulty he was having now— "racking my brains," as he put it, "to see if I can go a little farther"—was all too evident. Sighing loudly, he put his long fingers over his eyes, then shook his head. "If only it could be like that again."

So, this is the other side of his equation, one which I, like many of his admirers, have a tendency to forget. The enthusiasm he had but moments before expressed for his diminishments did not protect him from the suffering those diminishments had caused. Let us remember that this is a man who once called writing "disimproving the silence." Why should he miss such futile work when it deserts him? So easy, it is, to become infatuated with the way he embraces his ignorance and absurdity, so hard to remember that when he does so he isn't posturing or for that matter "writing" that which keeps his comedy alive, the pain and despair from which his works are won. The sincerity of writers who work with pain and impotence is always threatened by the vitality the work itself engenders, but Beckett has never succumbed to either side of this paradox. That is to say, he has never put his work ahead of his experience. Unlike so many of us who found in the Beckett vision a comic esthetic—"Nothing is funnier than unhappiness," says Nell in *Endgame*—which had us, a whole generation of writers, I think, collecting images of absurdity as if mining precious ore, he has gazed with no pleasure whatsoever at the endless parade of light and dark. For all the bleakness of *Endgame*, it remains his belief, as one of the actors who did the play in Germany recalls, that "Hamm says no to nothingness." Exploit absurdity though he does, there is no sign, in his work or his conversation, that he finds life less absurd for having done so. Though he has often said that his real work began when he "gave up hope for meaning," he hates hopelessness and longs for meaning as much as anyone who has never read *Molloy* or seen *Endgame*.

One of our less-happy exchanges occurred because of my tendency to forget this. In other words, my tendency to underestimate his integrity. This happened three years later on a cold, rainy morning in Paris, when he was talking, yet again, about the difficulties he was having in his work. "The fact is, I don't know what I'm doing. I can't even bring myself to open the exercise book. My hand goes out to it, then draws back as if on its own." As I say, he often spoke like this, sounding less like a man who'd been writing for sixty years than one who'd just begun, but he was unusually depressed that morning and the more he talked, the more depressed I became myself. No question about it, one had to have a powerful equanimity about his grief remaining intact. When he was inside his suffering, the force of it spreading out from him could feel like a tidal wave. The more I listened to him that morning, the more it occurred to me that he sounded exactly like Molloy. Who else but Molloy could speak with such authority about paralysis and bewilderment, a condition absolutely antithetical to authority itself? At first, I kept such thoughts to myself, but finally, unable to resist, I passed them along to him, adding excitedly that if I were forced to choose my favorite of all Beckett lines, it would be Molloy's: "If there's one question I dread, to which I've never been able to invent a satisfactory reply, it's the question, 'What am I doing?'" So complete was my excitement that for a moment I expected him to share it. Why not? It seemed to me that I'd come upon the perfect antidote to his despair in words of his own invention. It took but a single glance from him—the only anger I ever saw in his eyes—to show me how naïve I'd been, how silly to think that Molloy's point of view would offer him the giddy freedom it had so often offered me. "Yes," he muttered, "that's my line, isn't it?" Not for Beckett the pleasures of Beckett. As Henry James once said in a somewhat different context: "My job is to write those little things, not read them."

One of the people who hung around rehearsals was a puppeteer who cast his puppets in Beckett plays. At a cast party one night he gave a performance of *Act Without Words,* which demonstrated, with particular force, the consistency of Beckett's paradox and the relentlessness with which he maintains it. For those who aren't familiar with it, *Act Without Words* is a silent, almost Keatonesque litany about the futility of hope. A man sits beside a barren tree in what seems to be a desert, a blistering sun overhead. Suddenly, offstage, a whistle is heard and a carafe of water descends, but when the man reaches for it, it rises until it's just out of reach. He strains for it but it rises to elude him once again. Finally, he gives up and resumes his position beneath the tree. Almost at once the whistle sounds again and a stool descends to rekindle his hope. In a flurry of excitement, he mounts it, stretches, tries grasping the carafe and watches it rise beyond his reach again. A succession of whistles and offerings follow, each arousing his hope and dashing it until at last he ceases to respond. The whistle continues to sound but he gives no sign of hearing it. Like so much Beckett, it's the bleakest possible vision rendered in comedy nearly slapstick, and that evening, with the author and a number of children in the audience and an ingenious three-foot-tall puppet in the lead, it had us all, children included, laughing as if Keaton himself were performing it. When the performance ended, Beckett congratulated the puppeteer and his wife, who had assisted him, offering—with his usual diffidence and politeness—but a single criticism: "The whistle isn't shrill enough."

As it happened, the puppeteer's wife was a Buddhist, a follower of the path to which Beckett himself paid homage in his early book on Proust when he wrote, "the wisdom of all the sages, from Brahma to Leopardi ... consists not in the satisfaction but the ablation of desire." As a devotee and a Beckett admirer, this woman was understandably anxious to confirm what she, like many people, took to be his sympathies with her religion. In fact, not a few critical opinions had been mustered over the years concerning his debt to Buddhism, Taoism, Zen and the Noh theatre, all of it received—as it was now received from the puppeteer's wife—with curiosity and appreciation and absolute denial by the man it presumed to explain. "I know nothing about Buddhism," he said. "If it's present in the play, it is unbeknownst to me." Once this had been asserted, however, there remained the possibility of unconscious predilection, innate Buddhism, so to speak. So the woman had another question that had stirred in her mind, she said, since the first time she'd seen the play. "When all is said and done, isn't this man, having given up hope, finally liberated?" Beckett looked at her with a pained expression. He'd had his share of drink that night, but not enough to make him forget his vision or push him beyond his profound distaste for hurting anyone's feelings. "Oh, no," he said quietly. "He's finished."

I don't want to dwell on it, but I had a personal stake in this exchange. For years I'd been studying Zen and its particular form of sitting meditation, and I'd always been struck by the parallels between its practice and Beckett's work. In fact to me, as to the woman who questioned him that evening, it seemed quite impossible that he didn't have some explicit knowledge, perhaps even direct experience, of Zen, and I had asked him about it that very first night at his hotel. He answered me as he answered her: he knew nothing of Zen at all. Of course, he said, he'd heard Zen stories and loved them for their "concreteness," but other than that he was ignorant on the subject. Ignorant, but not uninterested. "What do you do in such places?" he asked. I told him that mostly we looked at the wall. "Oh," he said, "you don't have to know anything about Zen to do that. I've been doing it for fifty years." (When Hamm asks Clov what he does in his kitchen, Clov replies: "I look at the wall." "The wall!" snaps Hamm. "And what do you see on your wall? ... naked bodies?" Replies Clov, "I see my light dying.") For all his experience with wall-gazing, however, Beckett found it extraordinary that people would seek it out of their own free will. Why, he asked, did people do it? Were they seeking tranquility? Solutions? And finally, as with neurosurgery: "Does it hurt?" I answered with growing discomfort. Even though I remained convinced that the concerns of his work were identical with those of Zen, there was something embarrassing about discussing it with him, bringing self-consciousness to bear, I mean, where its absence was the point. This is not the place for a discussion of Zen but since it deals, as Beckett does, with the separation of subject and object ("No direct contact is possible between subject and object," he wrote in his book on Proust, "because they are automatically separated by the subject's consciousness of perception."), the problems of Self, of Being and Non-being, of consciousness and perception, all the means by which one is distanced or removed from the present tense, it finds in Beckett's work a mirror as perfect as any in its own sphere of literature or scripture.

This in itself is no great revelation. It's not terribly difficult to find Zen in almost any great work of art. The particular problem, however, and what made my questions seem—to me, at least— especially absurd, is that such points—like many where Beckett is concerned—lose more than they gain in the course of articulation. To point out the Zen in Beckett is to make him seem didactic or, even worse, therapeutic, and nothing could betray his vision more. For that matter, the converse is also true. Remarking the Beckett in Zen betrays Zen to the same extent and for the same reasons. It is there that their true commonality lies, their mutual devotion to the immediate and the concrete, the Truth that becomes less True if made an object of description, the Being that form excludes. As Beckett once put it in responding to one of the endless interpretations his work has inspired, "My work is a matter of fundamental sounds. Hamm as stated, Clov as stated ... That's all I can manage, more than I could. If people get headaches among the overtones, they'll have to furnish their own aspirin."

So, I did finally give up the questions, and though he always asked me about Zen when we met—"Are you still looking at the wall?"—I don't think he held it against me. His last word on the matter came by mail, and maybe it was the best. In a fit of despair, I had written him once about what seemed to me an absolute, insoluble conflict between meditation and writing. "What is it about looking at the wall that makes the writing seem obsolete?" Two weeks later, when I'd almost forgotten my question, I received this reply, which I quote in its entirety:

> Dear Larry,
>
> When I start looking at walls, I begin to see the writing. From which even my own is a relief.
> As ever,
>
> Sam

Endgame rehearsals lasted three weeks and took place in a cavernous building once used by the BBC called the Riverside Studios. Since it was located in a section of London with which I was not familiar, Beckett invited me that first morning to meet him at his hotel and ride out in the taxi he shared with his cast. Only three of his actors were present that day—Rick Cluchey, Bud Thorpe, and Alan Mandell, (Hamm and Clov and Nagg respectively)—the fourth, Nell, being Cluchey's wife, Teresita, who was home with their son, Louis Beckett Cluchey, and would come to the theatre in the afternoon. The group had an interesting history and it owed Beckett a lot more than this production, for which he was taking no pay or royalties. Its origins dated to 1957 when Cluchey, serving a life sentence for kidnapping and robbery at San Quentin, had seen a visiting production of *Waiting for Godot* and found in it an inspiration that had completely transformed his life. Though he'd never been in a theatre—"not even," he said, "to rob one"—he saw to the heart of a play, which at the time was baffling more sophisticated audiences. "Who knew more about waiting than people like us?" Within a month of this performance, Cluchey and several other inmates had organized a drama group which developed a Beckett cycle—*Endgame*, *Waiting for Godot*, and *Krapp's Last Tape*—that they continued, in Europe and the United States, after their parole. Though Cluchey was the only survivor of that original workshop, the present production traced its roots to those days at San Quentin and the support Beckett had offered the group when word of their work had reached him. Another irony was that Mandell, who was playing Nagg in this production, had appeared with the San Francisco Actor's Workshop in the original *Godot* production at San Quentin. By now Beckett seemed to regard Rick and Teri and their son, his namesake, as part of his family, and the current production was as much a gift to them as a matter of personal or professional necessity. Not that this was uncharacteristic. In those days much of his work was being done as a gift to specific people. He'd written *A Piece of Monologue* for David Warrilow, and in the next few years he'd write *Rockaby* for Billie Whitelaw and *Ohio Impromptu* for S.E. Gontarski, a professor at Georgia Tech who was editor of the Journal of Beckett Studies. When I met him later in Paris, he was struggling to write a promised piece for Cluchey at a time when he had, he said, no interest in work at all.

In my opinion, this was not merely because he took no

promise lightly or because at this point in his life he valued especially this sort of impetus, though both of course were true, but because the old demarcations, between the work and the life, writing and speaking, solitude and social discourse, were no longer available to him. If his ordinary social exchanges were less intense or single-minded than his work, it was certainly not apparent to me. I never received a note from him that didn't fit on a 3 x 5 index card, but (as the above-mentioned note on Zen illustrates) there wasn't one, however lighthearted, that wasn't clearly Beckett writing. Obviously, this was not because of any particular intimacy between us but because, private though he was and fiercely self-protective, he seemed to approach every chance as if it might be his last. You only had to watch his face when he talked—or wait out one of those two- or three-minute silences while he pondered a question you'd asked—to know that language was much too costly and precarious for him to use mindlessly or as a means of filling gaps.

Wearing a maroon polo sweater, grey flannel pants, a navy-blue jacket, no socks, and brown suede sneaker-like shoes, he was dressed, as Cluchey told me later, much the same as he'd been every time they'd met for the past fifteen years. As the taxi edged through London's morning rush hour, he lit up one of the cheroots he smoked and observed to no one in particular that he was still unhappy with the wheelchair they'd found for Hamm to use in this production. Amazing how often his speech echoed his work. "We need a proper wheelchair!" Hamm cries. "With big wheels. Bicycle wheels!" One evening, when I asked him if he was tired, his answer—theatrically delivered—was a quote from Clov: "'Yes, tired of all our goings on.'" And a few days later, when a transit strike brought London to a standstill and one of the actors suggested that rehearsals might not go on, he lifted a finger in the air and announced with obvious self-mockery, "Ah, but we must go on!" I'm not sure what sort of wheelchair he wanted, but several were tried in the next few days until one was found that he accepted. He was also unhappy with the percussion theme he was trying to establish, two pairs of knocks or scrapes that recur throughout the play—when Nagg, for example, knocks on Nell's ashcan to rouse her, when Hamm taps the wall to assure himself of its solidity, and when Clov climbs the two steps of his ladder with four specific scrapes of his slippers. For Beckett, these sounds were a primary musical motif, a fundamental continuity. It was crucial that they echo each other. "Alan," he said, "first thing this morning I want to rehearse your knock." Most discussions I was to hear about the play were like this, dealing in sound or props or other tangibles, with little or no mention of motivation and none at all of meaning. Very seldom did anyone question him on intellectual or psychological ground, and when they did, he usually brought the conversation back to the concrete, the specific. When I asked him once about the significance of the ashcans Nagg and Nell inhabit, he said, "It was the easiest way to get them on and off stage." And when Mandell inquired, that morning in the taxi, about the meaning of the four names in the play—four names that have been subject to all sorts of critical speculation, Beckett explained that Nagg and Clov were from "noggle" and "clou," the German and French for nail, Nell from the English "nail" and Hamm from the English "hammer." Thus, the percussion motif again: a hammer and three nails. Cluchey remembered that when Beckett directed him in Germany in *Krapp's Last Tape*, a similar music had been developed both around the words "Ah well," which recur four times in the play, and with the sound of Krapp's slippers scraping across the stage. "Sam was obsessed with the sound of the slippers. First we tried sandpapering the soles, then layering them with pieces of metal, then brand new solid leather soles. Finally, still not satisfied, he appeared one day with his own slippers. 'I've been wearing these for twenty years,' he said. 'If they don't do it, nothing will.'" More and more, as rehearsals went on, it would become apparent that music—"The highest art form," he said to me once, "it's never condemned to explicitness."—was his principal referent. His directions to actors were frequently couched in musical terms. "More emphasis there ... it's a crescendo," or, "The more speed we get here, the more value we'll find in the pause." When Hamm directs Clov to check on Nagg in his garbage can—"Go and see did he hear me. Both times."—Beckett said, "Don't play that line realistically. There's music there, you know." As Billie Whitelaw has noted, his hands rose and fell and swept from side to side, forming arcs like a conductor's as he watched his actors and shaped the rhythm of their lines. You could see his lips move, his jaw expanding and contracting, as he mouthed the words they spoke. Finally, his direction, like his texts, seemed a process of reduction, stripping away, reaching for "fundamental sound," transcending meaning, escaping the literary and the conceptual in order to establish a concrete immediate reality beyond the known, beyond the idea, which the audience would be forced to experience directly without mediation of intellect.

What Beckett said once of Joyce—"his work is not about something. It is something"—was certainly true of this production. The problem, of course, what Beckett's work can neither escape nor forget, is that words are never pure in their concreteness, never free of their referents. To quote Marcel Duchamp, himself a great friend and chess partner of Beckett's, "Everything that man has handled has a tendency to secrete meaning." And such secretion, because he is too honest to deny it, is the other side of Beckett's equation, the counterweight to his music that keeps his work not only meaningful, but (maniacally) inconclusive and symmetrical, its grief and rage always balanced with its comedy, its yearning for expression constantly humbled by its conviction that the Truth can only be betrayed by language. Rest assured that no Beckett character stands on a rug that cannot be pulled out from under him. When Didi seeks solace after Godot has disappointed them again—"We are not saints, but at least we have kept our appointment. How many people can say as much?"—Vladimir wastes no time in restoring him to his futility: "Billions."

But more than anyone else it is Hamm who gets to the heart of the matter, when he cries out to Clov in a fit of dismay, "Clov! We're not beginning to ... to ... mean something?"

"Mean something!" Clov cries. "You and I, mean something! Ah that's a good one!"

Hamm responds, "I wonder. If a rational being came back to earth, wouldn't he be liable to get ideas into his head if he observed us long enough? (Voice of rational being.) 'Ah good, now I see what it is, yes, now I understand what they're at!' (Normal voice.) And without going so far as that, we ourselves ... we ourselves ... at certain moments ... to think perhaps it won't all have been for nothing!"

As promised, Nagg's knock was the first order of business after we reached the theatre. This is the point in the play where Nagg has made his second appearance, head rising above the rim of the ashcan with a biscuit in his mouth, while Hamm and Clov—indulging in one of their habitual fencing matches—are discussing their garden ("Did your seeds come up?" "No." "Did you scratch the ground to see if they have sprouted?" "They haven't sprouted." "Perhaps it's too early." "If they were going to sprout they would have sprouted. They'll never sprout!"). A moment later, Clov, having made an exit and Hamm drifted off into a reverie, Nagg leans over to rouse Nell, tapping four times—two pairs—on the lid of her bin. Beckett demonstrated the sound he wanted using his bony knuckle on the lid, and after Mandell had tried it six or seven times—not "Tap, tap, tap, tap," or "Tap ... tap ... tap ... tap," but "tap, tap ... tap, tap" — appeared to be satisfied. "Let's work from here," he said. Since Teri had not arrived, he climbed into the can himself and took Nell's part, curling his bony fingers over the edge of the can, edging his head above the rim, and asking, in a shaky falsetto that captured Nell better than anyone I'd ever heard in the part: "What is it, my pet?

Time for love?"

As they worked through the scene, I got my first hint of the way in which this *Endgame* would differ from others I'd seen. So much so that, despite the fact that I'd seen six or seven different productions of the play, I would soon be convinced that I'd never seen it before. Certainly, though I'd always thought *Endgame* my favorite play, I realized that I had never really understood it or appreciated the maniacal logic with which it pursues its ambiguities. Here, as elsewhere, Beckett pressed for speed and close to flat enunciation. His principal goal, which he never realized, was to compress the play so that it ran in less than ninety minutes. After the above line, the next three were bracketed for speed, then a carefully measured pause established before the next section—three more lines—began. "Kiss me," Nagg begs. "We can't," says Nell. "Try," says Nagg. And then, in another pause, they crane their necks in vain to reach each other from their respective garbage cans. The next section was but a single line in length (Nell: "Why this farce, day after day?"), the next four, the next seven, and so on. Each was a measure, clearly defined, like a jazz riff, subordinated to the rhythm of the whole. Gesture was treated like sound, another form of punctuation. Beckett was absolutely specific about its shape—the manner in which, for example, Nagg's and Nell's fingers curled above the rims of their cans — and where it occurred in the text. "Keep these gestures small," he said to Cluchey when a later monologue was reached. "Save the big one for 'All that loveliness!'" He wanted the dialogue crisp and precise but not too realistic. It seemed to me he yearned to stylize the play as much as possible, underline its theatricality so that the actors, as in most of his plays, would be seen as clearly acting, clearly playing the roles they're doomed to play forever. The text, of course, supports such artifice, the actors often addressing each other in language that reminds us that they're on stage. "That's an aside, fool," says Hamm to Clov. "Have you never heard an aside before?" Or

Clov, after his last soliloquy, pausing at the edge of the stage: "This is what they call ... making an exit." Despite all this, Beckett wanted theatrical flourish kept to a minimum. It seemed to me that he stiffened the movement, carving it like a sculptor, stripping it of anything superfluous or superficial. "Less color, please," he said to Alan while they were doing Nagg and Nell together, "if we keep it flat, they'll get it better." And later, to Thorpe: "Bud, you don't have to move so much. Only the upper torso. Don't worry. They'll get it. Remember: you don't even want to be out here. You'd rather be alone, in your kitchen."

Though the play was thirty years old for him and he believed that his memory had deteriorated, his memory of the script was flawless and his alertness to its detail unwavering. "That's not 'upon.' It's 'on.'" He corrected "one week" with "a week," "crawlin" with "crawling." When Cluchey said to Thorpe, "Cover me with a sheet," Beckett snapped: "The sheet, Rick, the sheet." And when Clov delivered the line, "There are no more navigators" he refined, "There's a pause before navigators." He made changes as they went along—"On 'Good God' let's leave out the 'good'"—sometimes cutting whole sections, but had no interest in publishing a revised version of the play. For all the fact that he was "wobbly," he seemed stronger than anyone else on the set, rarely sitting while he worked and never losing his concentration. As so many actors and actresses have noted, he delivered his own lines better than anyone else, and this was his principal mode of direction. When dealing with certain particular lines, he often turned away from the cast and stood at the edge of the stage, facing the wall, working out gestures in pantomime. For those of us who were watching rehearsals, it was no small thing to see him go off like this and then hear him, when he'd got what he wanted, deliver his own lines in his mellifluous Irish pronunciation, his voice, for all its softness, projecting with force to the seats at the back of the theatre:

"'They said to me, That's love, yes, yes, not a doubt, now you see how easy it is. They said to me, That's friendship, yes, yes, no question, you've found it. They said to me, Here's the place, stop, raise your head and look at all that beauty. That order! They said to me, Come now, you're not a brute beast, think upon these things and you'll see how all becomes clear. And simple! They said to me, What skilled attention they get, all these dying of their wounds.'"

To say the least, such moments produced an uncanny resonance. Unself-conscious and perfectly in character he was, one felt, not only reading the lines but writing them, discovering them now as he'd discovered them thirty years before. And that we, as audience, had somehow become his first witness, present at the birth of his articulations. If his own present tense—the act of writing—had always been his subject, what could be more natural or inevitable than showing us this, the thoughts and meaning "secreted" and rejected, the words giving form, the form dissolving in the silence that ensued. For that was the message one finally took from such recitations, the elusiveness of the meanings he had established, the sense of the play as aging with him, unable to arrest the flow of time and absolutely resolved against pretending otherwise. Why should Hamm and Clov be spared the awareness of Molloy: "It is in the tranquility of decomposition that I remember the long confused emotion which was my life."

Perhaps it was for this reason that he was never far removed from what he'd written, that if an actor inquired about a line, his answers could seem almost naïve. When Cluchey asked him why Hamm, after begging Clov to give him his stuffed dog, throws it to the ground, Beckett explained, "He doesn't like the feel of it." And when he was asked for help in delivering the line "I'll tell you the combination of the larder if you promise to finish me," he advised, "Just think, you'll tell him the combination if he'll promise to kill you." Despite—or because of—such responses, all four members of the cast would later describe the experience of his direction in language that was often explicitly spiritual. "What he offered me," said Cluchey, "was a standard of absolute authority. He gave my life a spiritual quotient." And Thorpe: "When we rehearsed, the concentration was so deep that I lost all sense of myself. I felt completely empty, like a skeleton, the words coming through me without thought of the script. I'm not a religious person, but it seemed a religious experience to me. Why? Maybe because it was order carried to its ultimate possibility. If you lost your concentration, veered off track for any reason, it was as if you'd sinned." Extreme though such descriptions are, I doubt that anyone who watched these rehearsals would find in them the least trace of exaggeration. More than intense, the atmosphere was almost unbearably internalized, self-contained to the point of circularity. In part, obviously, this was because we were watching an author work on his own text. In addition to this, however, the text itself— because *Endgame* is finally nothing but theatre, repetition, a series of ritualized games that the actors are doomed to play forever— was precisely about the work that we were watching. When Clov asks Hamm, "What keeps me here?" Hamm replies, "The dialogue." Or earlier, when Hamm is asking him about his father, "You've asked me these questions millions of times." Says Hamm, "I love the old questions ... ah, the old questions, the old answers, there's nothing like them!" If the play is finally about nothing but itself, the opportunity to see it repeated, again and again for two weeks, offered a chance to see Beckett's intention realized on a scale at once profound and literal, charged with energy but at the same time boring, deadening, infuriating. (A fact of which Beckett was hardly unaware. While they were working on the line, "This is not much fun," he advised Cluchey, "I think it would be dangerous to have any pause after that line. We don't want to give people time to agree with you.") To use his own percussion metaphor, watching these rehearsals was to offer one's head up for *Endgame's* cadence to be hammered into it. Finally, after two weeks of rehearsal, the play became musical to a hypnotic extent, less a theatrical than a meditative experience in that one could not ascribe to it any meaning or intention beyond its own concrete and immediate reality. In effect, the more one saw of it, the less it contained. To this day the lines appear in my mind without reason, like dreams or memory-traces, but the play itself, when I saw it in Dublin, seemed an anti-climax, the goal itself insignificant beside the process that had produced it. If *Waiting for Godot* is, as Vivian Mercier has written, "a play in which nothing happens, twice," it might be said of *Endgame* that it is an endless rehearsal for an opening night that never comes and therefore, that its true realization was the rehearsals we saw rather than its formal production later in Dublin. Could this be why, being one reason at least, Beckett did not accompany his cast to Ireland or, for that matter, why he has never attended his own plays in the theatre?

He left London the day after rehearsals ended, and I did not see him again until the following spring in Paris. At our first meeting he seemed a totally different person, distant and inaccessible, physically depleted, extremely thin, his eyes more deeply set and his face more heavily lined than ever. He spoke from such distance and with such difficulty that I was reminded again of Molloy, who describes conversation as "unspeakably painful," explaining that he hears words "a first time, then a second, and often even a third, as pure sounds, free of all meaning." We met in the coffee shop of a new hotel, one of those massive gray skyscrapers that in recent years have so disfigured the Paris skyline. Not far from his apartment, it was his favorite meeting place because it offered a perfect anonymity. He wasn't recognized during this or any subsequent meeting I had with him there. Early on in our conversation I got a taste of his ferocious self-protection, which was much more pronounced here, of course, where he lived, than it had been in London. "How long will you be here?" he said. "Three weeks," I said. "Good," he said.

74

"I want to see you once more." Given his politeness, it was easy to forget how impossible his life would have been had he not been disciplined about his schedule, how many people must have sought him out as I had sought him out myself. What was always amazing to me was how skillful he was in letting one know where one ranked in his priorities. Couching his decision in courtesy and gentleness, he seemed totally vulnerable, almost passive, but his softness masked a relentless will and determination. He left one so disarmed that it was difficult to ask anything of him much less seek more time than he had offered. Though he promptly answered every letter I wrote him, it was three years before he gave me his home address so that I would not have to write him in care of his publisher, and he has never given me a phone number, always arranging that he will call me when I come to town. Why not? Rick Cluchey told me that whenever Beckett went to Germany, a documentary film crew followed him around without his permission, using a telephoto lens to film him from a distance.

As it turned out, however, there was now another reason for his distance. In London, the only unpleasant moment between us had occurred when, caught up in the excitement of rehearsals, I'd asked if I could write about him. Though his refusal, again, had been polite ("Unless of course you want to write about the work ... ") and I had expressed considerable regret about asking him, it would soon become clear that he had not forgotten my request. Even if he had, the speed with which I was firing questions at him now, nervously pressing all the issues I had accumulated since I'd seen him last, would have put him on his guard. Beckett is legendary, of course, for his hatred of interviews, his careful avoidance of media and its invasions (The Paris Review has tried for years, with no success, to interview him for its "Writers at Work" series), and the next time we met, he made it clear that before we continued, he must know what I was after. "Listen, I've got to get this off my chest. You're not interviewing me, are you?"

We had just sat down at a restaurant to which he had invited me. The only restaurant he ever frequented, it was a classic bistro on the edge of Montparnasse where he kept his own wine in the cellar and the waiters knew his habits so well that they always took him to the same table and brought him, without his having to order, the dish he ate—filet of sole and french fries—whenever he went there. Though I had my notebook in my pocket and upon leaving him would, as always, rush to take down everything I could remember about our conversation, I assured him that I was certainly not interviewing him and had no intention of writing about him. At this point in time, there was nothing but truth in my disclaimer. (And I might add that he obviously trusted me on this score, since he gave me permission to publish this article, and as far as I can see, has never held it against me.) Since I was not yet even dimly conscious of the ambiguous, somewhat belligerent forces that led to this memoir, the notes I took were for myself alone, as I saw it, a result of the emotion I felt when I left him and the impulse, common if not entirely handsome in a writer, to preserve what had transpired between us. Taking me at my word, he relaxed, poured the wine and watched with pleasure as I ate while he picked at his food like a child who hated the dinner table. "You're not hungry?" I said. "No," he said. "I guess I'm not too interested in food anymore." And later, when I asked if he'd ever eaten in any of the Japanese restaurants that were just beginning to open in Paris: "No. But I hear they make good rice."

Considering how thin he was, I wasn't surprised to hear that the desire for food—like almost all other desires, I believe, except those which involved his work—was a matter of indifference to him. What did surprise me, as the wine allowed us to speak of things more commonplace, was the view of his domestic situation—evenings at home with his wife, and such—which emerged during the course of the evening. He told me that he'd been married for forty years, that he and his wife had had just two addresses during all their time in Paris, that it had sometimes been difficult for them—"many near-ruptures, as a matter of fact"—but that the marriage had grown easier as they'd gotten older. "Of course," he added, "I do have my own door." Since I'd always thought of him as the ultimate solitary, isolated as Krapp and as cynical about sex as Molloy, I confessed that I couldn't imagine him in a situation so connubial. "Why should you find it difficult?" he said with some surprise. In fact, he seemed rather pleased with his marriage, extremely grateful that it had lasted. It was one more correction for me, and more importantly, I think, one more illustration of the symmetry and tension, the dialectic he maintains between his various dichotomies. Just as "can't" and "must" persist with equal force in his mind, the limitations of language no more deniable than the urgent need to articulate, the extreme loneliness he's explored throughout his life—the utter skepticism and despair about relationships in general and sexuality in particular—has had as its counterpoint a marriage that has lasted forty years. But lest one suspect that the continuity and comfort of marriage had tilted the scales so far that the dream of succession had taken root in his mind, "No," he replied, when I asked if he had ever wanted children, "that's one thing I'm proud of."

For all my conviction that I did not intend to write about him, I always felt a certain amount of shame when I took up my notebook after I left him. For that matter, I am not entirely without shame about what I'm writing now. One does not transcribe a man like Beckett without its feeling like a betrayal. What makes me persist? More than anything, I believe, it is something I began to realize after our meetings in Paris—that the shame I felt in relation to him had not begun with my furtive attempts to preserve him in my notebook, but rather had been a constant in our relationship long before I'd met him. To put it simply, it began to strike me that Beckett had been, since the moment I discovered *Molloy*, as much a source of inhibition as inspiration. For all the pleasure it had given me, my first reading of the trilogy had almost paralyzed me (as indeed it had paralyzed any number of other writers I knew), leaving me traumatized with shame and embarrassment about my own work. It wasn't merely that in contrast to his, my language seemed inauthentic and ephemeral, but that he made the usual narrative games—the insulated past tense, the omniscient narrator, form that excluded reference to itself and biographical information—seem, as he put it in *Watt*, "solution clapped on problem like a snuffer on a candle." More than any other writer I knew, Beckett's work seemed to point to that which lay beyond it. It was as if, though its means were Relative, its goals were Absolute, its characters beyond time precisely because (again and again) they seemed to age before our eyes. And such accomplishment was not, it seemed to me, simply a matter of talent or genius but of a totally different approach to writing, a connection between his life and his work, which I could covet but never achieve. It was this union—the joining, if you like, of "being" and "form"—that I envied in him and that caused me finally to feel that the very thought of Beckett, not to mention the presence of one of his sentences in my mind, made writing impossible. And once again: it was not merely a matter of talent. I could read Joyce or Proust or Faulkner without such problems, and I had no lack of appreciation for them. It was just that they were clearly writers, while Beckett was something else, a sort of meta-writer who, even as he wrote, transcended the act of writing.

Oddly enough, if there was anyone else I knew who stood in such relation to his own work it was Muhammad Ali, who seemed to laugh at boxing even as he took it to higher levels of perfection, who not only defeated but humiliated his opponents, establishing such possession of their minds that he won many fights before the first round even began because he stood outside the game in which his adversary was enclosed. One cannot play a game unless one believes in it, but Ali managed such belief without the attachment to which it usually leads. You could say that he found the cusp that separates belief from attachment, concentration from fixation and, on the other hand, play from frivolity and spontaneity from formlessness. And it seems to me that Beckett has done the same. No writer has lived who took language more seriously, but none has been more eloquent about its limitations and absurdities. Like Ali, he shows us where we are imprisoned. The danger is that, in doing so, he will imprison us in his example. If some fighters tried to imitate Ali by playing the clown and had ended up by making fools of themselves in addition to being defeated, writers with Beckett too much in mind can sound worse than the weakest student in a freshman writing class. After reading Joyce or Proust one can feel embarrassed about one's lack of music or intelligence, but in the wake of one of Beckett's convoluted, self-mocking sentences, one can freeze with horror at the thought of any form that suggests, "Once upon a time," anything, in fact, that departs from the absolute present. But if you take that notion too far you lose your work in the ultimate swamp, the belief that you can capture both your subject and your object in the instant of composition: "Here I am, sitting at my desk, writing, 'Here I am, sitting at my desk.'"

None of this, of course, is historically unprecedented. Every generation of artists has to do battle with its predecessors and each such battle has its own unique configurations. What made it so vivid for me was that now, twenty years after that first reading, his presence affected me much as his work had. Happy though I felt to see him, however amazing I found our time together, I always left him with an acute sense that I'd come up short, failed him somehow, as if the moment had passed before I had awakened to it. As if my conversational and psychological habits had stood between us. Or more to the point, as if the form of my social habit had violated the nature of his Being in much the same way that literary form, as he'd concluded years before, violated the being it excluded. Sitting across from me in the cafe, his eyes fierce in their concentration, his silence so completely unapologetic, he seemed to occupy, according to my reverential opinion, a present tense—this space, this moment in time—that I could merely observe from afar. Despite—no, because of—his humility, his uncertainty, the "impotence" which, as he'd once put it, his work had set out to "exploit,"[1] he manifested for me as for years he had for Rick Cluchey, a kind of ultimate authority, a sense of knowledge very near to Absolute. Neither egoism nor self-confidence—the opposite, in fact, of both—seemed a by-product of suffering, the pain that was so evident on his face an earned if not entirely welcome result of having explored and survived an emptiness that people of less courage, if they acknowledged it at all, considered by means of intellect alone.

Exaggerated and romantic though all this seems, I'm sure it's not entirely unjustified. Beckett is indeed an extraordinary being, a man who has travelled in realms that most people don't want to hear about much less explore. A true writer, an artist who pursues his vision so courageously and with such disregard for easy gratification that his work becomes, in the purest sense, a spiritual practice. What my responses showed, however, in light of my idealization of him and the self-criticism it evoked, was that such authority was nothing if not a hazardous experience. Like all great wisdom it could bring out the best or the worst in you, challenge or intimidate you, toughen you or make you self-effacing. Finally, if you were a writer, it could inspire you to listen to your own voice or trap you into years of imitating his. Like Joyce or Proust, or for that matter any other great artist one adopts as a teacher, Beckett is an almost impossible act to follow, but more so than most, I think, because his work is so subjective, so seductive in the permissions it grants because his apparent freedom from plot and character and his first person present tense can draw you into a swamp in which art and self-indulgence

---

[1] "The kind of work I do," he explained to Israel Schenker in a New York Times interview in 1966, before he'd closed the door to media, "is one in which I'm not master of my material. The more Joyce knew the more he could do. He's tending toward omniscience and omnipotence as an artist. I'm working with impotence, ignorance. I don't think impotence has been exploited in the past."

begin to seem identical. It is so easy to think that he opens the gates for anything you're feeling or thinking at the moment you sit down at your desk. How many writers could I count who had books like mine — the one I'd shown him, the one he'd criticized because the voice was "not believable"—which would not be written until the Beckett had been removed from them? The great irony is that, for all his rejection of authority and knowledge— precisely because of such rejection, in fact—Beckett is almost too much an authority, he knows too much that one must discover on one's own. If you aren't to go on imitating him, you either face the fact that there is nothing you really need to say and find yourself another vocation, or you dig for something truer in yourself, something you don't know, at the bottom of all you do. In other words, you start where he started after meeting his mother in Dublin. The trouble is that since most of such digging, if you're an ordinary mortal, is surely doomed to fail, it can seem as if he's taken you out of the game you're capable of playing and signed you up in one for which you've neither the courage, the talent, nor the appetite. Finally, his greatest danger—and his greatest gift—may be his simple reminder that writing is not about reiteration.

But of course there is also the other side to it, the one that has explicitly to do with the nature of his vision, the "being" he allows into the work, the void he's faced, the negation he's endured, the grief he's not only experienced but transformed with his imagination. "Yes, the confusion of my ideas on the subject of death," says Molloy, "was such that I sometimes wondered, believe me or not, if it wasn't a state of being even worse than life. So I found it natural not to rush into it and, when I forgot myself to the point of trying, to stop in time." Once we'd gotten over our laughter and exhilaration, how were we to deal with such a statement? For Beckett, such negation had fueled the work, but for many who presumed to be his successors it had often become an easy, a facile nihilism, less a game you lost than one you refused to play. Indeed for some of us, true disciples, it could become one you were ashamed to play. As if, having finally been enlightened as to the absurdity of life, you were too wise to persist at its illusions, too wise to allow enthusiasm, occupy space, to feed the body you knew to be disintegrating. In effect, if you misread him well enough, Beckett could turn you into a sort of literary anorexic, make you too cool or hip, too scared, too detached and disenchanted to take, by writing, the only food that nourished you. But the irony is that he himself, as he'd shown me in London in our very first conversation, is anything but anorexic. That's obvious, isn't it? This man who writes, in *Molloy*, "you would do better, at least no worse, to obliterate texts than to blacken margins, to fill in the holes of words till all is blank and flat and the whole ghastly business looks like what it is, senseless, speechless, issueless misery," has published six novels and fourteen plays during his lifetime, not to mention a great body of short prose, poetry, criticism, a number of television and radio plays, and a film script. Just fifteen pages later in *Molloy* he writes, "Not to want to say, not to know what you want to say, and never to stop saying, or hardly ever, that is the thing to keep in mind, even in the heat of composition." Much as he can recognize the tyranny of hope or meaning, he cannot deny that there is hope and meaning within such recognition and he cannot pretend that this hope and meaning is any less exciting or more enduring than the others. It's all part of the equation, however absurd, of being alive, and he's never rejected that condition for its alternative. After all, when Nell says "Nothing is funnier than unhappiness," we laugh at that statement, and—if only for an instant—are less unhappy as we do so. In a sense, Beckett is the great poet of negation, but what is poetry for him can easily become, if we use him incorrectly, if we make him too much an authority or if we underestimate the integrity of his paradox, a negation so extreme and absolute that it threatens the very source of one's energy and strength.

Of course, it's not easy to speak of these things. It's always possible that his greatest gift, not only to those of us he's challenged but also to the readers we might have enlisted, is the silence toward which he's pressed us. If you can't accept his example and allow Being into your work, why add your lies to the ocean of print already drowning the world? In my opinion, most writers deal with his challenge in one of two ways. Either they ignore his example, go on making—as I had, for example, in writing journalism—forms that exclude Being, accepting the role of explainer, describer, or else they try—as I was trying with my novel—to play his game despite the astronomical odds against any possibility of success. For those who take the latter path, the entry of Being into the form often means the entry of self-consciousness, writing about writing about writing. Too late we discover that Beckett, Molloy, Malone, et al., though they may be mad, haven't a trace of neurosis or narcissism about them, that their present tense is shaped and objectified by an inherently classical, concrete mind, a sense of self that differs radically from our own. In effect, that the present tense, which becomes, inevitably, an imperfect tense for them, remains a merely present—a merely reductive, a totally self-absorbed—tense for us. If you can't take the leap from present to imperfect, you remain rooted in the present. An honorable intention, of course, but if you're honest about it, you have to admit that writing and being in the present are not necessarily compatible, that in fact you're always flirting with contradiction and dishonesty. Tantalized by what amounts to a desire to write and not-write simultaneously, you may be equally loyal to form and being, but you may also be a mother who would keep her child forever in her womb. It's the sort of game in which defeat can lead to farce that's not only hypocritical but blasphemous toward the master one has pretended to revere.

These are just a few of the reasons, I think, I took notes when I left him, and despite my disclaimer, am writing about him now.

Why? Perhaps because Beckett himself, as I said earlier, freed me from the Beckett myth. Not entirely, for sure, but enough at least to help me resume a voice that differed from the one he once inspired in me. Not for nothing did he show me that he enjoyed my journalism. "Look here, Larry," he said to me once in London, "your line is witnessing." By that I understood him to have meant: Take your object and be done with it. Be content to write what you know without acknowledging every moment that you don't. So here I am, witnessing him. Maybe this is all just rationalization, but getting him down like this may be the best homage and the best revenge, the only weapon I have against the attack he mounted on my mind. I can't forget him, and I can't think of anything else to do with his example but reject it. Just as Buddhists say about their own ultimate authority, "If you meet the Buddha on the road, kill him," I say of Beckett that a writer can only proceed from him by recognizing that he is, having taken his work to all of its ultimate conclusions, now utterly emptied of possibility. As Hamm says, "All is absolute. The bigger a man is, the fuller he is ... and the emptier."

The next time we saw each other, a year later in Paris, our conversation continued, where it had begun and where it had left off, with the difficulties of writing. Because my work (the same novel) was going as badly as his, there wasn't a whole lot of joy in the air. For a moment, in fact, it became a sort of sparring match between us, agony versus agony, but then remembering whom I was in the ring with and how much he outweighed me, I backed off. "It's not a good time at all," he sighed, "I walk the streets trying to see what's in my mind. It's all confusion. Life is all confusion. A blizzard. It must be like this for the newborn. Not much difference, I think, between this blizzard and that. Between the two, what do you have? Wind machines or some such. I can't write anything, but I must." He paused a moment, then suddenly brightened, once again repeating a famous Beckett line as if he'd just come upon it, "Yes, that's it! Can't and must! That's my situation!"

He spoke of a sentence that haunted him. "It won't go away, and it won't go farther: 'One night, as he sat with his head on his hands, he saw himself rise, and go.'" Except for this, however, there was nothing. "It's like the situation I spoke of in my book on Proust. 'Not just hope is gone, but desire.'" When I reminded him—quoting the line I mentioned earlier ("The wisdom of all the sages ... consists not in the satisfaction but the ablation of desire.")—that according to the book he'd remembered, the loss of desire was not an entirely unwelcome development, he replied, "Well, yes, but the writing was the only thing that made life bearable." Sighing as if in tremendous pain, he seemed to drift off for a moment. "Funny to complain about silence when one has aspired to it for so long. Words are the only thing for me and there's not enough of them. Now it's as if I'm just living in a void, waiting. Even my country house is lonely when I'm not writing."

Occasionally when he talked like this there was an odd sense, absurd as it seems, that he was asking for help, even perhaps advice, but this time was different. Now seventy-eight years old, he appeared to have reached a sort of bottom-line exhaustion. He seemed smaller to me, the lines in his forehead more deeply etched, like a grid. Every gesture seemed difficult, every word a struggle. His blue eyes were shy, gentle, youthful as ever, but incredibly pained and sorrowful. I told him that sometimes I found it amazing that he went on. "Yes," he replied, "often I think it's time I put an end to it. That's all through, the new work. But then again ... there are also times when I think, maybe it's time to begin." He said there had always been so much more in the work than he'd suspected was there, and then added, in what seemed an almost unconscious afterthought, a phrase I've never forgotten, which may have summed up his work as well or better than any other: "Ambiguities infirmed as they're put down ... "

"Which is more painful," I asked him, "writing or not writing?"

"They're both painful, but the pain is different."

He spoke a little about the different sorts of pain, the pain of being unable to write, the pain of writing itself, and—as bad as any—the pain of finishing what he'd begun. I said, "If the work is so painful when one does it and so painful when it's done, why on earth does anyone do it?"

This was one of those questions that caused him, as I've mentioned already, to disappear behind his hand, covering his eyes and bending his head toward the table for what must have been two full minutes. Then, just when I'd begun to suspect that he'd fallen asleep, he raised his head and, with an air of relief, as if he'd finally resolved a lifelong dilemma, whispered, "The fashioning, that's what it is for me, I think. The pleasure in making a satisfactory object." He explained that the main excitement in writing had always been technical for him, a combination of "metaphysics and technique." "A problem is there and I have to solve it. *Godot*, for example, began with an image— of a tree and an empty stage—and proceeded from there. That's why, when people ask me who Godot is, I can't tell them. It's all gone."

"Why metaphysics?" I said.

"Because," he said, "you've got your own experience. You've got to draw on that."

He tried to describe the work he wanted to do now. "It has to do with a fugitive 'I' [or perhaps he meant 'eye']. It's an embarrassment of pronouns. I'm searching for the non-pronounial."

"'Non-pronounial'?"

"Yes. It seems a betrayal to say 'he' or 'she.'"

The problem of pronouns, first person versus third, which had been so much explored and illuminated throughout his work, was also the one he addressed in mine. That morning, as always, he was extremely solicitous, asking me question after question about the progress of my novel. Though the book continued to defy me, so much so that I'd begun to wonder if brain damage, as I wanted to approach it, might not be beyond the limits of art, he seemed to know exactly what I wanted to do. It wasn't surprising, of course, that the man who'd once described tears as "liquified brain" should be familiar with the subject of brain damage, but his questions were so explicit that it was difficult to believe that he hadn't considered, and rejected, the very book I wanted to write. The chapters I'd shown him in London had been written in the first person, which he had considered a mistake. "I know it's impertinent to say this, please forgive me ... but this book, in my opinion, will never work in the first person." When I told him, here at the cafe, that I had now moved it to the third person, he nodded, but he knew that problems of point of view were never resolved with pronouns alone. "Still," he said, returning to the point he'd made when we met in London, "you need a witness, right?"

He excused himself from the table—"pardon my bladder"— but when he returned it was clear that he'd taken my book with him. "Well, do you see the end of it?"

"No," I said, "not at all."

He sighed. "It's really very difficult, isn't it?"

He sipped his coffee, then homed in on the principal issue in my book as in so much contemporary fiction—the need for objectivity and knowledge in conjunction with the need for the intimacy and immediacy of a naked subjectivity. "You need a witness and you need the first person, that's the problem, isn't it? One thing that might help ... you might have a look at an early book of mine, perhaps you know it, *Mercier and Camier.* I had a similar problem there. It begins, 'I know what happened with Mercier and Camier because I was there with them all the time.'"

After I returned from Paris, I looked at *Mercier and Camier* again but found no place for his solution in the problems I had set myself. Still, I wrote an entire version of my novel in the third person, and I can say without a doubt that there were very few days I didn't feel him looking over my shoulder, whispering, "It's really very difficult, isn't it?" or when things were going worse, commenting on me as Nagg comments on Hamm, "What does that mean? That means nothing!" Halfway through, I knew it wasn't working, suspecting strongly that my only hope, despite what Beckett had said, was in the first person, but I pushed on. Certainly, it wasn't merely his recommendation that kept me going in that direction, but how can I pretend it didn't matter? When finally—a year and a half and an entire manuscript later—I turned it around and started over, in the first person, I could not, though I wrote him more than one letter about the book, bring myself to mention it to him. To my mind, the book worked, not only because it was in the first person but because I had finally succeeded in weaning myself from him. Given all this, I felt no small trepidation when I sent him the manuscript, but as before, he read the book at once and replied with generosity and enthusiasm. There was no sign of his original disappointment and none of his position vis-a-vis my point of view. His note, as always, was confined to a 3 x 5 index card, and his scrawl, which had grown progressively worse in the years that I'd corresponded with him, was not completely legible. To my chagrin, in fact, its most important sentence was only half accessible to me. After offering his compliments and appreciation, he concluded with a sentence that drifted off into a hopeless hieroglyphics after beginning with "And on with you now from . . ."

After "from" was a word that looked like "this," but might have been "thus" or "phis," then a word that looked like "new" but might have been "man" or "ran," a word that looked like "thought" or "bought" or "sought" and finally a word that looked like "anew." "And on with you now from this new thought anew"? It didn't sound like Beckett at all. I asked several friends to have a look but none could read his writing any better than I. What absurd apocryphy that a note from Beckett should conclude, "And on with you now from [illegible] [illegible]

[illegible]." Finally, unable to stand it any longer, I wrote to ask if, by some chance (after all, more than three weeks had passed since he'd written the note) he could remember what he'd written. Again, he answered promptly, ending our dialogue, as I will end this memoir, with a note that was characteristic, not only in its economy and content, but in what it says about his (failing?) memory and the attitude with which he approached his correspondence:

Dear Larry,

I believe I wrote, 'And on with you now from this new nought anew.'

As ever,

Sam.

7. KLONDIKE NEUROLOGY

A few years ago, working on a novel about brain damage, I realized that it could not go farther until I met up with those who'd experienced it. This meant working in a hospital of course, face-to-face meetings with one of the worst of all clinical disasters. At first, I encountered all the barriers lawyers set up to ward off nosy writers, but eventually I wrangled permission of authorities at a VA hospital in the Bronx to spend time with a severely dysfunctional patient whom I'll call what those on the staff did—the professor. I was granted access because he was a dull and helpless patient who would never leave the hospital, did not require a great deal of care, and had not yet excited any researchers. He needed company, and no one else wanted to be with him so they were happy to let me hang out with him. 'Professor' was not just a moniker but a link to his past life. Until viral encephalitis damaged his brain, he'd headed the sociology department at a large northeastern university.

He was a stocky man in his mid-sixties who, despite the fact that he got no exercise beyond his walks around the ward, looked to be in pretty good shape. His face retained just enough of his past authority and intelligence to make it possible, though certainly not easy, to forget his condition. He was an unusual patient because he retained his verbal and motor function but had lost his short-term and most of his long-term memory. He spent most of his time trying in vain to recover biographical information such as—despite the fact that his wife and daughter visited him once or twice a week—whether he was married, had children, and, most obsessively, why such questions stumped him. Again and again, as if with revelation, he said, "I think I have problems with my memory." He usually ended his investigations by concluding that such problems were caused by acid indigestion, which in turn was cased by candy bars. After I understood this and began to bring him a stash when I visited, he was always glad to see me, but he never recognized me. If I left his room for even two or three minutes, he'd greet me when I returned as if he'd never seen me before. He liked to cover his deficit with one of two long-out-of-date expressions that, despite his amnesia, he must have retained from his adolescence.

"See you later, alligator!"

"After awhile, crocodile!"

Obsession with my own brain had brought me to the book I was writing, and endless frustration with the book had brought me to this research. Since he was obviously a great research opportunity, I met him at first with the detachment and curiosity that is the researcher's privilege as well as his self-protection. Though my book was driven by the view that the human brain, "healthy" or "damaged," is basically capricious, demonic and tyrannical, I felt safe from too much identification with him until I realized we shared an addiction. Klondike solitaire was the only activity that interested him, and it interested me a lot more than I liked to admit.

I could not match him for frequency of course. He played hour after hour, all day long, every day, with fixed concentration that repetition and boredom never diluted. Like visits by me or others, each candy bar I brought him, each breakfast of each day when he woke up, and each realization that he had "memory problems," every game was his first. Since he did not, like me, own a computer, he played with real cards, spreading them carefully on his tray table, which he rolled back and forth as he moved between his bed and the lounge chair in the corner of his room. Visible in his face and posture, the attention he gave to the game was fierce and unequivocal, locating him so completely in the present moment that any hint of his tragic circumstances disappeared. Like anyone who plays a game—any game—wholeheartedly, his life dissolved in its temporal arc. Its outcome was the only future that concerned him. Outside the game, he could not bear his memory deficit, but while he played, he forgot it. The fact that nothing mattered but the next card was a State of Grace to which he constantly returned. His disease, of course, was an accident of his past visited upon his future, but since the game freed him of past and future, it was impossible to doubt that, as long as he played, he was free of disease.

Much though I wished to, I could not deny that the interest and concentration I felt when I played were every bit as avid as his. Nor could I pretend, since interest and concentration, not to mention the organization, logic and sensory-motor control the game required, are clear measures of neurological health, that the game's effects on my brain were entirely different from their effects on his. Furthermore, I had to deal with the parallels between the game and Zazen. Resistant though I was to the idea that meditation was a form of play, I could not deny that both took me to a state of mind that was not unlike what they offered him.

Unlike him, I did not play with cards. These were the early days of the personal computer. It was only a year since IBM had brought their first PC to market. The internet was fairly new, but solitaire, which had begun more than 200 years before as a form of fortune-telling—e.g., whether or not a game "came out" supposedly indicated whether or not the player's desire would come true—was already the most-used program in the Windows universe, the perfect means by which to develop fluency with a mouse and, as a Microsoft programmer put it, "soothe those who are intimidated by the Operating System." (As an article in Salon reported, "The Game's pedagogical elements were also a handy cover story. When a Minnesota state legislator got caught playing solitaire during a 1995 debate on education funding, she claimed she was merely doing 'homework to improve her mouse dexterity.'") If, like the professor, I'd had no computer, I'd have had to clear my desk of the notebooks, research material, envelopes, bills, shopping lists, etc. that usually covered it, and then play the game as he did. In contrast to its lightning speed on a computer, Solitaire with cards would seem manual and plodding, super-slow-motion, a slide-show rather than a movie. After shuffling and spreading my cards, I'd have had to endure— what? a time-lapse!--between each brain-hand-eye coordination. In comparison to the effort required by my mouse, my physical actions—shuffling cards, laying them out, placing one on another, etc.--would seem almost aerobic. With no discernable gap between visual perception, logical association and the clicks they produced, the temporal arc in which I played was so compressed that it seemed to eliminate separation between cause and effect, not to mention move me at breakneck speed toward the gratification that eluded me everywhere else in my life. While the professor had to put one card on another, thus deal with two separate entities, I put them together so fast that it seemed as if they'd never been apart. Day by day, I was more startled by my speed and facility, the spontaneity of my response to the cards. Was it possible I was getting smarter? It was as if my brain were constantly being upgraded with smaller and faster chips and a better Operating System. Needless to say, I'd failed to notice how much the game had changed my work environment. I took it for granted that it was always available on my desk, accessible through the same instrument I use for composition, allowing me with a single click on the same keyboard I'm using to write this sentence to shift from temporal, purposeful, endlessly complex and anxiety-producing work for which coherence and beauty, not to mention truth, are always uncertain and gratification highly unlikely to the immediate gratification of a game I play with the same hand and almost the same mind I'll use to edit, save or delete this sentence or, if I get too anxious or frustrated or angry at myself and can't bring myself to play the game again, escape through the computer's rabbit hole to play other games like checking my email, surfing the 'net, calling up a newspaper, magazine or pornography or ordering a book I'll never find time to read. So powerful and dependable, so comforting and ventilating is such escape that resisting it order to hang in with my work can seem masochistic. No need here to explore how all this—digital speed and ease versus typing or hand-writing, the difference between the absolute-solitude-no-escape in which I used to work and the constant escape offered me now, etc.— affects my writing or that of countless others who use this technology, not to mention our longed-for readers who use it as well and are thus, like us, becoming so habituated to immediate gratification and intolerance for anxiety that a sentence like this tries their patience as much as shuffling and spreading cards for solitaire instead of playing it on a computer, tablet or smart-phone.

I often wondered how the professor's game, and brain, might have been affected if he'd had a computer. By accelerating his perceptions and hand-eye coordination, would it have affected his amnesia? What if he'd been able to Google himself? He'd published books and articles, and his biography was accessible. What would happen to him if he met himself on Wikipedia?

Interesting though they were, such questions were dwarfed by my curiosity about his solitaire addiction and more, its parallels with my own. As the game replaced his impossible desire for memory with possible desire for another ace or king, it replaced my never-completely satisfied desire for clarity and truth with the easily realized goal that captivated him. I'd never taken anti-depressants but how could I doubt that the game was one for me?

Anyone who has read the above and knows something about meditation will not be surprised to hear that the brain that had led me to solitaire had also led me to Zen. In fact, it was Zen, which in its pure form, sitting meditation, or Zazen, is inescapably a kind of neurological research, had led to the book I was writing and the research that led to the professor. The parallels between Zazen and solitaire—game-playing in general, for that matter—were troubling and mysterious to me. Both are practices in concentration and present-moment-awareness, both take aim at anxiety, obsessive thought, long-term desire and other neurological oppression, and despite Zen's reputation for austerity and self-denial, the need for meditation is not completely antithetical to the need for play which is primal for animals as well as humans. Zazen, however, is not a game. It provides no measure of achievement, no loss or victory, no object of attention except the present moment which is always, of course, transient and ineffable, appearing and disappearing simultaneously. I think it's inaccurate to call it play without a game, not too far from solitaire without real or digital cards. Rooted as it is in the Buddha's understanding that birth is sure to generate desire, which in turn is sure to generate suffering, it would seem to be completely antithetical to a game organized around desire for a specific goal.

Still, if there's one thing you can say about Zen and other so-called "spiritual" practices, it's that they are not what they seem to be. I can't deny that, once the cards appear on my screen and with the usual, absurd, stupid excitement, I feel that I'm escaping my problems by placing one on another, the feelings I get from solitaire have much in common with those I find in Zazen. Doesn't solitaire, like Zazen, simplify my life? Bring me into the present moment? Make me feel, at least for a moment, that dread is not immutable?

For a moment, yes, but not forever, not even for awhile. What do I gain from consolidating my cards except a need to consolidate them again? Once my game is done, I'm still trapped by the same impossible desires—for security, say, or tranquility, not to mention eternal youth or freedom from illness and the certainty of death—that haunted me when I began. It is these ultimate, impossible desires that Zen addresses. More exactly, it addresses their neurological roots, the synaptic polarities that create and fuel them. You don't have to be a neuroscientist to know that such polarities generate negative-positive discriminations—bad and good, pain and pleasure, dark and light, etc.—and you don't have to be a Zen student to know that if the brain did not produce such information, desire would disappear. You do have to be a student of Zen or some other practice we'd call 'spiritual' to know that synaptic polarities occur in time but not in the present moment. Just then, sure, they occurred. Just now, they do not. It's only because of what happened then that the professor retains an idea of memory, thus a capacity to discriminate between memory and its absence, and only because of this that he suffers from his amnesia. And it's only because the game locates him entirely in the present moment that it frees him of his agony. That's the real joy of games but, since they always come to an end, it is their principal difference from Zazen.

Early on in Zen, one is dangerously vulnerable to over-excitement, belief in ultimate, perfect, never-to-diminish breakthroughs. Powerful and ecstatic, the feelings they produce are not unlike total victory in the only game one ever wanted to play. Since one is practicing, reaching for, and now and then experiencing absolute attention to the present moment—just sitting—it seems as if the brain is silent or at least unobtrusive. At one such moment, soon after I met the professor, it seemed to me I'd totally escaped identification with my brain. Though it continued to produce thought, memory and random mood and emotion, I saw all such as transient flashes that had no more to do with me than a blink of an eye or a muscle cramp. This is not an uncommon experience for those who embark on the practice, but I was new enough to it that it seemed unique and amazing. Just sitting, just in the present moment, I saw time itself as a flash, all my desires as laughable delusion, and understood for the first time why the Buddha (who after all, devoted his life to what I was doing just then), said "the first mark of enlightenment is contentment."

Later that morning, I visited the professor again. Since the hospital was a long subway ride from my home, I had plenty of time to contemplate my revelation. Among other things, it seemed to me I'd finally unpacked the conundrum of Zazen and solitaire. In *Zen Mind, Beginner's Mind*, Shunryu Suzuki, quoting the great Zen patriarch, Ehei Dogen, writes: "To study Zen is to study the self; to study the self is to forget the self." More than once, however, he also notes that "losing the self"—by which he means any form of escape—is antithetical to Zen. Like most beginning Zen students, I'd thought a lot about this point of view, but it seemed to me I'd only now understood it. What I'd known earlier, sitting in the present moment, was "forgetting" myself, but what I knew in solitaire, fixed on external objects, following a set of rules and aiming for a specific goal (all cards brought to perfect order) that gathered my attention and focused it on external objects, was "losing" myself. The latter was tranquilizing and restorative, of course, but it was also—as the professor and I had constantly discovered—transient, seductive and addictive, a respite from suffering that, like any drug or escape, left you, in the end, exactly where you'd been before with the probable exception that you were more anxious, probably desperate, to play again. All junkies—crack, weed or anti-depressants, alcohol, money, sex, TV or video games—know this trap. Losing the self solves nothing, forgetting it, everything. Where would I see better proof of this than in the professor and me, addicted to a game that left us, every time, exactly where we'd begun?

When I arrived that morning, he was in the midst of a game, sitting up in bed and, as usual, fixed on his cards like a child on a favorite toy. I knew at once that things were looking good for him. He glanced at me when I arrived but almost at the same moment turned another card. Standing at the foot of his bed, I knew it was just the one he needed. His smile was almost contagious. His victory was assured. One by one, he moved his cards until they were arranged in four horizontal lines near the top of his tray table. After enjoying for a moment this perfect order he'd achieved, he swept the cards into a single pile and with a dexterity I'd often noted, arranged them in a tight deck he gripped at the edge as if to test its geometry. Finally, nodding in my direction, he noticed the bag of candy I'd brought and, with almost as much interest as he showed in his cards, examined its contents. Extracting one, he unwrapped it slowly and, with serious, concentrated pleasure, took a small bite and chewed slowly, purposefully, as if to extend his pleasure as long as possible. How many times had I noted the similarities between the impulse toward solitaire and desire for food or drink, not to mention sex or, to bring it around to its obvious parallel, masturbation?

"Hello, professor."

"Hi."

"How are you today?"

He shakes his head. "No good."

Abrupt mood-shifts were hardly uncommon for him, but I'd never seen his face go dark so quickly. "I'm having problems with my memory."

"I'm sorry to hear that."

"Am I'm married? Do I have children? I'm trying to remember, but I can't!"

So much without thought did I answer him that I've never understood where my words originated. I thought I'd learned to handle the anxiety and the odd anger his condition could produce, but I saw now that I hadn't. Why else did my brain seem suddenly to split off from me, producing words I felt I'd not processed at all?

"Instead of trying to remember, why don't you try to forget?"

"What do you mean?"

"You spend so much time trying to remember things … why not try to forget them? 'Am I married? What's my wife's name? Do I have children?' Why not give it up? You're an amnesiac! You should be able to do that easily!"

He stared at me expressionless for minute. Then he laughed aloud. "Ha, ha, ha!" He wasn't smiling. The sound he produced could not by any stretch be confused with humor. Mirthless, hollow, it resembled nothing so much as the "Ho! Ho! Ho!" you hear from a professional Santa Claus. He'd always been mild, congenial, no threat to anyone, but as the laugh grew louder, it seemed aggressive, raging, not a little intimidating. I left the room quickly but even at the far end of the long hall between his room and the nurses' station, I could hear him bellowing. "Ho! Ho! Ho! Ho! Ho! Ho!" I don't know that I've ever heard a more frightening sound.

8. MADISON SQUARE GARDEN

Written on assignment for Esquire Magazine.

Ascend from the subway at 8th Avenue and 50th Street and the Garden is in view—a cavernous barn of a building, its marquee suitable for porn movies, its stonework badly in need of cleaning and repair. No one will mourn it when demolition crews move in next summer and, a few years down the road, no one will remember that the excitement it generated could once be felt even by those who did not know what is going on inside, four or five blocks away. Since its rush of events will continue, almost uninterrupted, in its new incarnation 16 blocks away, its 42-year reign as the greatest playground on earth will drift with the tides of history. Its games and events have been witnessed by an estimated 130 million people. They have ranged from what the building's booking records call "Hockey, Professional" to the game we call religion -- "May 14, 1947, Billy Graham" -- and further, since every American president or candidate for president has appeared on its stage, to the one we call politics. It is the home of the New York Knicks basketball team, the New York Ranger hockey team, the scene of circuses, track meets, dog shows, cat shows and horse shows, prize fights, of course, 6-day races (on bikes and roller skates), dance marathons and roller derbies, bridge tournaments, ice shows, ski shows, tennis and wrestling matches, ballets and concerts, rallies for every cause, race and nationality that booked it for a day. Preparing now for the last of its 12,678 events, it is, as always, a workaday world for the riggers, ushers, cleaners, vendors, and managers who constitute the army of support play and games require.

May 26, 1939

PADEREWSKI COLLAPSES AT GARDEN AS 15,000 GATHER FOR CONCERT

Ignace Jan Paderewski, the distinguished 78-year-old pianist, collapsed from what is officially announced as a "slight heart attack" last night in a dressing room in the Madison Square Garden a few minutes before he is scheduled to give the 21st concert of his present American tour.

* * *

Of all its departments, the one with which the Garden has been most identified is boxing. It isn't its most profitable division anymore, and surely it doesn't have the stature it had when the fighters were Joe Louis and Beau Jack and Sugar Ray Robinson, or the promoters Tex Rikard and Mike Ja- cobs, but the Garden was built by Rikard—a gold prospector from Texas who had promoted two fights before he came to New York—and built for boxing (thus its bad sight lines for events like hockey and track), so last February. the fact remained that if you wanted to get to the center of the Garden, if you wanted to smell the way it smelled when it was new, you had to go up to the boxing department and sit around for a couple of days at least.

From the Booking Records:

Feb. 23, 1938: Joe Louis vs. Nathan Mann, Heavyweight Champ.
Jan. 25, 1939: Joe Louis vs. John Henry Lewis, Heavyweight Champ.
Feb. 9, 1940: Joe Louis vs. Arturo Godoy, Heavyweight Champ.
Mar. 29, 1940: Joe Louis vs. Johnny Paycheck, Heavyweight Champ.
Jan. 31, 1941: Joe Louis vs. Red Burman, Heavyweight Champ.
Jan. 9, 1942: Joe Louis vs. Buddy Baer, Heavyweight Champ.
Jan. 27, 1942: Joe Louis vs. Abe Simon, Heavyweight Champ.
Dec. 5, 1947: Joe Louis vs. Jersey Joe Walcott, Heavyweight Champ.

It is a matter of image. If you ask anyone anywhere in the building where the boxing department is, they will tell you, "In the back." Because times are bad in that area. In the fifties there was a notorious anti-trust suit against James Norris (then director of Garden Boxing) and the International Boxing Club, and, recently, the tragic death of Benny Paret, after his fight at the Garden with Emile Griffith. Then, too, the state of the heavyweights, the Cadillacs of the business, is something less than wholesome. First Floyd Patterson brought neurosis into the ring, and then Sonny Liston turned out to be not only disreputable but discourteous. As if this hadn't been enough, Liston seemingly quit in his second fight against Muhammad Ali, then known as Cassius Clay, and the latter turned out to be, as he likes to put it, "the baddest" of all. He joined the Muslims, insulted white men, and finally, with innocence no draft board could tolerate, declared that he had "nothing against no Vietcongs." Nowadays, the Garden is a huge, diversified corporation, and image—hardly a word Tex Rikard fancied—is a thing that matters. That's why the boxing department, which is in fact located in the front-north corner of the building, overlooking 8th Avenue, with a perfect view of the diner on the comer of 8th Avenue and 51st Street, is said to be "in the back."

You have to let yourself in through a door with a complicated latch on the inside, but that is the last pretense at privacy. As John F. X. Condon, the publicity director, likes to put it, the four rooms that make up the department have "their own stink." The odor—a rather complicated mixture of stale leather and forgotten cigars leaning against cigarette packages in ash trays—is actually not uninteresting. These four rooms are open territory, and the openness is systematically abused, all day most every day, by a parade of

characters who look to have stepped without pause from the pages of Runyan or Leibling, or both. They are old fighters and young fighters, and managers of old fighters and young fighters, and most of the writers who write about fighters. When Joe Louis is in town, you'll often find him sitting on the radiator in Teddy Brenner's office. You might run into Sugar Ray, Emile Griffith, or Ali's manager, Angelo Dundee. The "Madison Square Boxing" on the door has an "Inc." after it, but for the "mob," as Leibling used to call it, this is a private club, the place where they come whenever they want to remember, or be remembered.

On this dismal, frigid day in February, there isn't much action. March 22, the next open date, is not yet filled, and there is more time than anyone wants to notice for talk. So much time, in fact, that Condon has recently tried to edit it. "I told them, 'No more talk about the old days.' For Christ's sake, how much can anyone talk about Ferlenbach and Delaney? I told them, 'The old days is NOW!'"

But there isn't much now to support Condon's edict. The telephone is hardly ringing, and the eight or nine people who staff the office are leaving early. There's a fight coming up between Frankie Narvaez and Ismael Laguna, but they are lightweights and that means plenty of working press tickets for everyone, no arguments for Condon, no sponges for Director Harry Markson to avoid. Since the biggest story about this one seems to be the riot everyone expects, and since no one writes about riots until after they're over, the reporters will do one pre-fight story and one post-fight, and even Condon can't convince them to do more. Without these distractions, the place is quiet, depressed, and reeking with anachronism. The boxing gloves hanging on the wall behind Condon's desk ("Save Water" inscribed on the fist of one) have as much authenticity as those pictures of Rita Hayworth that used to come with new billfolds.

But on February 16, Harry Markson calls booking manager John Goldner down to the booking office and imparts a piece of information that allows him to make the records more specific. Previously the schedule (prepared as always six months in advance) had signified "Boxing" on March 22, nothing more, but now Goldner will be able add the names of the combatants: "March 22 ... Boxing: Cassius Clay vs. Zora Folley, Heavyweight Championship."

It will be the first heavyweight championship fight since January 12, 1961, when Ezzard Charles knocked out Lee Oma. That bout drew 55,000 and earned less than $200,000. Markson is predicting a $400,000 gate for this one. Muhammad Ali, as the Garden has agreed to call him, will earn more for this fight than Joe Louis earned for all his Garden defenses. Between them, Markson and Brenner and Condon are already dispensing this information to the world, over telephones that hardly stopped ringing. The club has come alive.

From the Garden Booking Records:

Oct. 26, 1941 ... Rodeo moves out
Oct. 27, 1941 ... New York Committee for Medical Aid to Russia
Oct. 28, 1941 ... American Labor Party Rally
Oct. 29, 1941 ... American Trucking Association
Oct. 30, 1941 ... American First Committee

Oct. 31, 1941 ... Boxing - Sugar Ray Robinson vs. Fritzie Zivic
Nov. 1, 1941 ... Communist Party Rally
Nov. 4, 1941 ... Horse Show moves in

At first it is mostly routine. Markson has to think about pricing the tickets and television time, and Condon has to come up with a way to sell the fight to a crowd that has obviously ceased to believe in any challenger's chances against Ali ("But think of it this way," Condon muses. "Zora's 34. He's got eight kids and he is a combat hero in Korea. It won't be as difficult as you think.") The boxing staff has been through it all up to 52 times a year in the past. They are giving Laguna and Narvaez equal time until a sudden rush of information forces them to forget their lightweights altogether. At their training camps in the Catskills, Ali and Folley have found too much snow on the ground for roadwork. Their trainers have decided to bring them to New York where they can run in Central Park and set up their camps in the Garden basement.

The day after this shift in location announced, Condon, in his office "in the back," has exchanged his business suit and tie for a polo shirt and a golf hat. The Catskills are coming to the basement, and he is dressed for the trip.

1932 - VENZKE BREAKS INDOOR RECORD—
RUNS 4:10 MILE AT GARDEN
1934 - CUNNINGHAM RUNS MILE IN 4:08.4—
NEW INDOOR RECORD
1938 - CUNNINGHAM BREAKS OWN RECORD
AT GARDEN —RUNS 4:07.4
1940 - FENSKE WINS WANAMAKER IN 4:07.4—
EQUALS CUNNINGHAM'S RECORD
1941 - McMITCHELL WINS BAXTER IN 4:07.4—
TIES RECORD
1944 - GIL DODDS SETS NEW RECORD
AT GARDEN—RUNS 4:07.3 MILE
1963 - BEATY RUNS FIRST SUB-FOUR

MINUTE INDOOR MILE—DOES 3.58.6
AT GARDEN
1964 - O'HARA RUNS 3.56.6 MILE AT GARDEN
1964 - O'HARA BETTERS GARDEN RECORD—
DOES 3.56.4

In the jargon of the building, Dick Donapria is in charge of
"the back of the house," but more precisely, he is the initial
source of the Garden's illusions, the man who hides the building
behind the various wardrobes it must don for the benefit of its
games. Before Markson can receive Ali and Folley, he has to
check with Donapria. Can a ring be set up in the basement? Do
we have a heavy bag in our equipment room? A speed bag? Can
we wire the joint for television cameras? Once Donapria okays
the project, word is relayed to the Catskills. By the time Ali and
Folley arrive at the Garden basement at 12:30 and 2:30
respectively, March 6th (there are four hundred people waiting in
line on 9th Street to see Ali work out), Donaprias's men have
transformed the 2nd floor into a respectable training camp. A
main ring is installed, a heavy bag suspended from two cables
stretched diagonally between four of the columns that support
the arena floor above, a speed bag and its 2-foot platform erected.
Blue and gold curtains surrounding the areas try in vain to hide
the basement's shabbiness, but there is enough temporary voltage
wired in from generators to satisfy all the television networks at
once.

* * *

You have to look hard to find the building itself behind the
illusion. Surely you won't recognize this as the place where—
elephants feeding where the ring stands now—you saw the circus
menagerie, installed as usual a floor below the arena where it
appears, last April, but there are certain constants, like the gray

yellow walls, or the round globe lights hanging from the ceiling, or the "EXIT TO 49th STREET" sign. Like scraps of reality creeping through the magic, gaps in the armor of the Garden's anonymity, they are no less present for Muhammad Ali than they were for the circus.

APRIL 17, 1948

SALUTE TO ISRAEL PACKS GARDEN

19,000 INSIDE; 75,000 JAM 49TH STREET

For Donapria, it is hardly an accomplishment to set up a training camp in the basement. He has been performing this sort of miracle for almost thirty years. Except for the Russian circus, whose riggers he found indecisive, and a ski show in 1947, he can't remember much that gave him pause. He still talks about the ski show with incredulity. "We had to build a ski jump in the arena and keep it covered with snow that wouldn't melt when the temperature of the building is raised to its normal 70 degrees. Which meant we had to study the temperature and texture and contours of ski slopes and jumps particularly. Had to make sure that when they jumped, they'd land at the proper tangent on snow which would support them. Etcetera, etcetera. Not being a skier, I had to go to the library and read up on the stuff. Which I did, and it worked out pretty good, believe it or not. They landed all right." Donapria and his crew of about 110 have set up for political rallies, the Bolshoi Ballet ("a nice, dainty, quiet arrangement ... their maintenance men know their business."), girls' softball tournaments, and, in 1946, a one-ring circus which, as far as he can remember, brought the Garden the only mice he's ever seen here. He is particularly proud of a method his crew devised for keeping flies out of the arena when circus is in residence. "You might see a couple up here in the office," he said, "but try to find one in the arena." When the New York Fire Department had its "Midnight Alarm" show in the building, Donapria's men built them a three-story building to use in demonstrating escapes, and when the rodeo came, they installed 600 cubic yards of soil for three weeks and removed it within six hours, after the last show was over. In addition to these "special situations," they performed two jobs once or twice a week during the season. For one thing, they changed the arena from a basketball court into a hockey rink, and, for another, they changed it from a hockey rink into a basketball court.

December 31, 1959

**CINCINNATI DOWNS IOWA IN GARDEN
FINALE AS ROBERTSON GETS
RECORD 50 POINTS**

March 28, 1967

**SAM JONES SCORES 51 AS
CELTICS BEAT KNICKS**

As a case in point take the weekend just before the arrival of the fighters. On Friday night the New York Athletic Club has a track meet beginning at 7:15 PM. This requires importing what Donapria estimates as "a couple of lumber yards" into the main arena. A wooden 220-yard oval running track occupies most of the main arena. It is bisected by a wooden dash track which, because space is short, continues into the main lobby, and it will often look to be crowded by a pole vault pit and runway, broad-jump and high-jump pits and their runways, etc., and others of the various assortment of track equipment (the hurdles alone are an achievement to install), not to mention the dozens of athletes milling about, waiting for their events. The meet ends at 11:15, which is about half an hour after Donapria's night crew comes to work. While the porters strip the seating areas of their assorted beer and soda cups, cigarette packages and stubs, peanut shells, crumpled programs and newspapers and popcorn boxes and half-eaten hot dogs, and the occasional dollar bill they find, others dismantle the track and pile it onto Bobcats that take it down to storage in the basement. The Garden keeps its running track and re-assembles it for every meet. This wasn't true of the track used in six-day bike races, which was much too big and heavy for storage. Each year a new one was constructed, the last in 1959, at a cost of $30,000. After races, it went to landfill.

At 11:30, the carpenters begin disassembling the track, and at the same time, the ice plant is switched on, the brine in its pipes pumping a cool 11-degree wave beneath the floor. By two in the morning, the floor is bare and cleaned and, at three, the floor is sprayed with hoses. There are five different sprays and a delay between each for the ice to harden. The ice is eventually built to a thickness of 5/8 of an inch. Between the next to last and last spray, it is painted white, a practice begun in the ice shows and carried over to hockey when Donapria realized it would make the puck show up more clearly. At 6 a.m., the men punch out and where the track meet took place a few hours ago, there now lies an expanse of ice that is not without re- semblance to a birthday cake. It wears the blue and red insignia of the New York Rangers near the blue and red line that bisects the ice, and "Rangers" and "Blackhawks" have been allotted their proper places on the scoreboards that hang from four different points on the mezzanine. Between the rink and the grandstands, there now stands a thick plastic shield which will protect fans from errant pucks. Awaiting its players and its spectators, the Garden itself, dressed as if for a masquerade ball in a brand-new wardrobe, is hid- den by its function once again.

For the maintenance crew, however, the most difficult part is yet to come. The house is full for the hockey game—more than 15,000 people—and except for those the ushers called the "late pissers," they're all gone within eight minutes after the game ends, at 4:10. The raucous bedlam of the crowd is displaced by the clacking of the writers' typewriters and the brooms of the sweepers, collecting piles almost identical with those left by track fans last night. By 4:30, the plastic shield has been removed. There won't be enough time to melt the ice, so the basketball court will be installed on top of it. Within minutes of the game's conclusion, two of Donapria's men stretch lines of green twine across to guide the men who lay out the court.

At 4:25, the first of ten Bobcats roll onto the ice, dragging the basketball court, piled in slats, behind them. Each slat is 3 feet by 10, and there are 150 slats on each truck. Laying them in place, the men might be working on a huge jigsaw puzzle. After the ends of the court are in place, the glass back- boards, on hand trucks, are rolled onto the court, and two mechanical hoists (there are six in the Garden ceiling) are lowered, hooked to each and activated by a foreman on the 50th Street side of the arena. Rising from the floor to their exact official height, the backboards seem to levitate but their rims are exotic birds, bright orange in color, rising in a narrow arc from the floor. Finally, two men mount ladders set beside the backboards to attach four cables -- two connected to the ceiling and two to the side balcony—that will hold them stationary during the game. By now the sweepers are finished, and the men Donapria calls "cleaners" are dragging barrels toward their piles, collecting them, and taking them down to the basement, where dump trucks will pick them up tomorrow. There are forty-three men at work on the floor. Painters with stencils appear and the iconography of basketball begins to take shape. Foul lines, the half court line, the black keyhole take shape beneath the basket. By 5:05, the floor is a court. Concession men and ushers are sleeping in the top balcony. Six men, working on the scoreboards beneath the mezzanine press boxes, replace "RANGERS" and "BLACKHAWKS" with "KNICKS" and "PISTONS." Carpenters set to work, connecting the boards of the court with screws. On normal days, which is to say those when there is but one event, Donapria estimates 2 ½ hours for this part of the job, but today, with a crew triple the normal size, it takes an hour. At 5:10, the overhead lights, which were dimmed at the end of the hockey game, are turned up to ¾ their level during events, and an electrician addresses himself to the game clock which—set to five minutes and timed as it moves to zero —is tested before each event. Done with the clock, he checks the buzzers on the control board, adjusts the "twenty-four second" clocks, which stand at the corners of the court. By now a good part of the end balcony is filled with white-jacketed vendors. Since basketball courts are smaller than hockey rinks, 356 extra seats have been installed.

The court is a bit short of half-finished when Howard Komives, a New York player who's been injured for several weeks, appears with a ball. As the carpenters work at the other end, Komives works out under the eye of a doctor and trainer. At 5:30, Torn Van Arsdale and Eddie Miles, two Detroit players, appear at the edge of the floor, stare idly at the carpenters for a minute, then leave for their dressing room. At 5:30, the doors are opened, and the first spectators emerge onto the upper balcony from the chutes that connect the stands to the great wide concrete ramps that encircle them. The sight of Komives, who has been on the injured list for several weeks, brings the sort of whoops of recognition that one might offer an old friend. "Hey, Butch! How's the ankle?" "Let's see the jumper, Howie!" So involved with Komives are they that they do not notice a sight rarely seen by fans—the maintenance crew at work, not yet done with constructing the office where Komives goes to work. Most days, disappearing into the wings like magician's assistants disappearing through a trap door, Donapria's men are nowhere to be seen by the times the doors are opened. By now, Garden security has taken positions throughout the stands, and two of them are chasing two kids who have come down to courtside for Komives's autograph. "Hey, kid. Where you think you are?" The vendors, of course, are gone, working concession stands in the walkway or loading up their trays to work the stands. Early evening games like this are gold mines for concession stands because man fans don't eat dinner before the game. At 6:00, the lights go to full power and there isn't a maintenance man in sight. Virginia Thomas, virtuoso of the Garden's organ, offers one of her specialties: "Once in Love with Amy." At 6:15, the teams come onto the floor to warm up, at 6:20 the referees, the timekeepers and the scorers are in place, and John Condon, who supplements his work in the boxing department as the P.A. man for basketball, is checking out the microphone. "Five, four, three, testing. Five, four, three." Near the benches, Knick assistants set out water coolers, and starting players remove their warm-up suits. At 6:30 the buzzer sounds, Miss Thomas stops playing, and Condon speaks into the mic: "Here are the starting lineups for tonight's game. For the Detroit Pistons ... at forward... number 16 ... " There are thirteen thousand people in the stands. They know Komives and Van Arsdale, of course, but how many have heard of Donapria?

September 25, 1938

20,000 IN GARDEN CHEER FOR CZECHS

CHAMBERLAIN IS BOOED

'HITLER MUST FALL, SAYS THOMAS MANN. THIS AND NOTHING ELSE WILL PRESERVE THE PEACE!'

Every day at 1, they came to watch the champ. The mob is there, of course, and any fighter who is in town, but you'll also see more than 200 African-American children from a Manhattan public school, no small number of beautiful women, a huge, vocal Muslim contingent, and—almost daily—some black-frocked, bearded students from a nearby Yeshiva who spend most of their time dodging photographers. Last week, this room was the site of an antique show where cultivated women browsed attentively. It was preceded by the Westminster Dog Show, which brought 800 dogs to lodge in cages where Ali and Folley now train, while upstairs the quietest of all Garden crowds remained in the arena as long as eight hours to watch the competition and listen to a professorial announcer who introduced the breeds with the solemnity of a priest: "The Dachshund is a serious worker, known for his great determination. He originated in Germany where he used to hunt the badger. He comes in three coats—smooth, longhaired, and wild haired."

Preparing for the fight, Condon has relinquished his duties as basketball announcer. You'll see him every day now, greeting fans arriving to watch the training sessions, reminding them that the fight is every day getting nearer, and that the Laguna-Narvaez fight is so eminent that they better purchase their tickets immediately after the workout. He is in the process of repeating it

113

all for latecomers, when he hears a commotion near the stairs. It can mean but one thing. "Here he is now! Ladies and gentlemen! The heavyweight champion of the whole world ... MUHAMMAD ALI!"

As Ali, in a white terrycloth robe and white shoes, shuffles into the basement, Condon turns his attention to the press. It is his job to disseminate the day's relevant information. This morning, there has been a medical examination, and the reporters will surely want to know the fighters' blood pressures, weights, pulses, etc. etc. For color, he recalls a few of the witticisms Ali has uttered since yesterday ("The man that's gonna whup me is 11 years old right now.") and then he reminds the writers that they can arrange interviews with either fighter on any day they choose. By now the champ is in his comer, combing his hair with one hand as Drew Brown, one of his trainers, tapes the other. Condon explained to the crowd why a boxer's hands are taped, how they are taped, and how workouts require a different sort of taping than fights.

May 27, 1928

TRANSCONTINENTAL FOOT RACE
ENDS IN GARDEN

SMALLEST CROWD IN GARDEN HISTORY

At 8:19 last night, fifty-five athletes, sunburned and weather-beaten to a cindery complexion, leapt from the Weehawken ferryboat, completing their 3,485 mile run from Los Angeles to New York on their 84th day out. Only 543 people, the smallest crowd in Madison Square Garden history, are there to observe the finish and to see Tex Rikard present Andy Payne, the winner, with a check for $25,000.

Eleven of the runners announced immediately after the race that they would remain in New York to compete in the dance endurance contest beginning June 11 at the Garden.

114

Four days after Ali and Folley begin their workouts, twelve cardboard cartons arrive at a side entrance to the Garden. Two armed policemen sign for them and take them to the box office. They contain the tickets to the fight, and the man who takes charge of them is Ernie Fontan, the box office director. In 1931, Fontan had a small electronics business that wasn't making much money. When a friend who worked at the Garden asked if he could help them out for about ten days, Fontan came over. He's been here ever since. He has seen the Garden itself change, but he is adamant in his belief that the crowds themselves haven't changed at all. "People change. Societies change. But when you get a group of this size together, it is always the same." If you disagree on this account, you'll want to find a different man to argue with. Fontan is an expert on crowds. He watches them, unit by unit, being born, the face peering through the bars, the fingers thumbing on the counter as they mull over available locations, the hand disappearing, then returning with cash. "Everybody is mad at the box office man," he says, "and why shouldn't they be? There is only one seat at the center of the house, and, up here, that one belongs to Ned Irish." It may be that box office men all over the world share a particular view of humanity, but this view is wider and more heterogeneous at the Garden. Fontan isn't selling one event but as many as a hundred, receiving and delivering, arranging and registering and, sometimes, discarding portions of the nearly 200,000 tickets circulating in the box office at a given time. One year, when the Rangers made the playoffs unexpectedly, they sold 18,000 tickets in one day. It had gotten easier, of course. When Fontan arrived, tickets were stored in cardboard boxes and his space was thirty feet by fifteen, but four years ago, the Garden took over the Childs restaurant on the comer and the box office grew to eighty by a hundred. Then too, old-timers will tell you that this building was put up in such a hurry that no one thought of box office windows. In the early days, they made do with temporary tables under the marquee or in the side lobbies.

There are twenty men working in the office when the tickets arrive. Since the box office will be charged with every ticket, they had to be counted and a report sent up to the treasurer's office. In the new Garden, now going up on 7th Avenue, at 33rd Street, there will be a special room for such counting, but here desks have to be cleared, special tables set up, tickets laid out in batches. First, the mail orders will be answered, then, on March 6, the window sale will begin. "You'll get all kinds of course," says Fontan. "After a while you get so you can tell what they want before they say anything. Oh, in some cases, of course, it's simple. When the Bolshoi is here, we get people who never come near the place otherwise, and obviously, you don't have to be too smart to recognize the wrestling fan or the lady who wants two for the Roller Derby. But by now I think I can predict when they'll want hockey and when basketball, and, mind you, that isn't too easy." Reporting on a Joe Louis fight at the Garden, A. J. Leibling wrote: "The box office man is po- lite, which is always a bad sign for the gate." But Ernie Fontan claims his men have been mostly polite over the years. He's proud of the fact that no man has ever been dismissed for accepting a bribe. Like Garden ushers, they've been offered everything from cigars to crumpled twenties, but they have their own "Ten Commandments" in the box office, and, courtesy and honesty are the first two, just ahead of "Thou shalt always sell off the top."

Every day the Ali-Folley tickets are passed through the bars, the money taken and stowed in the wooden drawers under the counter. One day before the fight, Fontan and his assistant will study the figures and estimate the house. This is an important number. The Chief of Security will use it to decide how many men to call for the fight, the concessions department to determine their hot dog, roll, and peanut orders. Unfortunately for the workers in these two departments, Fontan's men are so good at estimates, hitting close to one percent as a rule, that few extra men had been called over the last few years. There is inter-Garden antagonism over this. It is also Fontan's job to make the house look good when it isn't. "I can make six thousand look like twelve, by killing off the right sections, or playing around with the lights and darkening some of the empty areas." Markson and Condon and Brenner are hoping with a relish that reached near prayer that Fontan would not have to call on this particular talent the night of March 22.

January 13, 1946

FOSTER BIDS UNIONS BE MORE MILITANT

20,000 COMMUNISTS RALLY AT GARDEN

Hands taped, robe removed, Ali dances and shadowboxes while Condon describes him to the crowd as if, for all his fame and singularity, he is un- known to them. "Muhammad Ali is twenty-five years old. He was born in Louisville, Kentucky. He began boxing at the age of twelve. In his six years as a professional, he's had twenty-eight fights and won them all, twenty-two by knockout. He is six foot two and one half inches tall and he weighs in currently at two hundred nine and one half pounds."

Constructed just a few days ago, this improvised training camp is a happy hunting ground for media—18 photographers are here today, two television crews, more than two dozen reporters. Roaming through the crowd, two men are selling autographed photos of the champ. After the schoolchildren arrive, Condon invites a photogenic eight-year-old girl to pose with Ali in the ring, and Ali enhances the situation by lying prostrate at the boy's feet while the flashbulbs explode all over the room.

Ali's sparring partner, James Ellis, is stretching and shadowboxing at the far end of the training area. Ellis is part of the undercard on the 22nd, scheduled for 10 rounds with Johnny Person. An Italian journalist asks if it gives him special incentive to fight in the Garden. "Oh, man, yeah," says Ellis. "These are fight fans here!" Most athletes will tell you that. Surely there isn't a basketball player in America who doesn't equate playing in the Garden with the highest available measure of success, and most fighters feel the same way. Johnny Green, a former Knick player now with the Baltimore Bullets, calls his first game at the Garden the greatest thrill of his life. "You have to play here before you know how good you are." But there are disadvantages, too. Green is with a losing team in Baltimore, as he had been in New York, but there is no comparison between losing in New York and losing anywhere else. "They expect you to win here, and they can be cruel if you don't. We're losing in Baltimore, but the fans haven't changed at all." A number of athletes will accept Emile Griffith's assertion that the Garden is "the place that turns you on," but there have been some who couldn't bear the pressure.

Alan Stanly, a hockey player now with Toronto, came up with the Rangers first, but, as Ned Irish remembers, "For some odd reason, the fans got on him. Every time he got the puck they'd call him Sonya from the balcony. He went to pieces on the rink, couldn't do anything for us. But here he is twelve years later on the All-Star team." Irish suggests that some players, particularly younger ones, are upset by the relentless impartiality of the crowd, and he can list the names of players who lost their careers to the Garden. "Darrall Imhoff, Walter Duke, guys like that can't take it here, and once the crowd picks up on their problem, they boo without mercy." Angelo Dundee, Ali's manager, has another slant on the matter. "The Garden is where the press is. What are we without the press?"

June 11, 1928

132 COUPLES START IN DANCE MARATHON AT GARDEN

Mayor Bossy Grille, of Newburyport, Massachusetts, fired a gun last night to initiate a dance endurance contest of indeterminate length at Madison Square Garden. As the first song, "Sweet Sue, I Love You," began, there were 132 couples on the floor and a brilliant variety of costumes in all colors. Standard dance derby rules will prevail during the marathon -- the contestants must dance for one hour and after that may take no more than 15 minutes rest.

June 12, 1928

ENDURANCE CONTEST LOSES 35 COUPLES

Thirty-five couples dropped out of the dance endurance contest at the Garden yesterday. 27 hours after the first dance, however, there are still 97 couples dancing.

June 15, 1928

TEMPERS CRACKING IN MARATHON DANCE

Heat, exhaustion and irritability, causing disregard for the rules, eliminated ten more couples at Madison Square Garden yesterday, leaving 34 couples still on the floor when the dance derby entered its fifth day. It is getting to be a battle of temperaments, as the couples try to discourage their rivals by looking their best and claiming total absence of fatigue.
Miss Patricia Salmon recovered her stamina yesterday after

119

dancing for 5 hours the previous day while unconscious. During the period of her semi-cataleptic state, she was carried about the floor by her partner.

Miss Gloria Patrick, 16 years old, was ruled off by the medical staff because her feet bad grown too big for the men's shoes she was wearing. Protesting vehemently, Miss Patrick begged that she be allowed to continue in galoshes, but she was ruled off anyway.

June 29, 1928

DANCE DERBY TRANSFERRED TO GARDEN BASEMENT NINE COUPLES REMAIN AFTER 425 HOURS

After 425 hours of continual dancing, 9 couples remained yesterday in the dance endurance contest at Madison Square Garden. Due to the previously scheduled boxing bout between Tommy Loughran and Armand Emanuel, the derby was moved to the Garden basement yesterday afternoon. The transfer went off without difficulty however, and the dancers were able to continue with no interruption.

June 30, 1928

DANCE CONTEST HALTED BY POLICE

NINE REMAINING COUPLES VOW TO CONTINUE ELSEWHERE

The Garden was named for its first location, on Madison Square, 23rd Street and 5th Avenue, New York. The original structure, opened in 1874, was owned by P.T. Barnum, who installed his circus there and found its principal capital in the horse show. Space limitations led to expansion in 1890—an impressive Stanford White design of mustard-colored brick and stucco. Like its successor, the new building quickly accumulated

120

its legend and scandal. One unscheduled event—the murder of White by Harry K. Thaw over the affections of Evelyn Nesbitt—achieved a greater notoriety than any other. Besides circuses and industrial shows and horse shows, the Democratic Party held its National Convention there in 1924. When the building's owner, Tex Rikard, was informed by the New York Life Insurance Company that they planned to build an office building on the site, he raised six million dollars (the new Garden, on 33rd Street, will cost an estimated $116 million) from a group he liked to call "my six hundred millionaires." In June of 1924, he announced purchase of a group of car barns on 8th Avenue and 50th Street, to build there what he called "the largest building in the world devoted exclusively to amusement." On November 19, 1925, an incredible six months after demolition had begun, the building opened with a six-day bike race. The New York Times exulted in its opening.

"A new clean Madison Square Garden, a garden of light and shining marble pillars in the lobby, a garden with modern ventilation which gives one the feeling of being in an enchanted oval. The building lacks but one thing -- the tradition, the aroma that the old Garden kept from its two generations of circuses, prizefights, and political meetings.

"Reputations will be made and lost in the Garden. The gay lights will look down on many a stirring scene of life and politics. Pugilists will achieve renown there and be battered out of championships, history will be made. But last night it was all new and fresh, with the future all before it - a Madison Square Garden with its face washed."

Workout finished, autographs dispensed, Ali and his entourage make their way back to a smallish room in the back of the building where Donapria and his crew have made a dressing room for him. Approaching it through one of the many cavernous ramps that make a maze of the Garden's interior, you pass the basketball court and the running track, still piled on the trucks that carry it to the arena. They are left here, in the open, because there is never time enough to take them down to the storage areas and bring them back for games and meets.

Ali's room is Number 29. It is ten feet by fifteen and at the moment there are forty-two people inside—photographers, fight people, reporters from all over the world. Yesterday, the champ's request for draft deferral, on the claim that he is a Black Muslim minister, was rejected, and he's been ordered to report for induction on April 11. Half in anger and half in deference to Madison Square Boxing Incorporated, since gate receipts have not yet developed momentum, Ali has announced that the fight with Folley will be his last. Which news has tripled both box office sales and the size of the press contingent. There are so many interviews going on in the room that the champion cannot move. His clothes are handed to him by one of his handlers over the outstretched microphone of a television newsman, and he does not bother to shower. Time and again he dispenses the now-famous remark that if someone can convince him that going to Vietnam will help to free 22 million Blacks, "you wouldn't have to draft me, I'd join tomorrow."

This isn't the room Ali will use on fight-night. That will be Number 28, and the Rangers are using it now. 29 is used mostly for emergencies. Twice already, during the National Invitation Basketball Tournament, the champ's equipment has been removed to the basement so someone else can use the room. John Goldner, who manages room assignments, likes to give this room to cheerleaders during the NIT, but with Ali in residence, he's invited cheerleaders to dress in his office, just as several years earlier he cleared it for Marilyn Monroe when she sang "Happy Birthday" to President Kennedy at his Garden birthday party. The Garden management had never been particularly obsessive about its records, but Goldner is something of an exception. If you press him, he'll tell you that Ali's dressing room is next door to the one the Boston Celtics prefer when they play the Garden, and that it is also the room where Paderewski had his heart attack, the room Benny Paret used the night he was fatally injured in his fight with Emile Griffith, the room Eisenhower favored when he visited the building. "When Ike came," says Goldner, "we made some changes—a couple of easy chairs and some flowers, you know. The phone to the White House and a couple of clean towels."

October 31, 1936

**ROOSEVELT DEFIES 'ORGANIZED MONEY'
PLEDGES CONTINUED FIGHT
FOR NEW DEAL**

**20,000 AT GARDEN:
GETS 13-MINUTE OVATION**

John Condon is a kind of Garden archetype. He's worked in the boxing department for seven years, but from the narrow plywood table at courtside, he's been surrounded by the Garden crowd for 17 years, and they, as well as the players, have come to know his voice as an essential part of the game. "You'd be surprised how I can control them. I can get them excited about a dull game, get them behind a player, or get them on his back. It all depends on tone of voice." Such intimacy with the crowd is not without repercussion. It has brought him embarrassment and physical danger. For one thing, since he announces referees' decisions, he is often held responsible for their decisions. Once, in an NBA game, a shot glass flew out of the top balcony and missed his eye by inches, and just recently Walt Bellamy, the Knickerbockers' six-foot-eleven-inch center, had seemed about to throttle him over what he considered a deliberate injustice by a referee. It was Condon after all who leaned forward, wearing dark glasses, gripping the microphone with absolute power, and informed the crowd, "The foul is on Bellamy." Once, in a St. John's-NYU game, he'd made such an announcement about a player who happened to have a fanatic supporter standing just behind the table. As Condon announced the player's foul, he heard a voice behind him snap, "Damn it, he didn't do it!" and before he could turn, he'd been hit with a karate chop on the back of the neck that knocked him cold. The game waited, of course, until Condon is revived.

On March 10, when Laguna fights Narvaez, Condon has to call on the steely nerves he has developed at the basketball microphone. The crowd that night is equally divided between Laguna partisans, many of whom have come up from Panama, and the supporters of Narvaez, who are well-known for their intolerance of decisions, just or unjust, against their man. Laguna's victory is decisive, but they smell a rat and set out to kill it. Seconds after the decision is announced, the anonymous heads at ringside are targets of debris which falls like bombs from the balcony—tomatoes first, then programs, bags of peanuts, coke and beer containers, all of it fairly benign until the bottles come. Once begun, they come from every angle, smashing against the ring post or the floor or the ringside seats and exploding in slivers that spray in all directions. Ringside customers, which is to say the press and celebrities or anyone comped for the fight, are trapped as if in ambush. Some claw their way to exits, but most take refuge under the ring. Security police hold chairs like shields over their heads. After it's over, 15 people (none seriously injured) will be taken to the hospital. The typewriter of a reporter hit on the forehead is streaked with the color of his blood. After the medics take him away, Condon—using the writer's blood-drenched notes—will finish his story: "Ishmael Laguna won a clear-cut decision over Frankie Narvaez in ten exciting rounds last night at Madison Square Garden. Narvaez's supporters rioted after the fight, hurling tomatoes, binoculars and bottles from the balcony ... "

February 21, 1939

22,000 NAZIS HOLD RALLY IN GARDEN

> Protected by more than 1,700 policemen, who made of Madison Square Garden a fortress almost impregnable to anti-Nazis, the German-American Bund last night staged its much-advertised "Americanism" rally and celebration of George Washington's birthday.

Even so, Condon thinks the crowds have grown more orderly. The professional basketball fan has always been blasé, and though the college crowd can get hysterical at times, it's easy ("... not by asking them, but by telling them what to do. They're used to being ordered around.") to control. Surely nothing of late has equaled the New York High School Championships, the notorious PSAL games which, like the Nazi party and the Laundry Workers' Union, whose meeting in 1947 developed into what ushers called "a riot-orgy," were finally barred from the Garden altogether. Of the PSAL games, Condon recalls, "As soon as the game ended, the chairs came out of the balcony. We'd hide under the courtside tables and cover our heads and pray.

After the chairs, came cherry bombs and finally the kids themselves, flying over the table. That one—yes, I guess you'd have to say it—was the worst of all."

One reward however makes Condon's job worthwhile. Every game is a chance to torture gamblers. The Garden's is a betting crowd, and he can al- ways discern the games that have drawn most interest. "Particularly the out- of-town games. If the money is big on a game, the joint is so quiet you can hear a pin drop when I report the score." Luxuriating in that kind of absolute power, he remains consistently inconsistent in his presentation. "I want them never to know whether I'll give the loser or the winner first. I'll say, 'Here is the NBA score from Philadelphia. At the end of the 3rd quarter, Philadelphia 73 ... then a good long pause to let them mull it over ... and Boston, 83.' Man, those guys want to kill me! One night there was a shocked silence after I finished and some guy up in the mezzanine screamed out so you could hear him all over the arena, 'What are you, some goddamn wise son-of-a-bitch?' Another guy comes up to me after the game and says I'm gonna give him a heart attack. Man, it's beautiful!"

September, 1957

BILLY GRAHAM CRUSADE TERMED
A RECORD

A report issued yesterday termed the Billy Graham crusade at Madi- son Square Garden - which lasted from May 13 until August 31 – "the longest and best attended drive in Garden history." 1,814,400 people attended and, according to a spokesman for Mr. Graham, 53,626 "made decisions for Christ."

Condon remembers a couple at a basketball game who attracted his attention because of the contrast between them. "The woman is raising hell and the man isn't moving at all. Sits there with his arms crossed the whole game, doesn't utter a sound. When the game is over, his wife stands to leave, straightens herself out and then turns to him. She gives him a tap on the shoulder and he topples out of his seat. He'd been dead, they estimated, since the first quarter."

According to Ned Irish, about six spectators—the great majority at wrestling matches—die every year at the Garden. A security guard remembers one string of 13 successive wrestling matches that produced fatalities. "You know," he explains, "those people get excited." Among performers and athletes, the danger has been less. Irish can remember only five athletes who have lost their lives in the building—one other boxer beside Paret, a circus aerialist, a parachutist from an event he can't recall who forgot to connect the rope that would catch him after a jump from the top balcony, and a cowboy who had taken leave from the armed forces to compete in the rodeo. The cowboy's funeral was held in the main arena, and it wasn't the first time they'd had a funeral there. When Tex Rikard died, of appendicitis in 1929, his body—in a $15,000 bronze coffin—lay in state for two days at that center of the arena. His funeral service equaled many of the prizefights he'd promoted by attracting a capacity crowd. The arena was draped with bunting, and policemen formed a line around the building to contain the crowds. The New York Times reported that it took several charges by the mounted police to make room for the procession when it left the building for the cemetery.

On the lighter side, Irish recalled the man who had strolled dreamily onto the ice during a Sonja Heine show, walked its full length, and left the building through the 49th Street entrance where he was picked up by the police and taken to Bellevue. The Garden's history, of course, is full of events in which the demarcation between game and reality fell away, and most of the ushers will tell you that their favorite is the fellow who set out to make his mark on the high wire, during a circus performance in the late 1950s. After stoking himself with several bottles of wine, he made his way through security and suddenly—so suddenly that most people thought he was part of the show—appeared on the wire, wobbling toward the center of the arena's ceiling. On little more than heart, for it was found he'd had no experience whatever, he made it for about ten feet, and then he fell, on the fattest, most malleable, and most resilient of the Ringling Brothers roustabouts. Though he escaped without an injury or even cuts and bruises, he was subjected to the embarrassment of being ejected from the premises.

March 9, 1943

40,000 HERE VIEW MEMORIAL TO JEWS

Madison Square Garden was filled twice last night for a mass tribute to 2,000,000 Jews slain in Europe. Actors, applauding Paul Muni and Edward G. Robinson, recited the record the Jews have written in History and on stage with them moved 20 of the rabbinate of European ghettos, most bearded and wearing black gowns and prayer shawls. The Kaddish prayer for the dead filled the arena and many in the capacity crowds remained in tears throughout the ceremony.

Ali himself seems more relaxed and confident every day. On the Tuesday before the fight, he doesn't leave the building after his workout but chooses instead to take the stairs two flights up to the Garden's main floor, where twenty or thirty people, spread out in the stands, are watching the Knicks practice for their first playoff game against the Baltimore Bullets, which will take place on this same floor three days after the fight. He knows some of the players personally but when he comes onto the floor in his street clothes, white dress shirt hanging loose over his jeans, he calls out to them as a group. "Gimme that ball! C'mon! I'll show you my game!"

At first they don't take him seriously, but when he persists — "You think I'm kidding? C'mon chumps...I'll show you how this game is played!" When Willis Reed passes a ball to him, he bounces it several times with two hands, awkwardly, in a manner that signifies clearly that this game is not his territory. It's hard to believe he's ever held a basketball in his life.

As anyone knows, however, humility is not Ali's style, and mind over matter has been his modus operandi as long, at least, as he's been in the public eye. Standing just a few feet in front of the half court line, he lifts the ball over his head and without interrupting his rap — "You think I'm kidding? Watch this!" — hurls it toward the basket for a swish. It won't be part of Garden history but you'd have a hard time convincing anyone watching that a more amazing event has ever occurred in this building.

As fight-night approaches, the gate is looking better. The Boxing Department gives a cocktail party for the press at Toots Schor's. It is clear by now that this fight will have more coverage than any event in Garden history.

Condon has distributed 350 working-press tickets and more than 100 photographers' passes. Two temporary darkrooms will be set up (one in Ali's temporary dressing room, the other in the room Paderewski used), thirty extra teletype machines installed in the basement.

Donapria's men get a break from the schedule because on Monday, March 20, the Golden Gloves is scheduled, and Tuesday the 21st, is what they call a "dark day." Since both Ali and Folley are working out for the last time on Sunday, the ring can be brought upstairs Monday morning and left there through the fight on Wednesday night. Even so, it is no small job to set up the ring for a championship fight. On Tuesday morning, after the Golden Gloves, the electricians work on the lighting frame. A steel structure that looks like an erector set, it is raised to the ceiling when not in use and lowered during fights to a point about 20 feet above the ring. They begin by lowering it almost to the ring ropes, and then they set about attaching the strobes and spots and remote-control cameras this sort of press requires. Many photographers bring their own lights and explain how they want them hung and, in most cases, the electricians comply. There are a few disagreements, but the absolute authority of the Chief Electrician, who always backed his own men, resolved them quickly. A scale is trucked in for the weigh-in, which will happen tomorrow, here in the ring. It's a huge bronze structure, antique and majestic and more than a little threatening.

One of the electricians climbs aboard to weigh himself. Muzak plays over speaker system. For the weigh-in the canvas-covered foam rubber pad that covers the ring during fights has been removed, revealing the painted but deeply weathered board that formed its floor. The Garden's ring was built in 1877, and it's been in constant use ever since. Its modernizations—the red velvet that covers the ring ropes, for example, the red lights over the corner post which flash when the bell ends rounds—have been improvised by maintenance crews. The red lights themselves are attached with friction tape. When the electricians are finished, the lighting frame is a high voltage monster that might have been built by a lunatic kid with an erector set—16 television lights, 31 strobes for individual photographers and, in two corners, the special Associated Press sequence cameras which, operated by pistol-like gadgets at ringside, take up to ten stills a second. It is from such technology that we are given morbid overhead shots of kayoed fighters flat on their stomachs. The AP man at ringside says that since he's been using the cameras, he hasn't missed a single knockout or the punch that did the job.

From each of the lights and cameras a cable runs to a comer of the frame and dropped to the ring post. The Chief Electrician has climbed into the ring and, with hand signals not unlike a referee counting a knockdown, he directs those in the control room to raise the frame gradually. As it rises, an electrician stands in each comer, and, winding the cables tightly, secures them with tape. Eventually, he snakes them under the ring to the power source. On one ring post alone, there are more than forty cables. Finally, the ring is swept and the scale dusted, and the speaker system interrupts the Muzak with "The Star-Spangled Banner."

November 29, 1954

13,000 AT GARDEN VOW McCARTHY AID
CRIES OF 'HANG THE COMMUNIST!'
RESOUND IN ARENA

Since heavyweights have no weight to make, their weigh-ins on the morning of the fight are about as meaningful as they are for the electrician who'd availed himself of the scale the day before. They are staged productions for the benefit of the press, good leads for the evening papers, and source of endless speculation such as, "At 204 he'll have more speed but less power" or "At 212 his punches have more snap, but what about his stamina?" At 10:50, Zora Folley is still in his dressing room and Muhammad Ali has not arrived at the arena, but there are 83 people in the ring. At 11:30, Condon is on the microphone, doling out the usual details and statistics. A note is handed to him. "Ali," he says, "has just arrived." A few minutes later, Ali and Folley, in entourages of fifteen and four respectively, find their way into the ring. The crowd inside is activated, cameras aimed, mics reaching for the ceiling. The ropes grow taut from the pressure of bodies. Condon begs them to make way for the fighters and somehow they do. Ali, in red and white trunks and rubber bath sandals, and Folley, in brown and yellow trunks, grey sox, bath clogs, and a huge gold watch glistening on his arm, shoulder their way through the mob and meet at the scale. They mount and dismount, and neither seems to hear as their weights are announced. Then there are interviews. Questions are hurled in their direction—"Are you ready, Zora?" "What round, Champ?"—and then the handlers lead them away to their dressing rooms. 15 minutes later, the arena is empty, and the ring, by the cleaner who swept yesterday, is swept again.

October 28, 1952

25,000 IN GARDEN CHEER STEVENSON

October 30, 1952

22,000 RALLY FOR IKE IN GARDEN

Dave Meck and Solly Mahel arrived at the building this afternoon at 4:00 sharp. The know a bit about the evening's event but they aren't all that interested because, though they'll work it from beginning to end, they won't see it at all. What concerns them is that the estimate isn't high and that, since it is boxing, they will sell twice as much beer as at hockey games, half as many programs as at track meets. They are the entrepreneurs of the Garden, the concessions men, a breed apart from the other employees. More than any of the employees here, they bear comparison to the athletes and performers they support, for they compete every night, with each other and with the reluctant appetites of their customers, and, after work, they will, like athletes, have an absolute measure of their performance. The measure is money, of course, percentage of the take, and it will tell them any evening how they did in their race. To be a good concessions man, Solly explains, "You need to be hungry first ...
and to have no shame." Each night you face the crowd and scream about your product, and you'd better be loud and uninhibited. Solly will tell you that nothing kills your customer's appetite like timidity. Garden ushers are mostly taciturn and a little depressed, and among the police there are few whose faces ask to be remembered, but there is color in a vendor's cheeks, and, even when he whispers, a hint of the crowd somewhere in his voice. You deal with him when you know what you want, but

what he offers is more than you think. Solly Mahel, selling programs at his stand inside the front doors, is your first contact tonight, your first taste of the experience you sought when you purchased your ticket. In 1965, the Madison Square Garden Corporation had a net of 10 million dollars. No one around the office could tell you how much of that was hot dogs, but Dave Merck can tell you how many he sold that year and how many he should have sold, because he knows his percentage. No salary, 26per cent on everything. Which means the faster he hits hit the frankfurter with his fork and slap it into the bun, the more often he'll get his 26, and all the better if it helped them upstairs to get their 10 million. After two years at the old building, Meck has worked here since 1923. He's seen the hot dog go from 15 to 35 cents and marveled at the paradox that sales went up with each increase. He's seen eating habits remain consistent through two wars, one depression, and more than twelve thousand events. "The only real difference I ever saw is between the City College crowd at basketball games and the crowd at, say, a St. John's game. St. John's is a beer-drinking crowd, but City College is soda. I guess it is the Jewish element." He has also seen his own salary increase at a happy pace. "In 1933, we could earn something like $1.14 a night. Some of the butchers on the floor could go as low as 18 cents. But in '38 we got the union and things changed. I can make anywhere from $60 to $100 a night for standard events and of course the sky's the limit at the circus. The parents bring the kids and the kids get bored, and the parents feed them to keep them quiet. If you work hard, you can make a thousand a week at the circus up here."

July 24, 1937

**22,000 CHEER MADRID DEFENDERS
AT GARDEN**

2,000 LOYALIST SUPPORTERS JAM
49TH STREET

The ushers and ticket takers arrive at 6:00, and the special police in their bullet-gray uniforms. Richard Esau, Chief of the Security, has called 75 men for the fight, or about 20 more than normal, Eddie Miller, the Chief Usher, a crew of 103, including porters and maids for the restrooms. For big fights such as this, or any event where there might be trouble, Esau also uses a 15-man "Flying Squad," which roams the building and tries to break up fights before they spread. He also posts men at the doors, to search anyone who looks suspicious. Over the years, such inspections have yielded ax handles, billy clubs, brass knuckles, garbage can tops, and beer bottles (108 at one college game). "Once," says Esau, "I opened an overnight bag this kid is carrying and saw two tiny green eyes staring up at me. 'What the hell is that?' I said. The kid wouldn't tell me of course, so we took him in the office. He had a goddamn skunk in there. 'Jesus Christ,' I said, 'What are you gonna do with it?' He said, 'Well, we had this idea we'd shout "St. John's stinks," and hold it up!'"

Both the concessions men and the ushers are groups that have seen little change over the years. "The money is good," says Andy Prince, director of concessions, "and besides, the work seems to get under their skin." Several of the ushers are over 70, and at least a dozen concession men have been on the job since the 50th Street building opened. Mike Jackowitz, one of the old- timers, died the previous year, at 78, while selling ice cream in the choice courtside seats at a hockey game, and one of the vendors had retired several years before at the age of 87. Both groups are proud of loyalties among their customers. "I've watched the hockey fans grow up," says Dave. "I had them when they were in the top balcony, when they moved to the mezzanine, and some of them now, they come with their kids and sit in the loge. They won't buy from anybody but me."

The last thing they do is cook up the hot dogs. On their new grills, installed three years ago, they can cook 300 in 20 minutes, and one of the problems Andy has with the new building is the City Building Department's ruling that they'll have to use roller grills which, though much slower, produce less of the odor that's their principal lure. His concerns will be tempered, however, by the new products they'll add to their stands. Next year, Dave and Solly will be selling ash trays and loving cups as well as hot dogs, and the souvenirs, with photos of the new building in heroic relief, will go for 10 or 15 times cost.

Hot dogs on the grill, Dave comes downstairs from his mezzanine stand to talk with Solly. It is 6:30. There are about 500 people waiting outside the doors but the lobby is as quiet as a private club. In clean white jackets, no trace of mustard or beer stains, 30 or 40 vendors lean on the counters and smoke on the stairs, and the ushers, in royal blue jackets with black epaulettes, drift around with vague indifference to their surroundings. Over at the Midtown Motor Inn, Muhammad Ali sits in his street clothes—jeans and a work shirt—and Angelo Dundee worries about Ali's "state of mind." "I didn't feel the edge," he'll say later. "He seemed a bit too relaxed to me." Back in dressing rooms 34 and 32, Pete James and Isaac Cole, the opponents in the first preliminary, which will begin in an hour-and-a-half, are getting their hands taped. At 6:58, Dave Meck glances at his watch and makes a hurried dash for the escalator. Two minutes later, as he's slipping under the counter to his stand, Eddie Miller, standing in the center of the lobby, lifts a police whistle and sends a shrill message to the world. The doors are open once again and, wardrobe in order, the Garden embarks on another masquerade.

March 23, 1972

ALI FLATTENS FOLLEY IN FOUR

9. ZELDA

Published in "Frequencies", Volume 3, Fall 2013

Vienna, 2002. On a warm wet evening in late October, Norman Mailer is greeted by a full-house rousing ovation as he parts the rear curtain and moves onto the stage at the Funkhaus Theatre. It is fifty-five years since his first book, *The Naked and the Dead*, propelled him into a celebrity that has so proliferated through the years that it seems to him now "an anchor I'm dragging through the sand." Next year, on his eightieth birthday, he will publish his thirty-second book, a collection of essays about writing called *The Spooky Art*, which includes this sentence: "If a writer is really good enough and bold enough he will, by the logic of society, write himself out onto a limb that the world will saw off." He likes saying that all novelists are actors at heart. Over the years, it's been a useful metaphor, completely subjective, of course, a reference to the voices and identities he explores at his desk, but tonight it is no metaphor. The writer is an actor and the role he plays is of another writer who may have been, on the public stage at least, as much engaged with acting as any writer who ever lived, including Norman Mailer. As Ernest Hemingway, Mailer is about to assume the voice he sought to emulate when he discovered it more than sixty years ago and, when it vanished with Hemingway's suicide some forty years ago, made him realize, as if for the first time, the immeasurable risk of the profession he had chosen.

In pursuit of his role, Mailer wears khaki pants and a matching jacket with epaulettes, an ensemble designed to make him look like a man embarking on safari—to hunt elephants, maybe, or no less an adventure, revisit a voice he had to jettison in order to find his own. Fatigue—a result of jet lag, a round of press interviews this afternoon and several official ceremonies in his honor the past two days—weighs on his posture, but his face is animated by the pleasure he derives from being on stage. Squeezed beneath his arm because his hands are occupied by the pair of canes his arthritic knees demand of him these days, he carries the script from which he'll read this evening. He is followed onto the stage by his wife, Norris Church Mailer, and George Plimpton, his longtime friend, once a good friend of Hemingway's, who happens to be the coauthor of the script from which they'll read. Left and center, schoolhouse desks are set up for Mailer and Plimpton and, to their right, a lectern and a higher stool for Church. When they're settled into their chairs, Mailer's canes neatly arranged in parallel on the desk beside his script, Plimpton addresses the audience:

"What you're about to hear is a collection of letters and prose that describes the arc of friendship between Ernest Hemingway, F. Scott, and Zelda Fitzgerald. You'll hear snippets from letters that Zelda wrote Scott and parts from twenty-nine letters between Fitzgerald and Hemingway. For reasons you'll see as we go along, Zelda and Hemingway did not exchange letters. They did not, it seems, like each other very much. The adaptation also includes short sections from Zelda Fitzgerald's novel, *Save Me the Waltz,* and a mention, toward the end, of a second novel she never finished. You'll hear a section from Hemingway's book on his days in Paris, *A Moveable Feast,* and one from *The Great Gatsby* and also a transcript of a painful conversation between Zelda and Scott that took place in the presence of a psychiatrist. You'll hear a shocking letter from Scott to Scottie Fitzgerald, his daughter with Zelda, which, in effect, condemns her mother for her effect on his writing. You'll also hear, from both Scott and Ernest, letters to someone called 'Max.' This is Maxwell Perkins, the legendary editor, who worked with both of them as well as Zelda. In case you're confused, Norman Mailer is Papa Hemingway. As you see, he's suitably attired. Norris Mailer is Zelda Fitzgerald, and I'll play Scott. That's why I'm wearing my orange Princeton tie which is alas somewhat shorter than it should be. Forgive me—it's the best I could do under the circumstances. OK, here we go. *Zelda, Scott, and Ernest.*"

* * *

Plimpton had once been my editor on a novel I published with Paris Review Editions. It was during lunch with him a couple of years ago, May 1999, that I first heard about this play. I knew that Mailer and he had long been friends, so I mentioned to him that Norman and I, who lived near each other on Cape Cod, had developed a happy ritual of quiet dinners now and then on bleak winter nights in Provincetown. As it happened, George said, he had plans to visit the Mailers in Provincetown that summer. "We'll be doing our play up there in August." He described the script as he'd describe it later, from the stage, in Vienna. They'd already performed it, he said, in Washington and New York and, after Provincetown, they were scheduled for Amsterdam and Paris. This trip to Vienna, which began two days ago in Fitzgerald's birthplace, St. Paul, Minnesota, and, after this stop, will take us to Berlin, Moscow, and London, was not yet planned, but in its wake the cast will be deluged with publicity and interest, invitations from Cuba, India, San Francisco, the United Nations, and other venues, a host of performances that will never happen because of Norris' cancer, which strikes just a few months after our return to the States, and Plimpton's sudden death, in his sleep, one year later. Three more times, after tonight, these six American archetypes will meet on stage, and then the play will succumb to the mortality and impermanence that are the unspoken heart of its matter.

Like those that preceded it, tonight's performance, in Vienna, is strictly noncommercial. Since the Hemingway and Fitzgerald estates own most of the material from which the play derives, all performances are philanthropic. Paris benefited the James Jones Society, Provincetown the Provincetown Repertory Theatre. The proceeds from tonight's performance will go to victims of recent floods in Europe. As always, the cast will not be compensated beyond its expenses. They do it for love of each other and the people they play, of performance itself, no doubt, and the mind-boggling contradictions—wisdom and ignorance, success and failure, love and hatred, joy and sorrow—they envelop as they perform. Then, too, none of them is oblivious to the mythic realm they are exploring. "When it comes to culture," Mailer says, "the U.S. is like an empty rich man who doesn't know what to do with his money. Mythos is culture, a nutrient. I would love to be able to do this play all over America. I'd take it to five towns in seven days, do it maybe twenty or thirty times a year. I think it could bring back the equivalent of Chautauqua."

Over that lunch two years ago, George explained that not a single word of the script had been invented. It was all an edit, searched out, composed, and organized with his coauthor, Terry Quinn, and fine-tuned by Norman, Norris, and himself. The play was a kind of Appropriation Art, suitable, perhaps even inevitable, at a time when the onslaughts of media and information had made the creation of new material a somewhat different proposition than it had been in the past—the days, for example, when Hemingway and Fitzgerald were publishing their masterpieces; when there was no such thing as a quality paperback; when 24,000 books were published in a given year, as opposed to the 120,000 that compete for shelf space today; and

Plimpton's Paris Review received less than 2,000 submissions annually rather than the 20,000 it received last year. Given that Plimpton had written or edited twenty-six books and appeared in thirty films, while Mailer, in addition to his thirty-two books, had directed four films and written ten screenplays and countless magazine articles, it struck me as both ironic and appropriate that they were involved, this time around, in what was essentially an act of recycling.

Since Plimpton had made a career of leaving his own for other identities, it was no surprise that the play had begun with him. As endless articles and newscasts reported after his death, his own myth no less celebrated than Hemingway's, Fitzgerald's, and Mailer's, his unique brand of participatory journalism had taken him into bullfighting, professional golf, basketball, football, baseball, and boxing. He'd explored the trapeze with the Ringling Brothers Circus and, by his own account, suffered one of the greatest traumas of his life when he missed Leonard Bernstein's cue while playing the gong in Mahler's Fourth with the New York Philharmonic. As a soccer goalie, he'd been scored on by Pele, as a hockey goalie, by Bobby Hull. As an amateur pianist, playing his own composition, he'd placed second at amateur night at the Apollo. Finally, however, it was his excursion into Edmund Wilson, during Wilson's epistolary argument with Vladimir Nabokov, that led to this night in Vienna. In *Dear Bunny, Dear Volodya*, an adaptation by Quinn of the Wilson-Nabokov letters, Plimpton was Wilson in colloquy with Nabokov's son, Dmitri, as his father. The form of that work had so captivated him that he'd turned his attention to the Hemingway-Fitzgerald letters and sought out Quinn to collaborate with him.

Over lunch, George described the happy coincidence that had set the play in motion. "Actually, we came together as a cast because of John Irving. Just at the time when Terry and I were working on our final draft, John asked the Mailers to do him a favor." Irving's children were attending a school in Manchester,

Vermont, which was about to hold a benefit, and he asked the Mailers if they would do a reading from Lanford Wilson's *Love Letters*. Sympathetic to the cause but not the role, Norman suggested that Plimpton might do it with Norris. "I told him I had a better idea—something the three of us could do together. I sent it to him in Provincetown, and he liked it a lot. Next thing I knew, we were working on it together in John's kitchen the day of the performance in Manchester. The audience response astonished us. I remember one guy crying out during the Q and A after the performance, 'This should be done in every high school in America!' Norman told John that the play ought to be done by professional actors, but John saw it differently. 'It's you three make it work—listening to you and thinking back to the originals. This is about history looking at itself.'"

Unlike the audience in Moscow, tonight's, in Vienna, does not require simultaneous translation. The laughs are less frequent than in St. Paul but, thanks no doubt to various collisions and intersections of English and Russian syntax, more abundant than they will be in Moscow three days later. Even so, the most striking discovery of this trip will be the stamina of American Literature as it travels the world. All performances—with minimal advertising—are sold out, and there is as much appreciation for the actors as those they portray. "It's nice to know," Mailer says, "that in Europe I'm probably read more seriously than in America. But that's an old story, of course. I'm sure many American writers could say the same. I get the same feeling in small American cities, like St. Paul. It's as if a sort of city patriotism takes over. People take a sort of pride that an author visits them." The owner of a restaurant in Potsdam, where the entourage will be taken for lunch the day after tomorrow (and treated, of course, to a tour of the rooms in which Stalin, Truman, and Churchill negotiated at the end of World War II), will confide that she named her son after Mailer. Asked what brings them here, more than one member of the audience will talk about reading *The Naked and the Dead* in high school. A young writer in Moscow talks about permission to read Hemingway ("the essence of America to us") as one of the happier results of Glasnost, and a secondary schoolteacher in Berlin says of Mailer that he "represents the American Left to us. And now, of course, because we are so afraid of the American Right, we're all the more anxious to hear what he's got to say." Most impressive of all was a talk given yesterday, the day after our arrival in Vienna, by Guenther Nenning, former publisher of the German magazine FORUM and founder of Austria's Green Party, on the occasion of Mailer's receipt of the Cross of Honor, which happens to be the highest distinction Austria can bestow upon an artist. Nenning addressed Mailer as a way to address America:

"Dear Norman Mailer, we small Austrians have a very clear position towards your great America. We are always for America and always against America. Always for America because we want to be protected and because, in the global clash of civilizations, we belong after all to the West. Always against America because in our Central-European souls, there is a lot of arrogance coupled with anger and envy. It is therefore a great relief when Mailer shoulders our anti-American burden, because you can't be more anti-American than this great American. Norman Mailer has a European concept of patriotism: he loves his country not how it is but how it should be."

* * *

Four days after we leave Vienna, Plimpton, his wife Sara and I, sharing a taxi from Moscow's airport to our hotel near Red Square, pass a soccer stadium that sports a banner advertising a local team called the Dynamite. "Hey," says George, "I played goalie against those guys! They scored on me!" He tells us how he was introduced to the Dynamite players as a veteran of renown, how impressed with themselves they were that they scored on him so easily. He talks about Bobby Hull and Pele and goal-tending in general, and then—another kind of goal-tending?—the night he introduced Hemingway—over dinner at the Colony Restaurant in New York—to thumb-wrestling.

As it happened, the whole thing came about because of Norman. Earlier that day, I'd had an idea that Norman might come to dinner with us. He'd been wanting to meet Ernest for years of course. As it happened, Ernest was interested. Not because of *The Naked and the Dead* but because of *The Deer Park*, which he'd just read, and liked. I set it up with Norman but for various reasons the meeting did not come off. As a matter of fact, they never met. But like I said, Ernest was interested in him, and at dinner he started plying me with questions. "What's he like? What's he interested in?" I told him that one of the things Norman was into was thumb-wrestling. "Thumb-wrestling?" Hemingway said. "What the hell is that?" I took his hand and set about demonstrating for him. I'd been warned that he was intense about any sort of physical confrontation, but before I knew it, we were into it for real. He was very bad at it. Very bad. He couldn't stand when I beat him. The table was shaking, dishes rattling. The mark of his fingernails stayed on my palm for a week.

I asked George what he was up to these days. He told me about three books—a biography of Ernest Shackleton (published in April 2003), a boxing anthology, and an account of a fifteen-year bird-watching project that had grown out of articles he'd written for Audubon Magazine. It had taken him to India, Antarctica, and thirty other countries. In addition, this seventy-four-year-old man who'd interrupted work at his desk, which was dominated, as it had been for nearly fifty years, by his editorial duties at Paris Review, who was traveling the world with a play he'd distilled from other writers' letters, was writing two New Yorker profiles and working on a children's opera, *Animal Tales*, with Lucas Foss. Participatory journalism? "Nothing planned just now, but I've got an idea. I want to manage a wrestler. Get this big guy—350, 400 pounds—call him 'The Grecian Urn.' He's got tattoos all over his body. 'Beauty is truth and truth beauty.' That sort of thing. I've got it all worked out. He comes into the ring strumming a little harp or lyre. When he's angry, he swears in Shakespearean odes. 'Devil damn thee black thou green-faced moon!' I took the idea to ABC. Thought maybe we'd do a sort of retrospective of all the things I've done, many of which are on film, you know. I wanted to intersperse it with story of the Urn. Seemed to me they were interested at first, but their pencils stopped when I started talking about the tattoos and the harp. They looked at me like I was crazy."

* * *

Zelda, Scott, and Ernest begins with a typically hyperbolic exchange between Zelda and Scott—tender expressions from the early days of the famous, high-octane romance that, if you know their biography, makes you wince with fear for them. Drawn from her own youth, in Arkansas, Norris's accent is a drawly suggestion of Zelda's Alabama roots; and if one had ever had the opportunity to hear Fitzgerald read aloud, one imagines he'd sound a lot like George, whose patrician accent is delivered so off-handedly that he might be addressing a small group of friends over dinner or, as was the case, with sad excess throughout most of Fitzgerald's adult life, drinks.

* * *

The play is set in motion by a 1919 telegram from Scott to Zelda: "Darling heart: ambition, enthusiasm and confidence. I declare everything glorious! This world is a game, and while I feel sure of your love, everything is possible." Scott finds himself in a "land of ambition and success" and declares that his "only hope and faith is that my darling heart will be with me soon." Zelda, matching Scott's mood, tells him that "[t]oday seems like Easter." "Everything smells so good and warm, and your ring shines so white in the sun—like one of the church lilies with a little yellow dust on it. Everyone thinks it's lovely, and I am so proud to be your girl."

Like no small number of women these days, Norris is captivated by Zelda's story, but there are parallels between the two women that push her interest toward an identification that's almost uncanny. Born just two months after Zelda died, she sometimes wonders if she's not a reincarnation of the woman she plays. "Maybe she came back to see if she could do it better this time." Both women were born in the South and married writers of renown, and both were themselves accomplished writers who abandoned their work for years. Both were talented painters and had aspirations—Zelda as a dancer and Norris as an actress and playwright— toward the stage.

Mailer's notorious battles with feminists had once made him a virtual archetype of male chauvinism, and, at first glance, it would seem that Norman/Norris will echo the destructive relationship evolving in the play between Scott and Zelda. The differences between the relationships are as significant as the similarities. While Scott raided Zelda's letters and diaries for his own work and was often mean-spirited in his attitude toward her writing—"You're a second-rate writer! Compared to me, you are—well, there is just not any comparison!"—Mailer has been unqualified in his support of Norris, who published her first novel, *Windchill Summer*, in 2000 and her second, *Cheap Diamonds*, in 2007. "Some of the dialogue between Scott and Zelda," Norris told me, "makes you want to cry. Part of it, of course, is the era she grew up in. Women didn't have the vote. They were totally subjugated to men." Norris reminds me that Zelda's problems were personal, not just institutional: "She was in and out of mental hospitals for the last twenty years of her life. But she once told Scott that she'd rather be in an asylum than living with him. 'At least they allowed me to write there.' It was if she had no right to her own life. Their life together was Scott's material. 'I'm the writer,' he said. 'How dare you use the name Fitzgerald?'" In the end, Zelda capitulated; she had no life of her own.

With Norman it was quite different. "Norman has been totally supportive. He's never held me back at all. He's not that kind of person." Norris acknowledges that Norman has made a number of inflammatory statements in the heat of the moment but feels that feminists have used him as a punching bag. "He's no enemy of women."

* * *

Mailer is 80 years old at this time. Talk to his friends these days and you'll hear—with amazement that mounts in proportion to the length of time they've known him—how age has mellowed him. About the man who used to be called "Stormin' Norman," who ran an eccentric, often bizarre, and distinctly unsuccessful campaign for mayor of New York City in 1969 and spent two weeks in Bellevue after a much-publicized stabbing of his wife in 1960, adjectives of the moment run from "kind" and "sweet" to "serene" and "avuncular." He's not always pleased to hear himself described like this but he can't deny the complexities to which time is introducing him. "One of the few benefits of old age is that I don't get nearly as exercised about questions I can't answer." Or: "It's hard to keep up the old vendettas because for the most part I've forgotten them." To my astonishment, I heard him, at one point on this trip, celebrate the benefits of short-term memory loss: "It makes you a better editor of yourself. You're much more objective when you come back to something you did the day before because you can't remember writing it."

My own experience confirms the endearing adjectives. I trace our friendship to a book I sent in search of a blurb. I barely knew him, but I'd heard about his generosity toward Cape Cod writers. Inundated though he is with such requests, he read the book and responded three days later. I know at least half-a-dozen other writers who've had similar experiences with him.

One thing that hasn't changed, however, is his passion for argument. The old vendettas may be forgotten but he is hardly reticent toward new ones. When The New Republic published a defamatory cover five years ago (a picture of Mailer in a loin cloth over a caption reading "He is Finished!") in response to his just-published *Gospel According to the Son,* he punched out its publisher, Martin Peretz, outside a Provincetown restaurant. He doesn't get to the gym these days, as he did for years when he was boxing or, in his mid-fifties, rock-climbing, but you only have to watch his eyes to see how sparring feeds his energy. Though at this time he'd been with Norris—his sixth wife, mother of the ninth of a brood of children that ranges in age from fifty-one to twenty-four—for twenty-eight years and, for the most part, seems content with their current life in Provincetown, their arguments are frequent and public, sometimes nasty, sometimes playful, often both, as if they're testing each others' tolerance and patience and, together, how near they can get to the edge of the cliff without going over. Norris describes such confrontations with a metaphor that seems to me appropriately mixed. "Kind of like dancing. He wins a few, I win a few." Norman? "Marriage is an excrementious relationship. One can take all that's bad in oneself and throw it at one's mate. She throws it back at you and you both shake hands and go on with your business—you can't do that when you're out in the world."

But even when he's angry, it's not clear how much he means to be taken seriously. Testing theories, risking offense, edging away from moderation and sometimes, as in the early days, even rationality, he seems at times to enjoy nothing so much as controversy. I suspect he'd not like to hear this, but I can't disabuse myself of the notion that his arguments are play, his interviews play, that an impulse toward play is always present in his work. Play—and gambling. As he says, "I'd classify myself and half the people I know as wicked. Gamblers. People just upping the ante." Needless to say, a writer's gambling is often solitary and not entirely confined to his work. For years, he's begun his work day with a long bout of solitaire, and ever since Norris got mad at him for losing money on football (she once remodeled their Provincetown kitchen to get even with him for his losses), he's pursued a sort of solitaire-football of his own invention, tracking the NFL and its weekly betting line but making "mind bets" against himself. Show me a better metaphor for a man who defines a novelist as a compendium of opposites, who once wrote, of Hemingway: "His contradictions are his unity. His dirty fighting and his love of craft come out of the same blood"; who writes in *The Spooky Art*: "To know what you want to say is not the best condition for writing a novel." While we were in Europe, he was hell-bent on the Monday Herald Tribune for the results of Sunday's NFL games, so as to see how he'd fared, against himself, the day before. Bad days bothered him not inconsiderably. Real bets or "mind-bets," sparring and argument were at once matters of import and games to be played with full intensity. What's more serious to a player than his game? At times, as in the fight with Peretz or some of his battles with feminists, he'd had real money on the line, but with Norris, the bets were always paradoxical. Not exactly safe but less about hostility than one's capacity to enjoy it. One played to win but the chips on the table were not the sort one expected to cash. He sometimes imagines Hemingway's suicide as an accidental loss of another sort of bet. "I think it was his need to be a man that killed him. He had all the male fears that were strong in those days—of being a coward, of ending up gay, of basic dread, etcetera. His solution was to dare death ... become a prizefighter, seek out the risks that frightened him. I can imagine him going into his study and putting a gun in his mouth, pulling the trigger in a sort of Russian roulette, just to test himself against his dread." On the other hand, mind bets have an ante like any other and, as he says, antes have to be upped if you want to keep the risk alive. He was particularly hard on Norris' Baptist background, perhaps because, as Norris suggested, he knew that nothing bothered her more. "Petty honesty" was what he accused her of. "It's worse than petty thievery. Where you come from, it's a big thing to find a way to pass the time without offending God." Anything but apologetic, he talked about their battles with no less abandon than he pursued them. A few hours before this evening's performance, for example, in a limo hired by our hosts in Vienna (heading out on a sightseeing tour that included, among other sites, the house in which Beethoven spent his formative years), he'd explained their game, apropos of nothing, like a first-time realization. "Norris and I are like two old gym rats. Fighting is our hobby." And then, a moment later, as if displeased by such benevolence, turned the screw in the other direction. "When you're my age and you've been married as long as we have, your wife can have half your IQ and twice your rage and you still argue like equals." Gazing out the window, Norris had not been paying much attention, but this last found her ear:

"Did you say half?"

"Well, maybe 55 percent."

"Fuck you, Norman."

"Fuck you too, baby. You act like my older sister. Christ, I've got to be the only eighty-year-old in the world who's treated like a six-year-old. When I leave you, I'll say it's 'cause you frustrated my late adolescence."

"If you leave me, who'll arrange for your wheelchair at the airport?"

Unsure how angry they were, I worried for a moment, but I was quickly reassured by the grin on Norman's face. I don't know that it had ever occurred to me that one can laugh and scowl simultaneously, but that's what he was doing, and I doubt he'll ever come closer to defining his love of play, and gambling and, come to think of it, his relation to his work, than he did with that expression.

* * *

Fitzgerald had already published *The Beautiful and the Damned*, and was close to finishing *The Great Gatsby* when he and Zelda made their way to Europe for the first time. It was a few months after that that he and Hemingway met for the first time. Drawing from *A Moveable Feast* in its description of this first meeting, Hemingway/Mailer says: "He had come into the Dingo Bar in the rue Delambre, where I was sitting with some completely worthless characters." He thought him, he (as Mailer) offers, "a man who looked like a boy, with a face between handsome and pretty. He had very fair, wavy hair, a high forehead, excited and friendly eyes—and a delicate, long-lipped Irish mouth that, on a girl, would have been the mouth of a beauty." Fitzgerald's features, he goes on, "should have added up to a pretty face, but that came from the coloring, the very fair hair and the mouth. The mouth worried you until you knew him—and then it worried you more. 'Ernest,' he said. 'You don't mind if I call you Ernest, do you? Tell me, did you and your wife sleep together before you were married?'"

"'I don't know,' I said."

"What do you mean you don't know?"

"I don't remember."

"But how can you not remember something of such importance?"

"'I don't know,' I said. 'It's odd, isn't it?'"

A few minutes later, Mailer/Hemingway confides in the audience at Fitzgerald's expense. The latter has loaned out his last and only copy of his new book but wants Hemingway to read *The Great Gatsby* as soon as he can get it back. As we know from their history, this reading changed everything for them. "He had many good, good friends—more than anyone I knew. But I enlisted as one more, whether I could be of any use to him or not. If he could write a book as fine as 'The Great Gatsby'', I was sure he could write an even better one. I did not know Zelda yet, and so I did not know the terrible odds that were against him."

* * *

Thus began a friendship that has generated as much interpretation and scholarship as any in American literature. Fitzgerald was already successful at this time; Hemingway just starting out. Supporting and advising him, Scott would introduce him to Maxwell Perkins, offer editorial help, and convince him to delete, from a preliminary draft of *The Sun Also Rises*, seventeen pages that would have badly weakened the book. Profoundly important to both, the friendship was passionate, perhaps homoerotic, increasingly colored, as the years wore on, by resentment, mistrust, and competition, not to mention the mutual antipathy between Ernest and Zelda. The mistrust increased as Hemingway's career outstripped Fitzgerald's. Here is Fitzgerald/Plimpton, summing it up in 1937, when he was forty-one: "I really loved Ernest, but of course it wore out like a love affair. We began trying to walk over each other with cleats ... I talked with the authority of failure, Ernest with the authority of success. We could never sit across the table again."

Mailer says he's never, himself, known a literary friendship like Hemingway's with Fitzgerald: "I'm not certain two writers of the same stature can really afford a profound friendship with each other. Imagine a marriage between a beautiful actor and a beautiful actress. How long's it gonna last? There's more imbalance than balance in the relationship." Even so, he and Plimpton have known each other for almost fifty years, and differ though they in vision and stature; the benefits of the friendship are apparent to both and anyone who knows them. If they don't completely mirror Fitzgerald and Hemingway, they surely offer, in their lives, an echo of the echo they're offering on stage. Norman counts the opportunity to work with George as one of the play's principal attractions, and on the same subject George can sound almost reverential. "Norman says 'Vienna' and I start packing. Even if I'm busy and tired of the play, I can't say no to him." Physically, they differ as much from each other as they do from Hemingway and Fitzgerald or, for that matter, as the latter two did from each other. At 5-7, Mailer is six inches shorter than the man he plays, and Plimpton, 6-3, nine inches taller. They're both Harvard graduates, but their backgrounds are as disparate as their bodies. Mailer was born in Brooklyn, his parents Jewish, his father an accountant who was a fairly chronic gambler. He went to public school before he went to Harvard. Plimpton, whose father, Francis Plimpton, was a Wall Street lawyer and a Deputy Representative to the United Nations, went to Exeter and, after Harvard, Cambridge.

No less different, the roads they took to their collaboration on stage tonight are a celebration of the endless tributaries that feed and branch off the river of their profession. Each was clearly influenced by the man he is portraying, and like any writer in the grip of major influence, including, of course, Hemingway and Fitzgerald, each has struggled to wean himself from it. Plimpton first tapped his literary voice in a class at Harvard with Archibald MacLeish. "I'd started a novel about murder—patricide, I think, or maybe fratricide—but suddenly I realized I had to do something different. I wrote a light piece, coming out of my work on the Lampoon. MacLeish praised it. My greatest influence, for sure, was Mark Twain, but in retrospect, I think that first piece was influenced by Fitzgerald. I'd just read *Diamonds Big as the Ritz*. In any event, I understood that I had to avoid the solemn at any cost."

Mailer was writing what he calls "crude imitations of Hemingway" eight or nine years before *The Naked and the Dead* was published. "I was sixteen or seventeen when I read that first collection of Hemingway stories, *The Fifth Column*. I read them over and over like a Bible. It was his style that moved me, of course, its manliness. I loved him the way some actors love John Wayne. I wanted to be like him as much as I wanted to write like him." After college, Plimpton turned to editing, founding (with Peter Matthiessen, Harold Humes, Thomas Guinzburg, and Donald Hall) the Paris Review in 1953 and interviewing other writers—E.M. Forster, William Styron, Irwin Shaw, and Hemingway, to name a few—for its famous "Writers at Work" series. Opting for journalism, he wrote occasional pieces and played small parts in film and on television until 1961, when he published *Out of My League*, a collection of his participatory journalism pieces for which Hemingway wrote this blurb: "Beautifully observed and incredibly conceived, this account of a self-imposed ordeal has the chilling quality of a true nightmare. It is the dark side of the moon of Walter Mitty." Though journalism remained his métier, he tried his hand at fiction in 1987 with a wonderful comedy called *The Curious Case of Syd Finch*. The story of a mystical baseball player whose spiritual realization leads to phenomenal success in the Major Leagues, it was critically and commercially successful. Many filmmakers have shown interest in it but, optioned by Warner Brothers and still their property, it has never been produced.

Mailer started with fiction, but of course, even more than Plimpton, he's worked in nonfiction too. Of his thirty-two books, twenty-six—including *Armies of the Night* and *Executioner's Song*, which won him Pulitzer Prizes—have been nonfiction. He differs from Plimpton in literary ego as much as he does in his work. In 1958, with a grandiosity that might embarrass him today, Mailer said: "I am imprisoned with a perception that will settle for nothing less than making a revolution in the consciousness of our time." Plimpton's ambitions, to say the least, are of a different magnitude. His nonfiction is subjective, his language and narrative skills sure-footed and original, but his self-image as a writer is almost diffident. If Mailer, in the view of almost any American writer, is the ultimate professional, Plimpton might be one of the few writers for whom "amateur" is a complimentary label. Say that he seems to risk himself at the typewriter the way he risked himself on the trapeze. As critic Gerald Clarke once noted, "It is Plimpton's triumph that he has restored the word amateur—which today is so often a synonym for bungler—to its original and true connotation: someone who takes up an art or craft not for gain but for love."

What Plimpton and Mailer share, and both of them share with Hemingway and Fitzgerald (at least the Fitzgerald who wrote *The Crackup*), is defiance of the life-work boundary and courage in the face of what Mailer calls the "perils" of their profession. Say that all four writers present on this stage in Vienna have struggled to reject Yeats' famous dictum that one must choose between perfection of the life and perfection of the work. Mailer could have been speaking for them all, no less than for Zelda and Norris, when he said of Hemingway, over dinner one evening in Provincetown, "Writing was a species of religion for him. He had a detestation of the abuse of English. I think he gave that to me as he did thousands of young writers. I can't think of a writer who was more aware of the danger implicit in language. He had plumbed its nature enough to know that it was not to be taken for granted." Mailer's "species of religion" claim is not mere exaggeration, but rather an open display of devotional understanding: "He was the ultimate master of 'show, don't tell.' It was implicit in the way he approached things. Everything was manifest for him. In that sense, he was an existential writer. More, he was a writer who was full of immanence, which is to say he was no less interested in the silence behind language than language itself." Mailer's performance at the dinner table is celebratory, but the dramatic engagement of *Zelda, Scott, and Ernest* opens up a different sort of communion, that of shared pain. On stage in Vienna, Mailer/Hemingway reads a letter written to Scott: "That terrible mood of depression, of whether it's any good or not, is known as Artist's Reward. Summer's a discouraging time to work—you don't feel death coming on the way it does in the fall, when the boys really put pen to paper. Everybody loses all the bloom—we're not peaches." This is the ultimate in writerly shop-talk, but the audience knows that Fitzgerald will die too young and that Hemingway, in a "terrible mood of depression," will end his life. The letter continues: "That doesn't mean you get rotten … you lose everything that is easy, and it always seems as though you could never write. You just have to go on when it is worst and most hopeless. You damned fool, go on and write the novel." Ecclesiastes tells us all is vanity but we should get back to the manuscript.

* * *

Thirty-five requests for interviews greet Mailer at the airport in Vienna. Pressed for opinions on George W. Bush ("the president we deserve—a man who can't stand a question that takes longer than ten seconds to answer"), Iraq, the 9/11 terrorist attacks, and, of course, the present state of American Literature, his presence here, as in Berlin, Moscow, and London, is close to Head-of-State news. Of course, the cameras and the questions bring out the gambler in him. Check this out for one of the mind-bets that, via this article in Berlin's Zeitung Am Sonntag, he wins:

WHEN I FIRST CAME TO BERLIN, I HAD AN ENORMOUS ERECTION

> Muhammad Ali once called him "the writing champion." And at 79, deaf and walking on crutches, the legendary American writer with the whiskey-colored voice has still got a crystal-clear mind and enjoys provocation and dirty talk. "When I arrived here first in 1959, I had an erection when I got off the plane.

As he sees it, his enthusiasm for interviews is a by-product of marriage. "When you've been married as long as I have, you'll do most anything to get yourself a situation where you don't get interrupted." Whatever the reason, it's clear that nothing caffeinates him like an interview or the random questions from the audience that follow these performances. Even after the Q and A—at the end of a day that began with a 10:00 AM press conference—he's witty and thorough and endlessly patient with the reporters who surround him before he leaves the stage. As it happens, our sightseeing tour this afternoon was an introduction to the main event. As it draws to an end, our guide directs our driver toward the outskirts of Vienna. We ascend till we reach the famous Vienna Woods that are said to have been a source of inspiration for Beethoven, Mozart, and Schubert. Rain came on a while ago and seems just now to be getting heavier. We park outside a restaurant in a lot already packed with cars and vans, equipment trucks, and media vehicles. Huddled beneath umbrellas, a crowd surrounds our car. As the Mailers emerge (the Plimptons are back at the hotel where, facing a deadline, he works on the galleys of his *Shackleton* book), cameras appear, and books—*The Naked and the Dead, Executioner's Song, The Gospel According to the Son*, and, to Norris's delight, several copies of *Windchill Summer*—are offered for autographs. We are joined by Norman's longtime friend, the Austrian journalist, Hans Janitschek, and a number of other luminaries: Austria's secretary of state, Franz Morak; Hans Dichand, publisher of the most widely read paper in Austria, Der Krona; and finally by Ernst Strasser, Austria's minister of police. A procession forms, and we set out along a hilly, graveled path. The rain continues. Snaking through the gloom, interrupted here and there by cameras, lights and sound booms, the reds and yellows and blues and greens of umbrellas are like a streak of color in a black and white film. Adapting its pace to Mailer's, even slower now because the terrain is hard on the knees, we shuffle along for fifteen or twenty minutes to reach a small, white, stucco building deep in the woods. It's fronted by a brick patio on which a pack of paparazzi are already encamped. Walking beside me, Janitschek, a buoyant fellow with an unwavering enthusiasm for history, politics, and, most of all, Norman Mailer, offers narration. He's been a close friend of Mailer since they met, more than twenty years ago, when Janitschek was president of the Second Socialist International. Presently the New York correspondent of Der Krona, he was Kurt Waldheim's chief deputy when he was secretary general of the United Nations, and he ran for president of Austria in 1992. He explains that the building we face is the famous Sissi Chapel, one of the great legends of Austrian history, built by Emperor Franz Joseph in the late nineteenth century in an attempt to win back the affections of his beautiful young wife, Elizabeth, or Sissi. She rejected him when she discovered he had syphilis. Assassinated by an anarchist in 1898, she was radically independent, so indifferent to the conservative principles of her day that she is often called "the first European feminist." Later I'll learn that Norman has no idea at this moment of the ceremony at which he's about to preside, but he conducts himself as if carefully rehearsed and perfectly cast. While most of us watch from the edge of the patio, he and Norris are seated at a picnic table facing the chapel's door. Janitschek explains that this tiny building was maintained by the Catholic Church until World War II, when it was plundered by the occupying Russians. Since then, its windows and doors have been sealed with brick to protect it from decay. Today's ceremony celebrates the bricks' removal and the beginning of its renovation, and the entire ceremony, as it happens, is built around Mailer. Dichand and Morak sit across from him. While cameras flash and search for angles, and aides hover with umbrellas, the speeches begin. Janitschek attempts a rough translation from the German but for the most part leaves the content to my imagination. Twenty minutes later, an elegant elderly woman in a yellow slicker approaches Mailer with a wooden panel containing an array of dials and lights and gauges. It looks something like a children's game but would not be out of place in the cockpit of a 747. At the top right-hand corner is a large, illuminated red button that Norman is directed to press. Immediately, as he does so, the doors of the chapel, illuminated by stage-lights, swing open dramatically. A great spray of smoke rises from the threshold and, amidst the applause, we hear the yearning chords of a Beethoven Sonata played by a cellist within the chapel. Mailer handles it all with calm and what seems to me a kind of amusement, but it's not a little moving to think of him, an American writer, here to portray one of his forebears opening doors on a new chapter in Austrian history.

* * *

Onstage, the shop-talk continues, and the relationship gets

rockier. Scott/Plimpton reads from a letter to Ernest, one in which Fitzgerald urges Hemingway to make cuts in *Farewell to Arms* because the story is, well, dull? Targeting pages 114–121 of the novel, Fitzgerald writes: "It's slow and it needs cutting—it hasn't the incisiveness of the other short portraits in this book or in your other books: the characters are too numerous and too much nailed down by gags. Please cut!" Fitzgerald complains that there's no psychological justification in introducing the singers— "it's not even bizarre." If the characters were consequential for the plot—if they got drunk with the protagonist and caused him to get tossed out of the hospital, say, "it would be OK. At least reduce it to a sharper and self-sufficient vignette. It's just rather gassy as it is." Fitzgerald goes on to say that pages 133–138 could also stand improvement. In general, says Plimpton for him on stage, "these conversations sometimes take on a naive quality that wouldn't please you in anyone else's work. Have you read Noel Coward?"

To which Mailer, as Hemingway, replies, "Kiss my ass!"

* * *

Mailer was seventeen years old and Plimpton thirteen when F. Scott Fitzgerald, a serious alcoholic down on his luck, writing screenplays in Hollywood three years after publishing *Tender Is the Night*, died of a heart attack at the age of forty-four. This was 1940. Hemingway did not go to the funeral. He and Scott had met twice, briefly, in 1937, but it was years since they'd pretended to be friends. Mailer reads a 1939 letter to Maxwell Perkins that sums it up for Ernest: "I always had a very stupid little boy feeling of superiority about Scott, like a tough, durable little boy sneering at a delicate but talented one." Hemingway was also, by this time, a serious alcoholic. For years, he'd taken pride in his drinking, bragging about his capacity and unequivocal about its value in his work. "We always called it the Giant Killer," he said of alcohol.

"Nobody who has not had to deal with the Giant many, many times has any right to speak against the Giant Killer." Other Giants for sure were the depression he'd been dealing with all his life and, as Mailer suspected, the fear of suicide that his father had bequeathed Hemingway by ending his own life. Whatever it was, the alcohol Giant was proving harder and harder to kill. By the time Lillian Ross wrote her New Yorker profile of him in 1949, he was less often sober than drunk. *The Old Man and the Sea*, published in 1952, was the last of his major work. He was after all a man who, as his son Gregory wrote, "could never develop a philosophy that would allow him to grow old gracefully." Physical problems—eyesight, liver, high blood pressure, much of it related to injuries he'd suffered in a 1954 plane crash, in Africa—cut into his writing, his sex life and eventually, the drinking itself. His marriage was so embattled that his Cuban doctor removed all the guns from his house because he and his wife were threatening to shoot each other. In addition to his father, his uncle was a suicide. Now he was on his way to his own. By 1959, extreme paranoia had him imagining phones tapped, government agents tracking him, and most of his friends allied against him. He was finally persuaded to enter Mayo's clinic under a pseudonym. After a series of shock treatments, he celebrated—in a telephone conversation with his friend, A.E. Hotchener—the fact that he was able, at last, to read again. The book he was reading was *Out of My League*, by the writer who, forty-three years later, will play Scott Fitzgerald opposite the man who is playing him. His wonderful blurb for it may well have been the last few sentences he'd write with ease. When he turned to his own work, attempting to finish *A Moveable Feast*, he was excruciatingly blocked. "There's no question," Mailer says, "that he devoted the best part of himself, not to love, not to his children, but his writing. I think one of the reasons he committed suicide was finally that he couldn't write well anymore. He was like a great lover who can't get an erection." Hemingway himself put it this way. "If I can't exist on my own terms, then existence is impossible. That is how I've lived, and that is how I must live—or not live."

When Plimpton—thirty-four years old—heard of his suicide, he walked around dazed for hours. Like many other writers, he felt as if he'd lost not only a "surrogate father" but also a friend with whom he'd fished, walked the beaches in Cuba, a man who always called when he came to New York. Though lacking such direct connection, Mailer, thirty-eight, was no less stunned. "It was as wounding to me as if one's own parent had taken his life. I can't call it life-changing, but it's something I've pondered ever since. I knew that, if a man with his strength, all the success he'd had, all the fame, could do this, then there is something seriously dangerous in being a writer. You better be aware of this danger. I think I have been, ever since."

* * *

Fitzgerald/Plimpton takes the stage and recites these well-known sentences: "And as I sat there brooding on the old, unknown world, I thought of Gatsby's wonder when he first picked out the green light at the end of Daisy's dock. He had come a long way to this blue lawn, and his dream must have seemed so close that he could hardly fail to grasp it. He did not know that it was already behind him, somewhere back in that vast obscurity beyond the city, where the dark fields of the republic rolled on under the night."

* * *

Neither Mailer nor Plimpton were as affected by Fitzgerald's death as they'd been by Hemingway's, and neither knew much of Zelda, whose reputation would remain a kind of subtext of Scott's until Nancy Milford published her wonderful *Zelda: A Biography* in 1970—The Paris Review gilded the lily with a feature on Zelda in 1983. For Norris, Zelda's influence is the dominant gift of the play. She will tell you that these evenings of inhabiting the always-surprising and often chaotic voice of Scott's wife—the woman who was a sort of demon for the man her husband plays—have changed her life. Focused as it is on the relationship between the three, the play's chronology ends with Scott's death. Zelda is forty at this time. It is ten years since she was diagnosed schizophrenic. She has spent most of the last decade in mental hospitals and is now confined to Highland Hospital in Asheville, North Carolina.

It's ghastly losing your mind and not being able to see clearly—literally or figuratively—and knowing that you can't think and that nothing is right, not even your comprehension of concrete things, like how old you are and what you look like ...

She and Scott have been separated for years. In the midst of her illness, she's finished *Save Me the Waltz,* had a one-woman show of her paintings at a New York Gallery, and experienced a soaring religious epiphany that Scott, like her doctors, takes to be one of her symptoms. "For God is the Actuality," Zelda writes to Scott. "God has evolved us from the beginning in Eden that we may ennoble our souls until they shall have attained a spiritual stature which can share His Beauty. That is the purpose of our lives, to increase our spiritual horizons." She will die eight years later in a fire that begins in the kitchen at Highland and spreads to her room through the dumb waiter shaft. Her last words tonight, delivered by Norris, are from the novel she was writing when she died:

"He was gone ... they had been much in love. He had been gone all summer and all winter for about a hundred years ... she wasn't going to have him anymore; not to promise her things nor to comfort her, nor just to be there as a general compensation...she was too old to make any more plans—the rest would have to be the best compromise."

But the final words of this drama are Hemingway's—a

summation of Scott and who knows how many other writers—from *A Moveable Feast*, the book he was trying in vain to finish a few months before his suicide. They are offered to the audience by Norman Mailer, who once said of him that "he was considerably more important, to those of us who wanted to be writers, than St. Paul was to Catholics."

"His talent was a natural as the pattern that was made by the dust on a butterfly's wings. At one time he understood it no more than the butterfly did and he did not know when it was brushed or marred. Later he became conscious of his damaged wings and of their construction and he learned to think and could not fly anymore because the love of flight was gone and he could only remember when it had been ... effortless."

Notes

The text of *Zelda, Scott, and Ernest: A Dramatic Dialogue* was shaped by George Plimpton and Terry Quinn in 2001, using a very select group of letters and fictional writings from the three authors. Those who wish to look into the Rashoman that was this friendship and those who wish to think about the enduring fascination of these vexed relationships can find more information in the following books:

Bruccoli, Matthew J. *Fitzgerald and Hemingway: A Dangerous Friendship*. New York: Carroll and Graf, 1994.

Some Sort of Epic Grandeur: The Life of F. Scott Fitzgerald, 2nd rev. ed. Cobia: University of South Carolina, 2002.

The Sons of Maxwell Perkins: Letters of F. Scott Fitzgerald, Ernest Hemingway, Thomas Wolfe, and Their Editor. Columbia: University of South Carolina, 2004.

F. Scott Fitzgerald on Authorship. Bruccoli, Matthew J. and Judith S. Baughman. eds. Columbia, SC: U of South Carolina, 1996.

Correspondence of F. Scott Fitzgerald. Bruccoli, Matthew J. and Margaret M. Duggan, eds., with the assistance of Susan Walker. New York: Random House, 1980.

Zelda Fitzgerald: Her Voice in Paradise. Cline, Sally. New York: Archive,

2003.

Hemingway vs. Fitzgerald. Donaldson, Scott. Woodstock, NY: Overlook, 1999.

Fitzgerald, F. Scott. *A Life in Letters*, ed. Matthew J. Bruccoli and Judith S. Baughman. New York: Scribner, 1994.

Ernest Hemingway: Selected Letters 1917–1961, ed. Carlos Baker. New York: Scribner, 1981.

Milford, Nancy. *Zelda: A Biography.* New York: Harper & Row, 1970.

10. CRANK'S PROGRESS

Written on assignment for Harper's Magazine

"It has become appallingly obvious that our technology has exceeded our humanity."

Albert Einstein

"Those who love their own noise are impatient of everything else. They constantly defile the silence of the forests and the mountains and the sea. They bore through silent nature in every direction with their machines, for fear that the calm world might accuse them of their own emptiness."

Thomas Merton

I'm sure there are neuroscientists who'll tell me I'm wrong, that we hear things without really hearing them, but until that morning, when I woke at 5:30 and realized that the mosquito in my dream was coming from the street below my window, it seemed to me I'd never really heard a backup beep. Maybe I'd heard a few beeps now and then, but until now the bird-like beep-beep-beep-beep, which is well on its way to becoming the sound-track of our environment, had somehow evaded my consciousness. How else explain my near-death experience, two days before, when a cable TV van, backing into a crosswalk, braked just inches from my knee and the driver jumped out screaming: "Don't you hear the beep, moron?"

When I realized the beep was not going away, I leapt out of bed and opened the window to locate it. Ten floors down, I saw a sanitation truck parked in one of New York's most beautiful streets, a cobblestoned Greenwich Village landmark called the Washington Mews. Gated at each end, just a block long and not much wider than the truck itself, favorite site for film, fashion and wedding photographers and architectural tours of the city, it was so little used by traffic that any truck, much less one of the dinosaurs we employ to save us from our lifestyle, seemed as incongruent and invasive as the alarm that was waking the neighborhood. If the truck was here for waste collection, it had yet to announce the fact. Its dreaded compactor was inactive. Smoking and reading a newspaper, its driver leaned against a rear fender. Free for once of the hopeless despair that industrial noise usually engenders in me, not to mention the cultural taboo that equates any sort of noise-protest with weakness, old age, or lack of patriotism, I threw on a jacket, raced 10 flights down to the street and addressed him in a voice he could not hear.

"Excuse me. Can you turn that off?"

"What?"

"Off! Is there a switch?"

"What?"

"The beep! A switch! Can you turn it off?"

"What?"

"THE BEEP! THE BEEP! FOR GOD'S SAKE, TURN IT OFF!"

"Oh, that. Sure, I can." He pointed to a red switch above the rear fender. "Right here."

"Why don't you then?"

"What?"

"Why don't you turn it off?"

His eyes spread with astonishment. "Violation!"

I suspect the same neuroscientist who explains how I'd long been hearing beeps I didn't hear will not be surprised to learn that I have rarely, since that morning, known a beep-free hour or, on bad days, quarter-hour. On really bad days, it can seem as if there is scarcely a minute free of the beep's announcement that the wonders of technology are at work nearby. After all, it's not just sanitation trucks and commercial vans that aim their beeps at us but, as I was soon to discover, almost every commercial or industrial vehicle or machine produced in the last 40 years. Even buses announce with beeps that they are kneeling for the handicapped or, in some cases, simply opening their doors. Since that morning, hearing them all is constant proof of my wondrous sensitivity and its debilitating cost. Clearly, my brain was altered by the sanitation truck, and whether you call such alteration "awakened" or "damaged" will depend, I suggest, on your noise-position at the moment you're asked. Do you hear the bombardment that assaults us more with every passing day? If so, do you hate it or fear its absence, consider those it bothers as your allies or your weak-kneed enemies? Do you prefer restaurants where conversation is possible or those in which the crowd and music make it a relic of the past? Despise or converse with those who talk during movies? Use a rake or a leaf-blower? An ordinary motorcycle or one on which your virility is confirmed by the absence of a muffler? In any case, I doubt you'll find it hard to understand that the sanitation truck forged a link between hearing and consciousness in my brain or that, as one neuroscientist explained to me, the frequency of the Backup Beep is such that frequent exposure will make you hypersensitive to it and thus a lot more likely to overcome the habituation that until now has made you unconscious of it. (Let us ignore, for the moment, the equally reasonable hypothesis that such overstimulation might cause certain brains—like those that don't just tolerate but prefer restaurants where conversation is impossible—to be so addicted to noise that a ubiquitous beep, if noticed at all, seems comforting). What I can say without doubt is that, since that fateful early morning backup alarm, few beeps escape my notice. Audiologically speaking, there is no separation between out-there and in-here. As far as this particular noise is concerned, my immune system is insufficient. The beep is so much part of my life that, hearing it before I hear it and waiting for it when it's gone, I often feel that the whole of the world suffers from Tinnitus.

This is not to say the world has not conspired with me. Later that same day, I heard a beep from the area of the Washington Square Arch which, despite being a block farther away, seemed even louder than the sanitation truck's. Venturing out to investigate, I found that it came from a boom-lift two stories high, maneuvering two workers in a small cab who were cleaning the arch with brushes and rags and what looked like buckets of soapy water.

I called from the ground. "Hey! Why are you beeping?"

"God knows!" cried one of the cleaners. "It's driving me

fucking crazy."

Only birds in flight or someone levitating above or below the cab would have been threatened by its movement but its beeps were close to constant and, as I discovered when I walked downtown, travelled through space with such efficiency and volume that on the other side of the park, at least an eighth of a mile away, they were almost as loud and shrill as they'd been when I stood nearby.

Not yet aware how much my new condition set me apart from at least a few others, I turned to a man standing beside me as we waited for a light to change. Bearded, wearing a tweed jacket, jeans, and work boots, he looked like he lived or worked in the neighborhood, so I felt a sort of comradery with him, so certain he shared my perception that he'd think I was belaboring the obvious.

"Can you believe that?"

"Beg pardon?"

"The beep! Over there! On the other side of the park!"

He did not respond. Friendly until now, his face took on the paranoid stare New Yorkers show toward aggression on the street. When the light changed, I'm pretty sure he waited to see where I was headed so he could go the other way. Why not? He hadn't noticed the beep any more than he'd noticed the shirt on his back or the feel of his sox on his feet. If he listened to me, the enemy of his habit, I'd ruin his day.

My own denial was not restored by his. Next time I passed the lift, which was still active and, as it would for the next three days, beeping steadily, I found the name of the manufacturer and, back at my office, searched out its phone number online. The woman who answered seemed almost thrilled to hear my voice, but she confessed that she did not exactly understand what I meant by "beep" or, once she did, why it bothered me.

"OK," she said finally, "I'll try to find someone to help you."

She called back a few minutes later. "Safety," she said. "It's a safety thing."

"For whom?" I said. "The lift is operating in mid-air. There's nothing above or below it."

"Yes, but you have to understand that these lifts are also used on ships or in high-rise construction where they move stuff between floors. People have to know when they're moving."

"But what about situations like this, where the alarm has no purpose and can be heard all over the neighborhood?"

"I can see that might be a problem," she says, "but we have to put safety first."

"Do they have a switch that can turn them off?"

"Oh no. None of our machines have switches."

"Why not?"

"Safety. It's always first for us."

* * *

Non-electronic back-up alarms were used as far back as the 1940s in the military. The version we hear now is typically 4-6 inches wide; 3-5 high; 2-3 deep. Four feet away, its beep is rated at 87 to 112 decibels, the latter of which is 12 above the level as which sustained exposure results in hearing loss. Activation, set in motion by a wire spliced to the backup light or the reverse switch wire, moves a diaphragm at a rate between 700 and 2,800 Hz to produce a narrow-band sound some have likened to the repetitive calls of birds in danger. Among those who particularly detest it—no small number in my informal survey—I've heard it equated with everything from dripping faucets to the obsessive flash of memory or thought on days when your brain is tormenting you. Myself, I think of it as a metaphor of information glut because the beep's meaning— "Watch out! Watch out!"—is nullified by its ubiquity as Mozart, say, would be nullified by the sound of ten or twelve marching bands playing John Phillip Souza or, for that matter, Mozart. Triton Signal Corporation claims that its founder, Matsusaburo Yamaguchi, invented the beeping alarm. It entered production in April 1963 and retails today for about $20. Many alarms we hear these days were probably manufactured by Preco Electronics, an Idaho company, which began shipping them in 1967 and, by the time it sold its High Frequency division (to Ecco, Inc. which continues to make them) in 2008, had built and shipped about 20 million. Consider that the field is highly profitable and competitive, companies all over the world making the alarm as fast as Preco did and Ecco, in all probability, continues to do now. Most contractors and manufacturers will tell you that they—and their insurance companies—insist on the beeping alarm because OSHA, the Occupational Safety and Health Association, requires it and, while this is an over-simplification of OSHA's current position, it's true that the alarm that woke me that morning and the one that announced to a neighborhood more than a half-mile wide that a boom-lift was moving its cab a few inches up, down or sideways was first mandated by OSHA, one year after it was created during the Nixon Administration in 1970:

> "No employer shall use any motor vehicle equipment having an obstructed view to the rear unless the vehicle has a reverse signal alarm audible above the surrounding noise level or the vehicle is backed up only when an observer signals that it is safe to do so."

* * *

The ruling was not unquestioned. At preliminary hearings, many contractors, manufacturers and government agencies worried about the expense. Representatives from the Georgia Power Company argued that their regulations, already requiring a "spotter to the rear who is more effective than a reverse signal alarm" made the ruling unnecessary, perhaps even counter-productive. "In our view, the [backup alarm] requirement will reduce our safety effort." A complaint from Deere & Company requested that machines such as loaders, tractors, bulldozers, and graders be excluded from the requirement "because these types of vehicles are often operated for considerable portion of time in reverse and the operation of the alarm in these cases contributes to excess noise and confusion on the job site." Finally, an agent from the Department of the Interior seconded the view from Georgia Power that a spotter was a safer alternative. "Based upon our experience, [Backup alarms] are difficult to maintain and frequently create distracting noise levels which actually constitute a hazard in some circumstances."

As we know, the people at OSHA were not—or not just then, at any rate—persuaded by such argument. Whether those who participated in the vote took into account the thousands of beeping vehicles they were unleashing on the world, the millions of sleepers they'd awaken, readers they'd distract or construction workers they'd subject to audiological torture, we will never know, of course, but it's clear that noise was not allowed to compromise the two great American dreams of technology unimpeded and safety at any cost. OSHA records since that time give no indication of efforts to define "audible above the surrounding noise level," not to mention establish any standard by which the volume and pitch of the beep might be regulated so that, say, an alarm meant to protect a worker in the path of a sanitation truck backing up at 3 AM would not awaken hundreds of people in the neighborhood. The U.S. Department of Transportation's Federal Highway Administration has noted that backup alarms are the biggest reported nuisance of nighttime construction. They were the single biggest complaint, by far, from those living near Boston's Big Dig project. Some vehicles, like the sanitation truck that woke me, have manual cut-off switches, but alarms without switches can be disengaged in minutes by anyone with a wire-stripper. Although OSHA's first priority is worker safety, neither their records nor those of the National Institute of Occupational Safety and Health (NIOSH) show any sign of concern for workers forced to hear backup alarms throughout their time on the job.

Given its brutal assault on the audioscape, one would suspect that the safety benefit of the backup alarm is inarguable, but such is not the case. For at least four reasons, there is a good chance that a worker in the danger zone of a backing truck a quarter mile away might not hear the beep that is driving you crazy. First, workers will tell you that it can be omnipresent, and when competing not only with other alarms but other machines on the work-site, more disorienting than protective. Second, the pitch of the beep, in most cases, happens to be almost identical to that which most ear-protection, also required by OSHA, is designed to mute. Third, despite its proliferation into surrounding neighborhoods and higher floors, the beep is far from efficient at its source. A study by Dr. Chantal LaRoche at the University of Ottawa demonstrated that because its single, narrow-band frequency reflects chaotically off solid material, it may actually become less audible to someone in its path as a vehicle moves in his or her direction. Finally, of course, there is the fact that workers habituate to the beep. How can a sound heard day after day for hours be any more noticeable than the shirt on your back? As far back as 2001, research by NIOSH stated that "commonly applied back-up alarms tend to be ignored after long-term exposure." The bottom line then is that the beep which has so proliferated in our environment that no silence, anywhere or any time, is safe from it can't be counted on to do the job for which it is designed.

Sad confirmation of this research can be found in accident statistics. Though not exhaustive, OSHA's numbers show that between 1984 and 2005, 45per cent accidents that mention the backup alarm occurred when it was operating. Dr. John Casali, director of the Acoustics Lab at Virginia Tech, has testified in numerous court cases where accidents occurred when the alarm was known to be beeping and the 'audiogram' of the worker showed that he heard it even if, like me in the days before the Sanitation Truck, he did not notice it. Casali has a video he won't let me see – "because, believe me, you wouldn't want to" – of a worker strolling idly into path of a truck whose alarm is beeping and whose engine alone is loud enough to be heard at 90 feet.

Another thing you might assume, given the various downsides of the beep, is that there are no alternatives to it. This is not the case either. The once ubiquitous flagman is still preferred by many safety experts. Another option, manufactured by Preco now, is a video monitor or audible alarm in the driver's cabin which is linked to a radar system that detects individuals in the vehicle's path and, if necessary, triggers an alarm of variable amplitude. An array of wireless backup cameras are also available to alert the driver. Though not all that expensive in relation to corporate costs, not to mention the community's Quality of Life, economics is probably the main reason this sort of technology is not more widely utilized. There is at least one audible backup alarm on the market, however, which is inexpensive and mercifully kind to surrounding neighborhoods. Brigade Electronics, an English firm, makes a broadband alarm which generates a sound like a quick burst of wind. Some call it a White Noise alarm. On-site workers have reported that it is more easily heard and located than the beep. Since it dissipates quickly and is focused on the immediate vicinity, it eliminates proliferating noise pollution. It's been endorsed, among others, by Les Blomberg, director of the Noise Pollution Clearinghouse, The Mine Safety and Health Administration, and the Society of Automotive Engineers. New York and Seattle, among other municipalities, are thought to be considering it for Sanitation use, New York City's recent noise code accepts it as "community friendly," and OSHA itself regards it as an acceptable option.

It should be noted too that some companies, like UPS, which has approximately 100,000 trucks on the road in the U.S. and internationally, abjure audible alarms altogether. All UPS trucks have rear-vision cameras. Drivers are given extensive training before they go on the road and then tracked with technology that monitors how often they put their vehicle in reverse and how long they backed up each time. As one UPS spokesman explained, "Audible alarms give the driver a false sense of security. We believe training is the best safety precaution. We do train our drivers to use their horn when backing, but since it is not an automated thing, it gets people's attention. We've known our lawsuits due to accidents, but even though some have been due to backing accidents, we've never known one that had to do with our backup technology. Our motto is, 'When in doubt, get out.'"

* * *

Most of us engaged with noise pollution issues think that everyone hates noise, but that's not exactly true. There is stubborn maddening argument on the other side. Noise is defined as "unwanted sound," but wanting and not-wanting, of course, are subjective variables. You have to hear sound—e.g., not be habituated to it—and not want to for it to become noise; this combination requires permeable psychological and neurological boundaries, appreciation of the quiet you enjoyed before sound invaded it and, most important, personal boundaries which, as you experience them, differentiate you from the source of that invasion. Finally, like any other discomfort, noise disturbs us only to the extent that we resist it. The first principal of the Lamaze childbirth method is that the more one resists pain the worse it becomes. John Cage, whom I, by the way, revere, used traffic noise in his compositions. If you can't manage his level of equanimity, you will often see yourself, as others do, as weak, excessively vulnerable, self-protective or self-important. No surprise then that, though my rage at the beep was reinforced at every turn, I often blamed it on myself. Do you have to hear it? Even if you do, why should it bother you? Is your comfort zone so fragile that it needs perfect silence to protect it? So precious that the whole of the world should accommodate it? It didn't help that (like Cage, I suspect) I'd heard and loved the story about the Zen master who liked to meditate under a wooden bridge while horse-drawn carts rolled back and forth above him. Asked by one of his monks why he subjected himself to the racket, he explained, "With so much noise outside, I don't have to listen to the noise inside." Like so much Zen, his reasoning made sense to me, but it neither disimproved my hearing nor dissolved the boundaries which the beep insulted. In fact, it seemed to me that trying not to hear it was like trying not to think of an elephant. As for trying not to be bothered by it – "accept it" or "embrace it" as that same Zen master would no doubt have admonished me to do -- that only made me more astonished that a truck a quarter mile away could at any moment, simply because its driver shifted into reverse, penetrate every ear in the neighborhood and, more important, since I was beginning to realize that the idea of the beep was even more pernicious than the sound, demonstrate the disrespect that the whole of my culture had toward its own audioscape.

As word spread about my unfortunate obsession, reinforcement came from all over the globe. A friend emailed from Bhutan that on her first morning in Paro, she was awakened by a beeping bulldozer across the street from her hotel. Another, calling from rural Vermont, held the phone near the window so I could hear a beeping bulldozer across the road. "I've heard it all day, every day, for the last two weeks." Another called from southern Colorado to say that for an hour or more every day he heard the beep of the loader at his town dump two miles away.

As noise pollution goes, the beep is fairly low on the totem pole. Even radical anti-noise organizations, like the Noise Pollution Clearing House or NoiseFree America, do not include it on the list of their primary complaints. Neither its decibel level nor its medical repercussions come anywhere near, say, aircraft or altered pipe motorcycles or, for that matter, major construction noise, and as an irritant, it arouses nothing like the rage of boomcars, jet skis, weather and sight-seeing helicopters or any of the other assaults the world is currently mounting on our sanity. We know from anthropologists that the human species has been at war with its soundscape since its earliest days, but of course the industrial revolution raised the stakes exponentially, and modern technology constantly refines and exacerbates both the sources of torture and our dependence on them. Playing defense, we write noise codes which (like the recent, tough-minded New York City code which is backed up by only 49 inspectors) are generally unenforceable, restrict construction hours or the number of sightseeing flights over national parks or set loudness and decibel limits for appliances, vehicles or even aircraft, but as anyone knows who's been kept awake by a dripping faucet or a cricket under his refrigerator, amplification is not the only reason noise can unnerve, and it always comes at the wrong time because there is never a right one for it. Invasiveness and repetition make decibels irrelevant, and when they combine with a ubiquitous narrowband frequency diabolically synchronized with the eardrum and the acoustic nerve, they make the backup beep unique in the noise spectrum, especially because its safety rationale makes it, of all forms of noise pollution, the least questioned. None measures better the degree to which we are not only habituated to noise but submissive to those who inflict it on us. If the audioscape were not the least relevant part of the environment, the beeping backup alarm would be treated like secondhand smoke and dog poop on the sidewalk. Yes, I have to admit I often blamed myself for hearing it and reflected on my inferiority to Zen Masters, John Cage or other realized beings who did not differentiate from the outside world, but in the end, it always seemed to me that rage at the beep was a vote for sanity in a world gone completely mad.

* * *

Two days after I came upon the Boom Lift, another beep arrived in the morning and continued through most of the day. Like the sanitation truck's, it came from the Washington Mews. Its source, I discovered, was the smallest of any vehicle from which, to this day, I've heard an alarm. Not much bigger than a golf cart, its view to the rear not at all obstructed (thus excluding it from the original OSHA mandate), it was driven, at the pace of a very slow walker, by a large, bespectacled man in a business suit and a Yankee cap who chauffeured a young woman with a long-lens camera fixed on the pavement below and ahead. Neither the beep nor the vehicle stopped when I approached so I walked alongside as I shouted the questions I could no longer resist.

"Excuse me. Can you tell me why this machine is beeping?"

Clearly annoyed to be interrupted, especially by a neighborhood crank with something so trivial on his mind, the photographer's stare was not accommodating. "Safety," she yelled. "Why do you think?"

"Right!" shouted the driver. "It's an alarm!"

"But you're going forward! You can see where you're going! There's no people or cars here. Why do you need an alarm?"

He shrugged. "Safety," he said again. "Don't want anyone to get hurt, do we? Anyway, we've got nothing to do with this thing. It's rented."

For all his impatience, he had shown me the root of the problem or at least one of them. Like the Boom-Lift and many other construction vehicles, his little cart came from a rental company that had sent it out into the world with no idea where or how it would be used. Before it got to the renter's lot and, let's not forget, satisfied the demands of its insurance company, it had been manufactured by another—probably huge, transnational, bottom-line-fixated—corporation with its own insurance policies and which was equally uninformed about its destination. Following what it incorrectly took to be OSHA's rigid regulations, it had automatically installed on this as on every other vehicle that came off its assembly line a backup alarm (which in this case was triggered by the forward as well as reverse gear), which had to be, as the mandate stated, "audible above the surrounding noise level," which could mean anything from the conversation in which we were now engaged to street traffic to construction site pandemonium, so who could wonder why the designer of this cart had interpreted his civic and legal responsibility to mean "so loud you can't not hear it, moron" so that, when the cart rolled off the assembly line, he'd not only be OK with OSHA but proud to have made the world a safer place, and who gives a shit about some neighborhood crank who thinks his own comfort is more important than the life of a construction worker?

But, of course, there are different ways to hear things and different ways of dealing with them if you do. When the cart drove off and I walked along the Mews, I came on one of the residents, a slender, whitehaired elderly man in bathrobe and slippers, standing in his open doorway not 20 feet from the noise. Yelling again to be heard above the beep, I could not resist the need to seek communion.

"AMAZING, ISN'T IT?"

"WHAT?"

"THE BEEP!"

The expression on his face reminded me of the photographer's, but he managed a patronizing smile. "Hey, it's New York, right?"

* * *

Like most people, I'd always thought of OSHA as an impenetrable bureaucracy, but later that day, casting about for relief after my encounter with the golf cart, it occurred to me that, if I meant to take on the beep, I had to begin where it started. As it turned out, a quick Internet search was all it took to get me there. By way of the phone number of OSHA's New York office, I connected with its media department and—one day later—an East Coast director. I expected him to be defensive or condescending, but he was sympathetic. "I hate the beep myself. When I was an inspector in the field and encountered violations of the mandate, I had to issue citations, of course, but if there was clearly no backup danger, I always did my best to accommodate them."

He knew about the quieter alternatives I'd discovered in my research, and he could not understand why they weren't more widely utilized. For that sort of information, he suggested I seek out a man named Ted Fitzgerald, the director of public affairs in the regional office in Boston and ask him to pass my questions along to Washington. I assumed I was sending my email into the bureaucratic void, but two days after I wrote Fitzgerald, I received an email from him which restated my questions and Washington's response to them. Though it restated the original mandate, it was anything but rigid. "OSHA," it said, "does not, in fact, mandate the use of backup alarms on construction sites. Employers have a choice as to whether they use a backup alarm or spotter. In addition, employers can choose what type of alarm they would like to use, so long as it is a reverse signal alarm distinguishable from [and] audible above the surrounding noise level." They were open to "emerging technologies" and saw no problem with "cameras, proximity detection systems, and broadband alarms, as long they meet the requirements of the original mandate." As for the narrowband alarm itself, "OSHA is aware of the problems it may cause. As announced on its regulatory agenda and mentioned above, OSHA will be publishing a Request for Information relating to preventing backover injuries and fatalities. As part of this, we are examining all aspects of backover prevention, including the types of alarms that are currently in use and possible alternatives."

I didn't realize it at the time, but this correspondence changed the game for me. Even though it took no position on noise pollution, it was the first indication that OSHA was neither inflexible nor insensitive to Quality of Life issues. Like so many who struggle with noise pollution, I had always assumed, consciously or not, that ours was a war against intransigent barbarity. It had never occurred to me that the debate could be anything but adversarial. But if the single despotic source of an absurd, avoidable, ubiquitous assault on quiet was not unequivocal about it, our argument had an outside chance of becoming a dialogue. In other words, it was no longer so clear that the other side was absolutely other. Not for no reason is the soundscape called the Commons. It belongs to us all, affects us all and, like it or not, connects us. Those on the other side, however much their definitions of noise might differ from ours, have ear drums and acoustic nerves that vibrate as much as anyone else's, and whether they know it or not, they can't survive without freedom now and then from such vibration. The taste and tolerance for silence may be relative, but as every religion or contemplative practice throughout history has indicated, the need for it is absolute.

* * *

A few days after the photographer's cart moved beeping through the Mews, the roar of heavy machinery announces why the pavement needed photographing. Looking down from my window, I watch an army of men in hard hats commence installation of a fence along both sides of the street while trucks of all sizes unload the armamentarium of tools, lumber, wiring and pipe we all recognize as industrial mobilization, a sure sign that our lives will be upended for the next few months or even years. In this diminutive space, there's no room for vehicles to turn around, so once they've unloaded, they back out with a chorus of beeps that, as usual, seems to rise above all other noise as the crash of cymbals can rise above the ensemble sound of an orchestra. Within a week, I'll see the cobblestones removed, the whole of the Mews stripped back to dirt and then, as if by autopsy, excavated and trenched to reveal the underworld of pipe and valve and wiring which hides below the surface.

Posters on the fence explain that this is New York University at work. The job will take a bit more than a year but when it's done, we're assured, the Mews will be restored to its original beauty, the whole of the neighborhood enriched by this wondrous project. Already the owner of a good deal of Lower Manhattan, a satellite campus in Abu Dhabi and a huge medical center on the East Side of Manhattan, much in the news of late because of its controversial 20-year plan to add three million square feet of new classrooms, dormitories and offices in the Greenwich Village area, a new engineering school in Brooklyn and satellite campuses in China and on Governors Island, the university (unbeknownst to many who live in this neighborhood) has owned almost all the buildings in the Mews for more than 50 years. Now it means to occupy them. The smaller buildings at the West End, which were stables for the wealthy before they became studios and homes for haute Bohemians, will be used for classrooms and faculty housing, and the two larger buildings at the east end, next to what are already the Deutsch Haus, the Maison Francais, and the Abu Dhabi Institute, will become the Africa Institute and the China Institute.

Within a week, all the buildings in the Mews are taped at window and door to protect them from dust. The sidewalks are fenced off from the street with thick green canvas screens into which have been cut small oval windows through which curious pedestrians can observe the violence within. One of the most enchanting streets in New York is not altogether distinguishable from a War Zone. Ten floors up, I have a terrific view of it all and, much though I try to resent it, cannot stop watching and appreciating how much thought and sweat goes into a job like this, how much coordination and skill it requires, how dangerous it can be, how much noise it inflicts on the community and, ruefully, how trivial and unavoidable such noise must seem to those who finance and manage the project.

The principal noise, however, is neither trivial nor unavoidable. It comes from a small Bobcat loader constantly in use for earth-moving, digging, or leveling. Like all Bobcats, it came out of the factory with a high frequency backup alarm that cannot be switched off. Since the work-site is narrow, excavated and trenched, thus close to impossible to navigate, it operates in reverse as often as it doesn't. Sometimes, it has to back up, beeping constantly of course, for five to ten minutes, from one end of the street to the other. Not infrequently, its beep sounds—at half-second intervals, of course—for three or four hours straight. Since the Canyon effect amplifies sound as it rises, the beep is actually louder on higher floors like mine and, of course, those in the three other high-rises within its range. Thus, am I astonished to realize again and again as if for the first time that on a megamillion dollar job financed and coordinated by one of the wealthiest educational institutions in the world, surely employed first-rate architects, designers and engineers and, in Plaza Construction, one of the most respected contractors in the United States, and has been monitored at every stage by the New York City's Buildings Department, Landmarks Department, Transportation Department and of course Environmental Protection Department, the major noise is produced by a $20 device that is wired to the reverse gear on a machine ten feet long and six wide and, when it's switched on, emits a narrow band beep that, as my on-the-ground research confirms, is audible at least an eighth of a mile north, south, east and west or, more exactly, to any one of the hundreds or even thousands of those whose brains, like mine, are both cursed with awareness of it and appreciative of the silence it destroys.

Monday mornings, of course, are the worst. Weekends are

quiet around here. I often take the silence for granted, but one morning, a few minutes before the onslaught begins, I don't. As if for the first time, I realize how nourishing and energizing it is, how it expands and clarifies space, how much hope and possibility it offers, how it slows time and so awakens one to the present that every moment seems a sort of re-birth. I am not unfamiliar with this sort of experience or the great range of poetic, philosophical and contemplative literature it has engendered, but what strikes me most about it this morning is its simplicity, its sanity. It's hard to believe there's anyone on earth who hasn't known what I know now and, consciously or not, sought it out again. When the Bobcat resumes its daily assault, it seems to me a crystallization of all the noise we create to deny this sanity, and the tremor it seems to send through the room is all the disorder that results from such denial. It's true that there are those like me who are hypersensitive to such disorder but just now it seems to me that even the noise-addicted must feel it. Who knows that the fear of silence is not exacerbated by the shock of its interruption?

A few days before, along with all residents of our building and, I assume, the others that surround the Mews, I'd received a "Hi All" email from a woman named Arline Peralta in the community relations department at NYU. The University, she wanted us to know, was very sorry about the disturbance we were experiencing, doing its best to mitigate it, and— "like all of you, I know"— hopeful that the job would be done as soon as possible. Meanwhile, if anyone had a particular complaint, we should not hesitate to send it her way and know with absolute certainty that she'd do her best to take care of it.

I'd ignored her offer because, despite my experience with OSHA, I did not believe that any noise problem, much less one as common and trivial and bureaucratically calcified as a backup beep, could be traced to an actual human being in a huge institution who would, first, take me seriously, second, accept responsibility, and third, have the authority and skill to do anything about it. In other words, I'd not bothered to answer because, like most anyone inclined to protest an institutional outrage, my state of mind had been adversarial, and I believed that she and her employers were entrenched on the other side of the barricades. After that morning, however, I could not doubt that Ms. Peralta and her employers had experienced, at some point in their lives, the sort of silence I'd just known. Was it not possible that they had heard the stupid beep they'd inflicted upon us?

I sent Ms. Peralta an email which summed up my position and research. Surprising myself with my civility, I asked her to consider why NYU had chosen to use a high-frequency backup alarm on the Mews project. "I can't believe you were unconcerned about the noise or contemptuous of the neighborhood or that you made this choice for purely economic reasons, but the fact is that this job, requiring extensive earth-moving in a confined and easily monitored space in a very dense neighborhood, is producing horrific noise pollution, that the worst of this pollution comes from the backup alarm, and that this alarm, unlike so many disturbing side-effects of major construction, doesn't have to be there."

Later that day, I had a telephone call from John Beckman, Ms. Peralta's boss. My letter, he confessed, had raised questions in his mind. He could not understand why NYU, "which by the way removed the backup beep from its mail trucks three years ago," had not done so on the Mews project. He'd called a meeting with his colleagues to discuss the issue and he promised to get back to me as soon as they'd done so. Two days later, I had a call from one of those colleagues, Beth Morningstar, whose title alone— "Assistant Vice President for Strategic Initiatives and Communications, Division of Operations, NYU"— would have convinced me a few days earlier that I was up against an impenetrable bureaucracy. Ms. Morningstar, however, was not just a bureaucrat but a human being with cheerful voice, a reasonable mind and a miracle to share. She wanted me to know that the Bobcat's beeping alarm had been replaced by a rear-vision camera and a White Noise Alarm, and though she hated to bother me, she wondered if I could meet her on the worksite to explore these new conditions first-hand.

Along with Ms. Peralta and a director from NYU's Community Relations Department, Sayar Lonial, we met next morning at the scene of my grief. Not allowed on the Mews because we did not have hard hats, we stood on the sidewalk and watched through the fence while the Bobcat, just on the other side, backed up, moved forward and backed up again. The "White Noise" alarm was a loud and focused blast of wind. It seemed impossible that anyone in the vehicle's path would fail to hear it. Pleased though she was, however, Ms. Morningstar was not completely satisfied. Though we'd convinced ourselves that the new alarm protected workers, we had now to investigate its effect on the world beyond. What she needed now, she said, was to hear how the noise proliferated. Would it be possible for her and her colleagues to come up to my apartment and check it out?

A few minutes later, the four of us stood at the window from which I'd looked down on the job. Ten floors down, the Bobcat shifted into reverse and backed up from one end of the Mews to the other.

Ms. Morningstar leaned out and, straining to hear, closed her eyes in concentration. "I can't hear it. Do you?"

Leaning over the windowsill, I focused the whole of my beep-fixated mind on the source of my rage and despair. "No," I said. "I hear nothing at all."

* * *

How sweet it would be if we could end the story there. Miraculous though it was, however, we must not believe our blessing unmixed. It's true that NYU, community conscious as it needs to be at this contentious moment in its history, has resolved that none of the 132 building projects it is currently planning will use the narrow band alarm, but the bureaucracy that gave us the beep remains in place. Though it welcomes public comment and is open to alternatives, OSHA neither supports nor rejects any alarm that satisfies its mandate, and as far as I can see, does not consider noise pollution a significant variable in the realm of "occupational health and safety." Since most real estate developers, contractors, manufacturers, insurance companies, and noise-enforcement organizations, like New York's Environmental Protection Department, use the OSHA mandate as their guideline, there is no explicit reason why any of the millions of beeping alarms which are already on the road should be deactivated or replaced with quieter alternatives and no reason why any developer, manufacturer or contractor—unless noise pollution is much higher on his list of priorities than it seems to be for most others in these fields—would seek a quieter form of safety. When I asked Richard Wood, the president of Plaza Construction, if he would continue to use the White Noise Alarm NYU had chosen, and which his own Safety Director had approved, he shook his head. "If someone gets hurt on a job where we aren't using a narrow-band alarm, we have to worry about litigation." Of course, one could answer his logic—as I did—with all the information I'd collected, but the fact remains that the beeping alarm is cheaper and louder than any alternative and backed by a culture that is not only habituated to it but obeisant to its safety rationale. The fact remains as well that the Office of Noise Abatement, which like OSHA was created in 1970, was defunded by the Reagan Administration in 1981, and to my knowledge has not appeared on the agenda of any president since that time. Until it joins toxic waste, secondhand smoke, acid rain, dog poop on the sidewalk and other pollutants we are neither afraid nor embarrassed to take on, the backup beep will remain a crucial blemish on the soundtrack of our environment.

11. LORD PROSTATE

In the late 1970's, when a group of women actors requested Samuel Beckett's permission to do a female version of WAITING FOR GODOT, he refused. Why? "Women," he explained, "don't have prostates."

When I heard that story years ago, the frequency and significance of urination in the play had slipped my mind, so I thought Beckett was being uncharacteristically perverse or, characteristically, purist about his work. Soon after that, however, when I joined a pack of men in the halftime rush for the bathroom at an NFL game between the Giants and the Eagles at Yankee Stadium, I discovered that his response, like the gland to which he referred, was both literal and inarguable. It's always dangerous to venture explanations about Beckett, but I don't think we can dismiss the possibility that the prostate gland was a crucial piece of the inspiration that led him to GODOT.

The line at the men's room snaked single file down the hall toward the concession stand. Inside, it split into shorter snakes behind each of 8 urinals. Like many others in the room, my hand was deep in my pocket, squeezing my dick at its root to keep me from pissing myself. Squeezing hurt, of course, but the idea of piss on my legs hurt more. Needless to say, the mood in the room wasn't good. Prostate metabolism united all the men in these lines in communion almost religious. Awakened to the tyranny of the gland we shared, we might have realized that we were allies, but of course, most of my fellow victims were probably as ignorant as I was of the fact that our discomfort was caused by a walnut-size gland which was wrapped around our urethras and squeezing them so as to maximize our urgency. It was also not unlikely that this tiny, diabolical gland had inhibited our last piss, causing our bladders to be close to full when the game began. Remember too that somewhere along the path of our neurological evolution, brain cells related to will-power and self-esteem joined those associated with urination to make the slightest piss-dribble on one's skin a source of humiliation and shame.

Though all of this united those in the Men's Room, there was no comradery in it. Impatience announced itself again and again as those in line tried to rush those at the urinals.

"Hey, jerk off at home, OK?"

"C'mon, man, it don't hurt to take a drop with you."

"Shake it off later, OK?"

Imagine being so helpless and frenzied when just a few minutes ago we were celebrating the speed and power of great male athletes whose prostates, we can safely assume, were no less dictatorial than ours. Imagine being humiliated by a gland that's enlarged by an excess of testosterone or, of all things, estrogen. Imagine what it feels like when, on arriving at last at the urinal, I find I…CANNOT PISS! Squeezing and pushing and holding my breath, I plead with my plumbing while throats clear and feet tap behind me. It's not difficult to imagine an arm around my throat. Nothing works of course. The urgency I felt just minutes ago is gone, and I can't doubt that it will return as soon as I zip up and move on.

None of this, as I say, is connected to my prostate because at this point in my life, I hardly know I have one. My urological education won't begin until a few days later when, on my GP's referral, I call the first of the five urologists who have guided me through six decades of prostate tyranny.

A mild-mannered preppy type in his mid to late 60's, U-1 is different from any of his successors for the simple reason that he doesn't have much technology at his disposal. Since these are the days before receptionists give us forms that ask, among other things, "How often do you dribble on the way to the bathroom?" first-hand observation is his initial source of information about me. There's a small bathroom in his office and he stands just outside the door in order to evaluate by sound the velocity of my stream while I piss into the small plastic container that awaits me on the sink.

Though the examination that follows is routine and painless, it seems to me, like so much I'll experience in Urologists' office, a first-hand measure of my pain-threshold and tolerance of anxiety. He directs me to drop my pants and kneel over his examination table so that he can push a gloved finger into my rectum and move it slowly from side to side. "Yep," he says, "that's a pretty big prostate you've got. No wonder you have an urgency problem."

It should be noted that while patients and urologists often speak of an intense need to piss as "urgency," the experience dwarfs the label. Physiologically speaking, enlargement of the prostate changes such need from analogue to digital. It does not arrive gradually, like hunger or thirst, but as a sudden inarguable force initiated by an-off switch, the announcement -- "Now!" -- allowing for no delay and, even if you manage to hold back till you get to a toilet or the nearest alley, wall or tree, humiliating your last illusion of self-control.

U-1 wipes my ass with a tissue and thoughtfully pulls my underpants over my ass. "Turn over, please."

Lifting my shirt, he spreads an ointment on my belly and rubs it with an object shaped like a cucumber which is actually, as I discover, a small video camera. On a monitor that stands next to the table, we now observe the flesh that drove me crazy at the football game. Working his keyboard, U-1 moves a cursor on the screen. "That's your prostate, see? And this is your bladder. This tells us how much urine remains in it after your last specimen. 37 milliliters. Not bad but not great."

A moment later, at his desk, he clarifies my situation. "What you've got is something called BPH. Benign Prostatic Hyperplasia. Sad to say, it's not uncommon, but you're young to have it. It hits about 1 out of 5 men in their 40s, 1 of 4 by age 55, 1 of 2 by age 75, and 4 out of 5 over the age of 80. As you know, its first symptom is urgency to urinate. It can also limit how much you empty your bladder so that you have to go more often than before. We can treat it with medication or surgery but you don't need either at this time.

"The prostate is a gland that surrounds the urethra. Normally, it's about the size of a walnut. Weighs about 11 grams. It grows in size because your hormonal balance -- testosterone and estrogen – changes as you get older. I'd say your prostate is about 13 or 14 grams. Big for walnut but small for a plum, which is what you'll probably have to deal with a few years from now. It's tough tissue, the prostate, a sort of muscle. It seems to get stronger as it expands, like your biceps when you lift weights. That's why you get the urgency that hit you at the game. But as you saw, BPH can also produce bladder retention and sometime, bladder spasm, which creates urgency or even incontinence. In some cases, it causes bladder infection because residual urine contains bacteria. Interesting fellow, the prostate, no? Don't judge it too soon! Without its help, you can't ejaculate! In medical school I got obsessed with it, and I'm still obsessed today. Yours? Well, it's not problematic yet. I'm sorry to tell you you'll never write your name in the snow again, but your frequency and urgency is still in the realm of self-control. Make it a habit to piss before you go out. If you can do that, you've got nothing to worry about."

When U-1, unfortunately, decides to retire, he refers me to U-2 and suggests that, given that the size of my prostate has steadily increased over the three years I've seen him, I try to get a urological evaluation every year. On my first visit, U-2 sees more or less what U-1 saw. Though he agrees I don't need medication, he advises me, as no other urologist has, that the best treatment for BPH is frequent ejaculation. "Jerk off, wet dreams, or fuck, I don't care how you do it. Come at least three or four times a week and you'll shrink your prostate back to normal."

He explains that the prostate's relation to orgasm is much more complicated than people realize. "For one thing, stimulation of it can by itself produce orgasm. It's not so well-known in our culture but in the Far East, countries like Thailand, it's the sort of thing whores have to know. If you're lucky, they'll offer you a back-end rub for a few extra bucks. Then too, some research relates frequency of ejaculation to prostate cancer. One study found that men who have 21 or more ejaculations per month have a significantly reduced risk of getting it. The theory is that seminal fluid that's kept in the body for long periods of time can undergo biochemical changes and become carcinogenic. It's kind of like milk that spoils if you keep it past its expiration date."

I don't know it, of course, but this is my last un-traumatic visit to a urologist. When I return the following year, he sees something he doesn't like on my sonogram. "I hate to say it, my friend, but I've got to cystoscope you."

Unfamiliar with the word as well as the procedure, I do not ask for the Valium that many urologists -- except those, like U-2, who are either happy about or unaware of the torture they're about to inflict -- automatically prescribe for cystoscopy.   He is also disinclined to arrange for the privacy that most urologists (as I'll discover) provide for this examination.

Calling for his nursing assistant, he disappears into his adjoining office. She is Edith, a tall Afro-American woman with short curly hair, broad shoulders, a steady, comforting smile and, obviously, no little experience with this ordeal.

"Pants down, please. Underpants too."

After directing me to lie back on the examination table, she lifts my dick, wipes it with a moist cotton pad and then, dipping a Q-tip into a bottle of purple liquid, offers me all the comfort she has in her repertoire. "Painkiller now. Sorry. Gonna sting a bit." When she inserts the Q-tip into my urethra – "Easy now!" -- the burning is so intense that the whole of my body convulses. "Easy!" she says again, and then, "Done now. Not so bad, right?"

A friend of mine named Harvey, who has a 5th Degree Black Belt in Karate, says that after his first cystoscopy he felt he deserved a promotion to 6th.   I'm sure there are worse examinations – actually, I've had a couple myself – but at this point in my life, I've never known anything comparable to it, and though I've had three since that first, I still can't think of it without a shudder. Cystoscopy is not just invasive. It's a mental and physical insult that seems like a wound which will never heal.

It doesn't help that U-2 thinks I'm overreacting. "Come on, it's no big deal. Just breathe deep and relax!"   Standing at his shoulder, Edith holds a large metal container to which is connected a rubber tube and a catheter he inserts in my dick. "Breathe deep!" he says again as I squirm. "Relax! Make it easy for yourself." Since the pain and fear are inseparable, one can't really focus on one or the other, but there's no doubt that both get worse with every movement of the catheter. For U-2, it's an object of passion. "This is an elegant instrument," he explains. "There's a light and Video camera on the tip. Amazing when you think of it, no? Invented maybe 12, 15 years ago. In a minute -- easy, deep breath, good, see, that's better, right? -- in a minute we'll have a clear picture of your prostate and bladder. Deep breath, good, that's right! Didn't I tell you it was no big deal?"

He's right that the worst is over but since the withdrawal is only slightly less bad than the entry, I'll only know that in retrospect. Between the two, he's got bad news. "There's a polyp on the tip of your bladder. We'll have to go in and get it."

While the surgery, three weeks later, requires just one night in the hospital, three weeks of cancer-fear follow. The surgery is not painful and pathology shows the polyp to be benign, but pissing burns for three days and on the fourth, a normal, no-burn piss produces a stream of blood that makes me sure I'm on the way out.

As it happens, it's just another mixed message from my urinary tract. "Scar tissue, don't worry!" says U-2 when I phone him in panic. "Be thankful! It shows you're healthy and healing!"

After a few solicitous questions, he reminds me to come in and see him a year later, then closes with news which, since I don't have cancer, seems the worst he could offer. Indeed, to me at that moment, the worst I've ever heard. "Of course, I'll have to cystoscope you once a year for awhile to make sure we got it all."

U-3 replaces U-2 because he is treating a friend who mentions in an off-hand way that he's just been cystoscoped and adds, "Thank God for Valium" before I can seek out commiseration with him. Though anticipation of the procedure will keep me awake for several nights before my first cystoscopy at U-3's office, Valium reduces the trauma by half at least and a good part of the rest is erased by the fact that U-3 does it alone and gently with no nurse hovering at his shoulder. Don't let anyone tell you that bedside manner is overrated or that any doctor of any sort can't help you along with awareness and sensitivity.

As it happens, U-3 is prominent in the field, professor at a prestigious medical school, internationally known and respected in his specialty. A few minutes into my first meeting with him, he makes it clear that he means to educate me on my prostate. He doesn't promise of course that such education will replace my treatment, but since the latter is always a personal choice on a spectrum that's changing fast, it usually comes to that. Behind him on a shelf stands a life-size plastic model of the urinary tract with the bladder at the top, the penis and testicles at the bottom, and the prostate, wrapped around the urethra and hovering between them like a cloud. "As a man gets older," he explains, "he makes less testosterone and more estrogen. By his mid 30's, the balance shifts altogether. You make more estrogen than testosterone. This is called a 'hormonal inversion.' As the years pass, it accelerates. An added problem is that an enzyme called aromatase converts more and more of what little testosterone you have into another hormone called estradiol which increases the risk of cancer. Estradiol is the main reason why prostate cancer is the most common for men. According to recent research, it strikes about 150 in every 100,000 men, but of course its fatality rates vary widely. Some research indicates that almost all men get prostate cancer after a certain age, but it's not always the cause of death. In many cases, it doesn't show up till autopsy."

Not long before my first appointment with U-3, something called PSA had become the Holy Grail of prostate screening. Though it is not inexpensive and so adds to the cost of the of prostate treatments and medications, not to mention the Health Care crisis which is rapidly bankrupting the U.S., almost every urologist in the United States has begun to prescribe it and will continue to do so even after research, a few years from now, shows it to be a source of many false-positives and a great deal of unnecessary treatment. PSA means "Prostate Specific Antigen". It's an enzyme secreted by the prostate which is produced for the ejaculate, liquefying semen and so permitting sperm to swim freely. Though present in small quantities in the semen of men with healthy prostates, it is often elevated in the presence of prostate cancer or other prostate disorders. It's unquestioned just now, in the first flush of its discovery, that if your PSA is over 4.0 or if it varies too much from one year to the next, you need a biopsy. Further complicating the issue is that PSA is a highly volatile enzyme which often overreacts to other irregularities in the prostate or functions (like the kidneys) which are interacting with it. My PSA is 4.2 the first time U-3 sends me for blood work (at a cost, to Medicare, of $140) but a year later, when I suffer a bout of prostatitis, my number shoots up to 42. As a result, U-3 is so concerned that he sets me up – at a cost of $2000 -- for a biopsy two weeks later.

Between that first PSA and the biopsy I face two more weeks of maybe-cancer, so it's a relief when the day for the procedure arrives. It is just a bit less uncomfortable than cystoscopy but by the grace again of medication, it's a lot less traumatic. By now, of course, certain parts of the drill are familiar – drop your pants and kneel with your ass facing your doctor, breathe deep, remind yourself that rectal invasion is neither painful nor a sign, if it doesn't make you too uncomfortable, that your heterosexuality is more equivocal than you think. The latter variable is more in play with biopsy than digital examination because the invading instrument is not a single probing finger but a thick hard tube about five inches long. Apparently, it has something like pincers on the end. Collecting samples of tissue, U-3 pushes it deeper or angles it from side to side so that, with a snapping sound and a slight burning sensation, he can gather tissue by which the pathologists will be able to discern whether the walnut which controlled my destiny at Yankee Stadium will end my days or ruin them or let me live a little longer in the grip of its tyranny and suspense.

Two weeks later, U-3 informs me that the news is good, allows me about 5 seconds to celebrate my luck, then clears his throat and, in a sober, apologetic voice, complicates my future again. "But it's clear your prostate needs attention. We can proceed with treatment as soon as we decide on our target and weapons." He pauses, shakes his head and turned to look at the model on his wall. " It's not an easy decision. We've got drugs that relax the bladder and drugs that shrink the prostate. There's a new drug that relaxes the prostate and another that blocks the nerve which causes bladder spasm and another which just relaxes the bladder. We can use them separately or together. Some people are using Microwave and heat procedures to dissolve prostate tissue, but I'm not impressed by their results. The Gold Standard, of course, is direct surgical resection, what we call TURP, for transurethral resection or – colloquially -- the 'Roto-rooter." It uses a mild electric current to remove tissue from inside the prostate and create an open channel that allows urine to flow from the bladder to the urethra.

That's heavy-duty surgery, of course, two or three days in the hospital, home with a catheter inserted for a week or more. Another option is something called a Green Light Laser. It's an out-patient procedure that vaporizes prostate tissue. For this too, you'd go home with a catheter, but if things go well, it should be out in a couple of days."

"Which do you recommend?"

"I'd like to start you on medication first."

"Which one?"

He reaches for his prescription pad. "Why don't we try to shrink your prostate?"

Stunned by all this information, I don't think to ask him about side-effects of the medication, but he offers them nonetheless. "We'll have to follow you closely. Some patients complain that the medication decreases libido, causes problems with ejaculation and erection. Not surprising, since it works on your testosterone. We can supplement it with testosterone injections, but the problem with that is that testosterone can increase the size of the prostate or exacerbate prostate cancer if you have it. Obviously, there's no easy answer here. If you don't want to risk the libido effect, we can just try to relax your bladder. Problem is, bladder drugs can decrease libido too. Sometime too, they'll block urination. They will almost certainly lower your blood pressure. We can't predict the effects of these drugs, but in my experience, most patients are able to tolerate them. It's up to you how we proceed."

Taking the obvious route, we begin with the medication that shrinks my prostate but, perhaps because the testosterone issue hangs heavy in my mind, I'm quickly convinced that this one-a-day pill is affecting my energy and darkening my mood. When I call U-3 to discuss it, he says, "Yes, we often get that. No problem. We'll go after your bladder instead." He prescribes an "alpha blocker" which is meant to protect against the sort of spasm that produces urgency to urinate. A month later, when I call to report that I see no sign of improvement, he moves on to another option. "No problem. Let's just try to relax your prostate."

Investigating my new medication on the Internet, I find that there's a government advisory against combining it with drugs that relax the bladder – which is to say the other pill I'm taking – but of course, as I should know by now, all is relative in Urology. "In my view," says U-3, "that warning is unjustified. I've yet to see a patient get in trouble with this protocol. Why don't we try it for a while and see how it works for you?"

A year later, when it's time for my annual checkup, I find that U-3 is out of town. Symptoms unimproved, I decide to see the younger urologist who is covering for him. U-4. I like him at once because, unlike all his predecessors, he has a sense of humor, and he commiserates with me.

"Believe me, I know first-hand what urgency feels like. The only time I don't have to pee is when I'm peeing."

He studies the information e-mailed from U-3's office, doesn't bother to examine me and says, "Let's be honest. It doesn't matter what medication you take. With a prostate that big, surgery's your only option. Without it, you'll have pissing problems all your life and sexual problems unless you become a monk."

Though my other urologists have offered to prescribe Viagra whenever I saw them, he is the first to address the sexual issues which may be, of all the effects of prostate problems, the most diabolical. It stands to reason that a gland which is crucial to your testosterone and your semen production will also affect your erections and ejaculations, but the interaction of such issues with the great range of medications in the urology repertoire can turn sex into a gamble which, like the fear of pissing in your pants, wreaks havoc in your mind. I'm feeling less desire for sex these days, and I don't know how much to blame that on psycho-sexual issues or, again, the walnut alone.

So much do I appreciate U-4 that a year later, when it's time for my next appointment, I decide to see him instead of U-3. When I walk into his office, I find a changed man, his sense of humor darkened by cynicism.

"What are you doing here?"

"It's a year since I last saw you. Time for another examination."

"What do you think I can tell you that you don't already know?"

"Well, among other things, whether I have prostate cancer."

"How can I tell you? The PSA doesn't mean shit and you've already had a biopsy. Anyway, cancer is no problem at your age. Something else would kill you before it does."

He watches my consternation with pleasure. "I know you're disappointed. Like any patient, you want to be examined whether you need it or not. 'I don't care, I don't care, just look at me and give me an answer and send the bill to Medicare.' What do you care if Medicare cuts our fees in half? Last week, I had a patient lose his temper because he thought I didn't examine him carefully enough. 'OK,' I said. 'Next time I'll use two fingers.'"

Despite the fact that my urgency increases, and I'm waking to piss three or four times a night, I resist the impulse to call him until a year later, when I run into my old friend, Harvey, the Black Belt who had warned me about cystoscopy. Karate keeps people in shape, of course, but it seems to me he's looking younger and stronger than the last time I saw him.

"What's happening?"

He lowers his voice as if sharing a secret. "Did you ever hear of the Green Light Laser?"

"Yes, what about it?"

"Had it last week!"

"How'd it go?"

He closes his eyes and takes a deep breath, as if he can't believe what he was about to say. "I'm pissing like a teenager!"

Say this for prostate issues. Perverse though they are, the very helplessness one feels when caught up in their mix of confusion, fear and despair tends to encourage spontaneous decisions. I call U-3's office as soon as I get home.

His secretary says he's just had a cancellation for the following morning. This time at least he's not surprised to see me, and he doesn't challenge me when I tell him I want the Green Light. "Sure, we can do it. It's expensive, of course, but the procedure itself is no big deal."

He allows me a moment to enjoy this rare moment of optimism. The dream of "pissing like a teenager" seems a kind of summary judgment on the Beckettian irony that began at Yankee Stadium. But of course this is the Prostate, the constantly changing, always ambiguous world of Urology.

"We'll need some screening first, of course."

"How much? What sort? When can we begin?"

"Well, we've got some interesting new stuff to try. A new diagnostic called a PS3 Urine test which seems to be pretty good at determining whether any cancer you might have is aggressive and dangerous or one we can ignore. If this is ambiguous, as it often is, we'll look at a prostate-specific MRI."

"And if you find no cancer?"

He turns in his chair and, as often, studies the urinary model on the shelf behind his desk. It doesn't tell him anything he doesn't know already, and he's not reticent about admitting it.

"Well, that's a tough question. Let's wait and see what we find."

Two weeks later, all his questions answered, he orders the Green Light for me. It's non-invasive, easy and fast, and actually entertaining -- so high-tech it seems like a visiting a Science Fair. My results however are nowhere near Harvey's. Withing a week, I find myself waking to piss three or four times at night and re-visited, during the day, by the sadly familiar double whammy – frequency and urgency. U-4 confesses he's at a loss. "There's no indication that you have cancer, but your frequency problem is following that pattern. Your prostate is just too big. If this continues, I'm gonna suggest that we get rid of it."

"What would that mean?"

"Well, there's a new procedure that looks kind of sexy. , Robotic surgery… not exactly my territory but it looks interesting, maybe perfect for you. It's minimally invasive but it permits removal of most of the prostate. From what I've read, recovery seems to be fast and unproblematic."

He turns again to his urinary model. As do I. Contemplating the enigma that's brought us together, both of us remain silent — and more than a little uncomfortable — for several minutes. Finally, he sighs loudly, turns back to his desk and scribbles a note for me. "Like I said, Robotic surgery is not exactly my territory. You can learn everything you need to know if you look it up on-line. Check out this web site when you get home, then give me a call tomorrow."

Like the other treatments I'd tried — indeed, like every step in my Urological melodrama — Robotic Surgery seemed a no-brainer. Three weeks later, cautioning myself about my excitement and hope, I walked into an Operating Room which, bigger and more hi-tech than any in my experience, looked like a movie-set. General anesthetic put me under, and I was kept me in the hospital overnight, but I knew from my research what had been done to me. Through four small (less than one centimeter) incisions in my mid- and low-belly, short, narrow tubes, called trochars, were inserted into my abdomen. Through these trochars, the surgeons inserted long, narrow instruments which permitted very precise cutting, sewing, and finally, removal of the tissue which, to one degree or another, had been dominating my life for more than five decades.

It's absence now would dominate me in another way. Since urination would not be possible for 3 or 4 weeks, I was now required to use a catheter and master the delicate process of inserting it on my own. One of the nurses gave me a lesson and, when I was dismissed, two boxes appeared with my belongings. Though the process of insertion was maddening at first, I mastered it in a few days and since the relief it provided was instantaneous, came to feel a kind of appreciation for it. Two months later, when I was able to depend on my own plumbing again, I found myself — YES!! — pissing like a teenager. Of course, as a Urology Veteran, I should have known to mistrust my excitement, but please — show me anyone who's been through five decades of prostate misery who'd find anything but joy in effortless urination.

More despair, however, awaits me.

If I'd done my research carefully, or chosen a more forthcoming urologist, I'd know that approximately 85% of men report difficulties with erection following radical prostatectomy, but since I didn't, and don't, I'm frightened and depressed when, after my convalescence, my once dependable dick, which has served me well through five decades of urological melodrama, is hopelessly unresponsive, a helpless victim of my perverse, sadistic Prostate or the Urologists who've treated it.

U-4 is not disturbed by this news, but when both Viagra and Cialis prove to be ineffective, he is humble and self-effacing.

Searching his desk drawer, he finds a card and hands it to me. "Sexual function is not exactly my strong suit. If I were you, I'd talk to this guy."

"This guy," is U-5, a professor at a well-known university medical center. This means that he has teaching as well as clinical responsibilities and, as anyone knows who's tried to reach prestigious clinicians, he is close to impossible to reach on the phone. After a number of tries, I finally get through to his office, and after 35 minutes of wait-time and music, I choose #5 of the eleven options (in Spanish as well as English) offered by the phone system and thus manage to leave a message with his secretary, who gets back to me the next day to tell me I can see U-5 at his next available appointment, two months later, at 10:00 in the morning.

To my amazement, he's waiting for me when I arrive. He's tall and lean, a surprisingly young African American with a soft voice and a comforting equanimity that allows him, among other things, to realize I'm about the age of his father. Since he's already studied my file, he's amazed as well at the uncanny parallels in our urological histories. Standing to greet me, he says, "I've got to examine you, of course, but your issues are so similar to my Dad's that I feel like I know what I'm going to find."

His initial examination is cursory and, of course familiar, the same front and back, visual and digital, the same nods and smiles and shrugs, and only one question I haven't heard before.

"Do you often miss your mark when you urinate?"

"Actually, yeah. I never know where it's going."

"You've got a yeast infection on the tip of your penis. I'll give you some powder for it. Just pull the foreskin back and squirt a little on the tip every night. It should clear up in no time."

He returns to his desk, and nods toward his laptop where, I surmise, my file is already uploaded for him. "We see your problem often these days...people get excited with surgical solution, but the prostate and the urinary tract can be unforgiving. My father had the same surgery you did and also suffered from erectile dysfunction."

He studies his laptop, moves his cursor with his mouse and clicks a few keys, studying what I presume are my X-rays and files. "You've been through it all, haven't you? It's sad to me, infuriating really, that they don't give patients more information before they put you through a surgery like that. Of course, we're all excited, patients and surgeons alike, to have non-invasive access to the prostate, but I've seen very few patients who were forewarned about the risk of erectile problems." He pauses to study my file again, sighing again and shaking his head. "Strictly speaking, you know, the prostate is not necessary for erections. It adds secretions to the ejaculate, which help sperm survive, but it doesn't control the ability to have an erection. The problem is that there are some fine nerves which trigger erections that lie close to the prostate, and they can be damaged by a procedure like you just had. Those nerves could be the source of your problem, but, but there's also the possibility, at your age, that this is a cardiological issue. The heart has to pump a lot of blood to make a penis hard. Over time, high blood pressure can diminish either the force of that blood or, if your blood vessels aren't healthy, the volume that gets to the penis. Think of it --how complicated and beautiful and fragile it is! And we're not mentioning the mind, right? All the issues that psychology and neurology generate. Psychiatrists, psychologists, neurosurgeons, neurologists – everyone speculates about erectile dysfunction but no one explains it conclusively."

Closing his laptop, he smiles. "You know, you're just the sort of patient that led me to Urology. Other specialties treat patients in passing. After an orthopedist corrects your knee problem, you may never see him again. But since urological and prostate problems persist throughout a patient's life, we treat people of all ages, often see them annually or bi-annually. In the process, we get to know them, I think, better than in almost any other specialty."

He stands from the desk. "What we need from you first is a Doppler study. It's the only way we can determine what kind of dysfunction you have. Fortunately, our Doppler technician is here this morning. If you've got time, I think he can work you in."

In a small room down the hall, I change into a hospital gown and lay down on a full-length examination table, my head raised on an angled slope. Next to the table stands a sizable main-frame computer with an impressive tangle of wires linking to instruments on the shelf below. Arriving a few minutes later, U-5 has changed into hospital scrubs. "Make yourself comfortable now. Our technician is already here. The two of you will be working together for a while."

From a pocket in his gown, he removes a small black case and from the case, a full-size syringe and a bottle about the size of his thumb. Filling the former from the latter, he lifts my gown, spreads my legs and leans between them, gripping my penis and stretching it slightly, then aiming the needle at its base.

"Little prick," he says. "Sorry."

The injection is slightly painful, of course, but tolerable.

"Our technician should be here soon. By then, hopefully, the medication should take effect. I'll see you in my office when you're done."

For the next 10 or 15 minutes, stretched out on the examination table, I watch my stubborn, unresponsive dick with hope not far from prayer and a horrific procession of self- pity.

As a veteran of the urological wars, I thought I'd accumulated a good reserve of detachment and cynicism but how can I deny that I'm looking at my mortality and impermanence?

When the technician arrives, my penis remains indifferent to U-5's injection.

He's a tall, thin Asian with long hair tied in a pony-tail and complicated tattoos on both arms. Pulling a stool close to the computer stand, he nods in my direction.

"Hi, I'm Abby. With your permission, I'll do your ultra-sound now."

"Thanks."

He asks me the familiar series of I-D questions — my name, birthdate, etc. — typing my answers as I offer them, then, removing a scanner from a drawer in the computer stand, presses a series of buttons on it and his keyboard, and explains,

"This is an ultra sound program. It allows us to estimate the blood flow through your vessels by bouncing high-frequency sound waves off circulating cells."

Eyes shifting back and forth between his screen and my penis, he places the scanner on my testicles, moves it slowly up and down, and then, typing all the while, up and down on my penis and back and forth and up and down on my low belly, my ribs, and finally my penis again.

"That'll do it," he says. "Thanks for your cooperation. You can dress and go back to the office. Doc will have your results in a few minutes."

I slip out of the gown, dress in my street clothes again, and return to U-5's office. Still at his desk, he stands to greet me, sits again and studies his screen again, and finally closes the laptop and turns to me. "Would you be interested in a penile implant?"

"I don't know," I said, and then, "No."

ABOUT THE AUTHOR

Lawrence Shainberg's books include the novels, *One on One, Crust,* and *Memories of Amnesia* and the non-fiction, *Ambivalent Zen, Brain Surgeon: an Intimate View of His World,* and *Four Men Shaking.* His articles and essays have appeared in The New York Times Magazine, Harper's, Tricycle, The Village Voice, Evergreen Magazine, and the Paris Review.

Made in United States
Orlando, FL
18 July 2023

35260398R00122